The
Bean and Bun

Amanda Leifeste

Available as an eBook

ISBN 979-8-9919072-9-3 (paperback)

ISBN 979-8-3124519-1-7 (hardcover)

Publify Publishing

Lampasas, TX 76550

contact@publifypublishing.com

For all those who dream of running away to the beach.

Chapter One

March 1, 2015

The day might come when Aggie Jeffries would be forced to trade her flip-flops back in for high heels and pencil skirts, but it wasn't today. She stirred the pan on her commercial stove, brown sugar and butter melding together as the January sun peeked over the Gulf of Mexico. Outside, the gas lamps lining the cobblestone streets dimmed, and life on Sandcastle Island began to stir. Tending the pan with one hand and sipping an oat-milk latte with the other, she hummed along to Edith Piaf's *La Vie En Rose* playing over the bakery's sound system. She felt like that here. As if she saw everything through rose-colored glasses. What a sharp contrast from a few short months ago.

She added cream and Mexican vanilla to the pan. The brown sugar she sourced from India gave her salted-caramel cupcakes the deep, nutty-sweet flavor locals and tourists alike raved about. Those cupcakes had earned The Bean and Bun not only a five-star Yelp rating, but a mention in the latest issue of Texas Monthly magazine. Surely business would pick up soon. Birding enthusiasts trickled in year-round to the nature preserve covering the southern third of the barrier island. But tourist season was just around the corner, and soon the town would come alive as holiday makers filled the candy-colored cabins that hugged the shore in neat rows.

The rich aroma of the caramel mingled with the scent of vanilla-almond scones cooling on the marble countertop and the cranberry-orange ones rising in the oven. Layered underneath everything floated the sharp smell of freshly ground espresso beans. Aggie surveyed her domain with pleasure. Despite her late start, the shop now smelled like a proper bakery should. Sort of like a hug. The bell near the delivery door buzzed. "It's open," she called over her shoulder.

"Morning, Aggie! Where do you want these?" Scott, the island's only postman, called, his face hidden behind the boxes balanced in his arms.

"Good morning! You're off to an early start. Those can go right over there." She gestured to a corner of the kitchen. Her face lit up when she spotted the green Mainland Printing logo on the boxes. She desperately needed another income stream, and hoped the t-shirts and coffee mugs packed inside would do well with the tourists.

"Alrighty, here ya go." Scott set the boxes down with a thump. "Smells amazing in here."

"Thanks, help yourself."

"I really shouldn't," he said, patting his stout midsection with one hand and reaching for a scone with the other. He took a bite, and shook the scone in Aggie's direction. "If heaven has a flavor this is it," he said with his mouth full. He swallowed. "Okay, gotta run. Trying to get done early today. Got a date with the missus for Maya's school play."

"Oh, that's right. Tell her I said to break a leg!" The family came in every Sunday morning, little Maya's nose in a battered copy of *Little Women*, her parents passing sections of the Houston Chronicle over their pastries and coffee.

"Will do. Thanks for the bite. See ya!" With a jaunty salute, Scott disappeared into the morning light, the door swinging closed behind him.

Aggie returned her attention to the pan. Wisps of steam drifted upward toward the ornate tin tiles lining the lofty ceilings of the 1920s sandstone building. Her phone buzzed in the pocket of the apron she wore over her unofficial uniform of white jeans and chambray button down. She fished it out, frowning at the interruption. But her lips curved into a smile as she tapped the screen, snugging the phone between her ear and shoulder, her spatula never leaving the pan. "Hey, you," she said.

"Hey, yourself," Shane replied, his familiar tone rich with his trademark enthusiasm. "How's island life?"

Shane was the first person she very literally bumped into at Tulane freshman orientation thirteen years ago. The two bonded over a mutual love of the New Orleans food scene. While their classmates slogged through Bourbon Street double-fisting Hurricanes, Aggie and Shane explored every dive in the city on a never-ending search for the best muffalettas, po-boys and gumbo. Aggie had been crushed to realize he preferred the tattooed blonde guy in their Poli-Sci class to her, but she'd gotten over it and had since happily played the Grace to his Will.

"Pretty fantastic!" Aggie responded. "Oh my gosh, I have the most amazing news! I got a write-up in Texas Monthly. Well, to be fair, my cupcakes got a write-up, but I'm good with riding their coat tails."

"Awesome, Ags! Congrats! I'll pick up a copy."

"I'll send you one. I have a whole stack. What's up? Talk fast though. I'm running late."

"You've never run late in your life."

"Yeah, well. Island time. Also, there *might* have been too many Proseccos involved in my celebration."

"What happened to that two-drink limit of yours?"

"Amelia happened. She has this lovely-terrible habit of refilling your glass when you're not looking. I'm not sure if it's sweet or pure evil."

Aggie put the phone on speaker and set it onto the counter, freeing her hand to massage her temples. "I woke up late with a dude shaking maracas inside my head, and he's working his way up to a full-blown mariachi band."

"Ouch. Which one is Amelia, again?"

"She owns the wine bar next door. You will love her. She's Armenian, and covered in floral tattoos, and wears so much jewelry she jingles when she walks. She also knows more about wine than anyone I've ever met."

"Well, that's saying a lot." Shane's voice flattened and dropped an octave. "Um, listen, I hate to be a buzzkill first thing in the morning, but we need to talk. Remember our deal?"

Aggie cringed. She remembered.

Shane plowed ahead. "I know I said I'd give you a year. I don't want you to think I'm rooting for you to fail down there, but I miss you. I want you to come back. We all do."

Of course, they do, thought Aggie. She wondered who was fielding client complaints and solving HR squabbles for the last six months. Shane, probably. No wonder he missed her. For six years she had shouldered far more than her share of responsibility running their Houston accounting firm. To be fair, Shane didn't realize this until she left. The thought of returning to tax projections and quarterly filings summoned an all too familiar tightening in her chest. She willed the sensation to relax, reminding herself that however much Shane would like her to abandon what he jokingly referred to as her early-life crisis, sell the beautiful building that housed her shop and apartment, use those funds to buy back into their partnership, and get her tail back to Houston, pronto — she had six more months to get The Bean and Bun on solid financial footing. According to their agreement, that is. She changed the subject. "How's Gregory?" Gregory was Shane's long-term boyfriend, and he and Shane were about the only thing Aggie missed about Houston.

"He's good, he misses your cooking. And you. Look, there's no easy way to say this, but I'm going to need an answer sooner. Mark Myers wants to buy into the business. He's putting a lot of pressure on me to make him a partner. He's all but said that if I don't, he's going to walk and open his own shop. And he's the point person on two dozen of our biggest accounts."

"He can't do that," Aggie interjected, her eyes focused on her pan. "He signed a non-compete agreement." The caramel was approaching the perfect color and consistency.

"Everyone knows those things don't hold water," Shane shot back. "We make everybody sign one, but at the end of the day it's up to me to enforce it, and I can't run this place and deal with a legal hassle at the same time. I know you technically have six months left, but I need an answer sooner."

The spatula in Aggie's hand shook and then stilled, hovering above the glossy confection. Sooner? Her mind flashed to her current financial statement. It was a sea of red. The purchase of the building and kitchen equipment ate up the cash from selling Shane her half of the practice, and her savings account became more anemic with every invoice that landed on her desk. The shop was inching its way steadily towards the black, but she needed more time.

"How soon?" she asked, her tone as flat as her spatula.

"Well, ideally now, but I think I can put him off for a month. Maybe two, tops. Look, I realize this is crappy. I'm sorry. I really am. But I'm going to need an answer. It's no secret I don't want to take your name off the letterhead. But if you're really going to stay down there, I need to know as soon as possible."

The ache in Aggie's head concentrated into an angry, pulsing pain at the back of her skull. Her voice became thin and tinny. "I understand. I've got to go. I'll get back to you." Her hand trembled, and she disconnected the call as the acrid smell of burnt sugar singed her nostrils. She dumped the pan in the sink and ran water over the sticky, ruined mess. Hot tears pricked the backs of her eyes. The short hand on the clock above the door pointed to eight. It was time to open. She shelved the conversation, boxing it up and shoving it into the far recesses of her consciousness. A month, he said. Two, tops. Could she figure this out in two months?

Crossing the honey-hued hardwood floors to the front of the shop, Aggie ran her hand over the marble topped bistro tables with their wrought iron bases. Light from the floor to ceiling leaded glass windows flooded the room, glinting off the stainless-steel espresso machine behind the counter. She flipped light switches as she went, several of which were in unexpected spots due to multiple phases of electrical work over the last century. She reached the heavy glass and iron door and, almost ceremoniously, flipped the Closed sign around to Open just as the oven timer dinged. Straightening her shoulders, she headed back to the kitchen to transfer the scones to a cooling rack and start a fresh batch of caramel.

As she reached for more butter, there was an insistent tapping at the front door. She rolled her eyes realizing she flipped the sign around but neglected to actually unlock the door. She was really batting a thousand today, she thought, wiping her hands on a clean dishtowel and hurrying to the front.

Peering through the door, one hand cupped around his eyes, stood a tall, extremely tan man in a Texas

Rangers baseball cap, gold rimmed aviator sunglasses, jeans, and a rumpled t-shirt that clung slightly to well-defined biceps. *Sheesh*, Aggie thought, *what a day to have a head full of dry shampoo.* Rubbing her temples again, she promised herself she would go find the Advil as soon as she dealt with this guy. And what was he holding at his side?

"Good Morning," she said, swinging open the door. "Sorry. We're having a few, um, technical difficulties this morning."

"No worries." He flashed a toothpaste-commercial smile. "I started to worry you were closed." He held up an orange paper cup with a black lid. "I was hoping to upgrade my coffee?" It took Aggie a nano-second to recognize the cup.

"Ah. You met Omar." she said, backing up and gesturing for him to come inside.

Aggie had vivid memories of her own first encounter with Omar. The first morning of her fateful vacation to the island nine months prior, she had gone in search of coffee. A Google Maps search had produced only one option, Omar's Fuel and Bait. *Hmm*, she thought. *Okay, when in Rome.* She pointed her Mini Cooper away from her beachfront Airbnb cabin and drove towards the ferry landing. A faded sign, that perhaps once had been red, perched atop a squatty gas station declaring itself simply - 'OMAR's". Her tires crunched on the gravel parking lot. When she pushed open the door, a bell jingled, and she was met with a friendly smile and an unpleasant odor.

"Um, hi. I was hoping to grab a coffee?"

"You bet, darlin'. Gimme two seconds while I pop these guys in the fridge," the man behind the counter said around the toothpick dangling from the corner of his mouth. '*These guys*' appeared to be a styrofoam box filled with tiny fish. Aggie wrinkled her nose.

"Okay." She wanted nothing more than to walk right back out. The man, presumably Omar, poured a dubious liquid from a stained coffee pot. Accepting the neon orange cup with trepidation, she held out her Visa.

"Oh, sorry ma'am. Cash only."

Aggie dug in her bag and handed over a five. "Thanks, keep the change." She had escaped out into the sunshine, gulping in the fresh air.

While Omar's was the first opportunity to grab a coffee after rolling off the ferry, the man in the Rangers cap wasn't the first to ditch the orange cup when The Bean and Bun came into view a few miles down the road.

"Yep, sure did. Nice guy," the man replied, bringing her back to the present.

"He is nice," said Aggie. It was a small island.

"But his coffee tastes like tar mixed with cigar ashes. Serves me right by buying coffee from a guy whose main business is gas and fish bait."

Aggie laughed. "What can I get you?" "Can you do an extra hot, double shot Americano?"

"Coming right up." Aggie moved behind the counter. The grinder whizzed to life as she ground beans into a fine powder for the espresso machine. The man cast a glance around the shop, taking in the glass cases and polished hardwoods.

"Did this used to be a burger joint?"

"I'm not sure. It was empty when I bought the building six months ago. I think it's been a lot of things. Most recently a pizza place if memory serves." She carefully added hot water to the espresso shots.

"I think I remember this being a burger joint when I was a kid."

"You're from the island?"

"Not exactly." Aggie passed the Americano across the bar. He handed her his black AmEx and accepted the coffee. He removed the lid and blew on the steaming liquid for a moment before taking an exploratory sip. He closed his eyes. "Hmm. Now that is coffee. You have saved me. Thank you."

"I'm glad we could upgrade your morning," she replied with a smile, handing back his card. "Come back soon."

The man started to leave but stopped and turned before he reached the door. He walked back over the counter. Aggie looked up, puzzled. "Is something wrong with your coffee?"

"No, it's fine. I just thought I should grab something to take to my Gran. A pastry or something?"

"That's a sweet idea. Grandmothers love that sort of thing."

"Yes, mine especially. She's famous for her sweet tooth."

"Maybe I know her. I sort of have the monopoly on town sweets. What's her name?" The man hesitated, and Aggie back tracked, waving her hand as if she could wipe her words away. "I'm sorry. That was rude."

"No, not all. Her name is Nell. Nell Schmidt."

"Oh, Nellie!" Aggie clapped her hands in delight. "I adore Nellie. We all do. She's wonderful! You're her grandson?"

"Guilty. And she'll shoot me if you tell her I've forgotten all my manners." He extended a hand, his face breaking into that Colgate smile again. His teeth had to be professionally bleached, Aggie thought, but his golden-brown eyes were warm and crinkled at the corners when he smiled. "Brooks Schmidt."

She shook his hand. "Agatha Jeffries. But absolutely everyone calls me Aggie."

"So, I can call you Aggie?"

"I would say you qualify as absolutely everyone, so sure." She smiled, something unfamiliar fluttering in her stomach. *Did he smile at everyone like this? Was he flirting?* She would be a terrible judge. She didn't think she remembered what flirting looked like. In Houston, aside from Shane and Gregory, her deepest relationship had been the front desk guy at her gym who called her Alice.

She dropped his hand and tucked a heavy chestnut lock behind her ear. "Nellie comes in with her bridge group on Tuesdays. The lemon-blueberry scones are her favorite. But I'm afraid I don't have any right now." And even though lemon-blueberry was not on today's menu, and Aggie had exactly zero spare minutes, her next words popped out fully without her permission. "I can have some ready in a couple hours though."

Brooks flashed those pearly whites again.

"I should have guessed that. She always did love lemon anything. She used to keep a glass bowl of lemon drops on the kitchen counter and a pitcher of lemonade in the fridge at all times."

"She still does! She invited me for tea right after I moved to the island. She's incredibly hospitable."

"That she is. Um, I really should know this, but do you happen to also know her coffee order?"

"I do." It was Aggie's turn to grin. "Her coffee order is an Arnold Palmer. Half tea, half lemonade."

Brooks chuckled. "I should have guessed that too. Okay, I'll be back for blueberry-lemon scones and an Arnold Palmer."

"Sounds good." She waved him off. She wished there was a way she could freshen up and wash her hair before he came back. But there would be no time for that.

No sooner did Brooks leave the Bean and Bun than the doorbell tinkled again in time to a squeal from Sadie as she barreled towards the counter. "Was that who I think it was?" Sadie pointed over her shoulder.

"Who? The guy who just left?" Aggie rubbed her temples. The mariachi band in her head was fully tuned up. She really needed to go find the Advil.

"Yes, the guy who just left." Sadie was looking at Aggie like she wanted to slap her forehead and hand her a V-8. "You don't recognize him?"

"No, should I?"

"Um, if you've picked up a People magazine anytime in the last year, then yes."

"Sadie, you know my knowledge of pop culture could fit on the head of a pin. Also, my actual head is still suffering from Amelia-itis."

"That's Brooks Jagger!"

Aggie frowned, cocking her head to one side. "Wait, no. He just introduced himself as Brooks Schmidt. He said he's Nellie Schmidt's grandson."

Sadie snapped her fingers. "Ah, well, yes. Same person." Her voice took on a staccato rhythm when she got worked up. "Yes, he's her grandson. He spent summers here as a kid. He was a few years older than me though. He owns a cabin on the North End, but I don't think he's been here in years. He's famous now. Brooks Jagger is a pen name. He wrote the Chester McCombs books."

Aggie gave her a blank stare.

"Seriously? I swear, you really do live under a rock. His books aren't really *my* thing - very MacGyver meets James Bond. But Mark reads all of them, and they're being made into movies. Mark and I saw the first one. I forget the name, but it was pretty good. Helen Hanes stars in them." Sadie's husband was a huge fan of action movies, and Sadie was a huge fan of any evening out that didn't involve changing pull-ups or one of their three-year-old twins smearing ketchup in her hair.

"Helen Hanes?"

"You have got to be kidding. You really do live under a rock." Sadie rolled her green eyes.

"Be nice, or I'll cut off your caffeine supply." Aggie smirked. Even she had heard of Helen Hanes. "What about her?"

"She stars in the Chester McCombs movies, and Brooks...," Sadie leaned over the counter dropping her voice to a conspiratorial whisper, "is her boyfriend. In real life, obviously. Not in the movie. Oh my gosh, I wonder if Helen's here too?" Sadie squealed again.

Something clenched in Aggie's stomach. Of course, he had a girlfriend on America's Most Beautiful list. "Well, he's coming back later for scones. If he shows up with anyone who looks like a movie star, I'll text you. Now, if you're going to behave yourself, do you want your usual?"

Sadie nodded, her auburn curls bouncing. "Better make it three shots."

"Amelia-itis?"

Sadie nodded again. "Not only that, but the twins both ended up in our bed last night, and I don't think anyone slept more than twelve minutes at a time." Sadie's excitement over her celebrity sighting dissolved into a yawn. Aggie handed her the coffee.

"This is on the house if you happen to have any Advil in that Mary Poppins carpet bag of yours." She pointed at Sadie's oversized tote.

"Oh, please." Sadie set her bag on the counter and began rifling through its contents. "I've got half a pharmacy in here." She extracted a rolled-up jewelry travel bag. She untied the string holding the bag together and unrolled it onto the counter, revealing a dozen compartments, each neatly labeled with its contents.

"I thought I was organized. You take it to a whole new level."

While extracting two orange pills, Sadie deadpanned, "When one has a real estate business on an island that has been labeled 'an undiscovered gem' in national travel magazines, two tiny humans who can't wipe their own patooties yet, and a husband whom one adores, but can't manage to pick up his own socks, one stays very, very, organized. Otherwise, one's life will dissolve into complete and total chaos. Trust me."

Aggie burst out laughing and accepted the pills Sadie dropped into her palm. Sadie slung the tote over her shoulder. "Thanks for the coffee. But you should really stop giving away things for free. This shop better make it. I can't go back to Omar's being my only source for caffeine."

Chapter Two

Brooks left the Bean and Bun and pointed his midnight blue 1966 Thunderbird towards the North End of the island. The houses up here sat on larger lots. You almost couldn't see one from the next. At the second to last drive, he turned in and pulled to a stop in front of his modest cabin. The house boasted two bedrooms, a bathroom, a slightly sad kitchen straight out of 1964, and a living room with green shag carpet. As soon as the ink had dried on the closing papers, he had plans drawn up for a full renovation. But before he could so much as rip out the green shag, Hollywood came calling. What he assumed would be a brief stay in California turned into a five-year hiatus from the Lone Star State.

The porch was his favorite part of the house, which even though weathered to gray, was still solid. It stretched across the front facade and was deep enough to offer a shady spot to read or nap any time of day. He climbed the steps and let himself sink down into one of the oversized Adirondack chairs facing the Gulf. He gazed out past the waving grasses and the worn, wooden walkway leading over the dunes and down to where the waves broke gently on the shore.

Brooks removed his cap and set it on his knee as he leaned his head back against the chair. He closed his eyes, inhaling the salty breeze and letting the wind ruffle his dark blonde hair. His shoulders lowered an inch and tension eased out of his tired body. Arriving on the island always had this effect on him. Why did he stay away so long? Hollywood seemed far away and suddenly unimportant. The rhythm of the waves breaking on the beach soothed his raw nerves. A gull called overhead. Two long days of driving and a couple nights of restless sleep caught up to him, and his eyelids grew heavy.

Brooks didn't realize he fell asleep until he was awoken by slow, heavy footsteps on the porch stairs. He jumped awake and rubbed his eyes underneath his aviators. He looked up and broke into a grin. "Ambrose!" he exclaimed as he stood.

The old man grinned back at him, his white teeth a sharp contrast to his leathered face. "Hey, kiddo. How's it goin', son?" The two men shook hands and embraced. Ambrose had functioned as caretaker for the Schmidt clan for as long as Brooks could remember and was considered one of the family. It was Ambrose who taught Brooks to fish, wading out into the waves in front of the big family beach house, catching crabs in the bay, and later, how to beat the pants off anyone in Texas Hold 'Em. Now Ambrose was the island's most popular general contractor, property manager and handyman. But he still personally handled anything Nellie needed at the beach house and had assumed responsibility for looking after her grandson's cabin.

Ambrose removed a bleached and frayed straw cowboy hat from his balding head and slapped his leg with it. "I can't believe it. James O'Henry called and said he thought it was you walking out of the Bean and Bun. I just had to come see if it was true."

Brooks laughed. He had forgotten how fast news travels on the island.

"Have you seen your Gran yet, son?"

"No, not yet. I think I need a shower first. And apparently, I needed a nap." He cast a sheepish glance at the chair where Ambrose caught him sleeping and rubbed the back of his neck.

"Don't tell her, okay? I'm headed over there as soon as I get cleaned up. Promise."

Ambrose settled his hat back on his head and started down the steps. "Alrighty, son. She won't hear it from me, but I'd go sooner than later if I was you."

"Yessir, will do. Thanks."

Ambrose turned around. "You need anything?"

"No sir. I haven't even been inside yet. Is the key still under the flowerpot?"

"Oh, nope. That pot blew over in a storm and broke a couple years ago. We've got a new system." Ambrose walked over to a keypad on the front door that Brooks hadn't noticed. He punched in a code and the lock clicked open.

"I'll text you the code." He pointed an arthritic finger at Brooks. "You get over to see your Gran lickety-split. You hear me?"

"Yessir," Brooks repeated with a grin. What was this? Sleepy little Sandcastle Island had a coffee shop with an actual espresso machine. And now Ambrose was texting from a cell phone and using electronic keypads? Brooks shook his head. He had been away a very long time indeed.

He returned to the car for his bag and carried it into the cabin. It looked exactly as he'd left it. Or probably a lot cleaner than he'd left it, thanks to Ambrose. Everything in the cabin was functional, with the possible exception of the oven, which he suspected was a fire hazard. But it could use a facelift. He would talk to Ambrose about it. First though, he had to start on the new book. The weekly email inquiries from his agent were becoming more insistent. Maybe here he could finally get to work on a manuscript. He would start first thing in the morning. Right now, he needed a quick shower and then he owed his Gran a much overdue visit.

Shortly after two, a clean shaven and less rumpled Brooks breezed back into the Bean and Bun. "Hi there,"

Aggie handed over a white cardboard box. "You clean up nice."

"Thanks. I try." He noticed her chestnut curls were escaping her ponytail and her face was flushed. Every table was full, and people were milling about. "It's hopping in here. Is it just you running this place?

"Sadly, yes. Just me, for now." Aggie poured an Arnold Palmer over ice into a to-go cup.

"Here you go. Please tell Nellie hello for me. We're all going to miss her so much when she leaves."

Brooks narrowed his eyes over his aviators. *What on earth did she mean by that? Leave?* As far as he knew, Nellie hadn't left the island in over a decade.

"Uh, okay, will do. Thanks again." He pushed his aviators back into place with his knuckle, paid, and headed back to the car. Brooks left the Bean and Bun confused. There was most certainly not more than one Nell Francis on the island. But Aggie must have her mixed up with someone else. He puttered along the road that led to the southern end of the island, the cool breeze carrying the briny scent of the Gulf in his face. The houses on this section of the island were older. Much older. Some dated back as far as the 1920s and claimed even larger lots than those on the North End. He passed a couple puttering along in a golf cart and then, there it was. Set far back from the shore, with a weathered walkway leading over the dunes and down to the sand, sat the original family beach house. Every one of his best childhood memories were rooted to this spot. Sun-soaked summers spent hunting crabs, collecting shells, and jumping waves in the surf. In the evenings, sitting at GranNell's knee on the porch, drinking ice cold lemonade and shelling peas while she spun half true tales of the pirates that sailed the Gulf in the days of his great-grandfather's grandfather.

In 1902, long after pirates died out as a breed, Brooks' great-grandfather hit it big in the Texas oil boom. Not long after, on a business trip to the East Coast, great gramps fell in love with the grand family camps of the Adirondacks and returned home to Texas hell bent on creating his own. He bought a thirty-five square mile uninhabited island and at astronomical expense turned it into a retreat for the Francis family. Then in 1913, in a move of exquisite legal footwork to extricate the family from a squabble with the Internal Revenue Service, the southern third of the island was donated to the federal government to be utilized exclusively as a nature preserve. Birders and a few tourists began to find their way to Francis Island. Slowly, plots of land were sold off to other families and a community sprang up, the local economy revolving around tourism and a robust fishing industry. Eventually, a bridge was built, connecting the island to the mainland.

In 1935, the Island Council held a sandcastle building contest to increase tourism. It became so popular that within a few years, the island became known to anyone within a hundred miles as Sandcastle Island. In 1954, the Island Council voted to officially adopt the name. And so, it has been called since.

Brooks' grandmother, Nell Francis Schmidt, affectionately known as GranNell to her children and grandchildren, still lived in the family home. She was Brooks' champion when he wanted to leave law school to pursue a writing career. She had succinctly pointed out to his parents, in words only she could get away with, that he could always go back to law school. His parents reluctantly acquiesced. GranNell also persuaded an editor friend at a publishing house in New York to read his first manuscript. He owed her a hell of a lot. And he couldn't remember the last time he called, much less visited. Well, there was no time like the present.

Brooks parked in the circle drive and took the wide steps two at a time. The boards of the deck creaked under his footsteps, but the grand old dame still stood proud, her white paint fresh, brass doorknob polished, the bay windows spotless like big square eyes. A wooden swing at the far end of the deep porch swayed in the breeze. On the opposite side two wicker rocking chairs stood guard, a small table between them. He straightened his shirt and threaded his aviators into his collar. A scone wasn't going to make up for years of absence, but if his good Southerner of a mother taught him nothing else, it was to never show up anywhere empty handed. A pastry couldn't hurt. He smoothed down his hair and knocked three times. There was the sharp scrape of wood on wood, a chair scooting away from a table. Someone making their way towards the door. He mentally chastised himself. He really should have called first. Surprising a ninety-one-year-old woman, even if it was the sturdiest ninety-one-year-old to ever walk the planet, could be shortsighted. It was too late now, he thought, as the door opened to reveal his GranNell. All four-foot ten-inches of her. Her snow-white hair was pinned up in a neat French twist. She wore a pressed shirt dress, white Sketchers, six carats worth of diamonds, and an expression of disbelief mixed with pure joy.

"Well! As I live and breathe. Brooks!" She briefly touched her hand to her chest, and Brooks' pulse quickened in panic. But her hand reached out toward him. "My darling boy. You've come home." Brooks did not point out that nine months out of every year home was his parents' house in Dallas, and more recently his own apartments in Dallas and then in L.A. But, on second thought, maybe she wasn't wrong. He just took her hand and gently folded her in a one arm squeeze.

Gah, she feels fragile, he thought to himself as he bent down and kissed her papery cheek. She still smelled the same, of lavender, and lemons, and the sea.

"Hi, GranNell," he smiled.

"Oh, my goodness, honey. Come in, come in! You must have got my letter?"

"Letter?" said Brooks standing stupidly rooted to the front porch as she held the door open. He thought back, trying to remember the last time he physically checked his mail.

All his bills were automated, and fan mail went to a different address and was handled by an assistant. "No," he said, shaking his head. "I'm sorry, what letter?"

"Oh, dear. Well, come in anyway."

He followed her into the cool house and set the bakery box on the scarred farm table in the kitchen. He handed her the cup from the Bean and Bun. "I understand you're still an Arnold Palmer fan." He smiled, hoping the cold drink and pastries would somehow make up for his lack of basic adulting skills, like checking his own mail.

"Ah, I see you've met our Aggie." Nellie cast a sidelong glance at the box. "Sit, sit, child."

"Yes, I did," Brooks said, bemused. "Our Aggie?" He took a seat, crossing an ankle over his knee.

"Yes, it's so civilized having a proper coffee shop on the island." Nellie sat across from him and opened the box. "Let's see what you've brought me, and I'll consider telling you what was in my letter, Mister Fancy Pants, bestselling author who's too important to read his own mail." Brooks' face flushed, as if he's been called out at school for misbehaving. "Ah, Blueberry Lemon." Nellie nodded in approval. "Either you have a good memory, or Aggie is generous with information."

"Both?" Brooks shrugged. "So, are you going to tell me what was in the letter?"

"Patience, child." Nellie selected a scone. "First, I want to hear all about your exciting life in California and that fancy actress I saw you with in People magazine."

"You read People magazine?" Brooks asked, his eyes wide.

"Indeed, I do! Far more entertaining than any of the garbage on television. And especially when it features my favorite grandson. I like to see what he's up to, since he doesn't seem to have the time to answer letters from his old Gran." She pursed her lips and shot him a sideways look as she took a decidedly unladylike bite out of the scone.

"GranNell, I really am sorry. It's just…" he trailed off.

"I'm kidding dear, sort of anyway." She patted his hand. "You are young, and you are doing exactly what young folk are supposed to. I do want to hear all about it though now that you're here." She settled into the chair with her drink and pastry, waiting for him to begin.

Brooks slowly told her about L.A. and about the movie set. He shared some funny stories about the cast and the crew and their shenanigans. He paused to reach for a scone. The smell was too much to resist, especially after two days of gas station tacos. He took a big bite, spreading crumbs all over the table. "Wow!" He exclaimed around a mouthful of scone. "These are incredible!"

"Yes, I know, dear. Aggie is a gifted baker. But for goodness' sake, don't talk with your mouth full. What about the girl?" GranNell prompted.

Brooks hesitated and set the scone back down, the pastry turning to sawdust in his mouth. The scene he kept trying to block out popped, unwelcome, into his head, playing out like a movie reel. He had been so excited, like a kid on Christmas, walking into Helen's dressing room three days ago. What a difference three days made. Three days ago, Brooks had the world on a string. The second book in his Chester McCombs series was in production as a major motion picture. Royalty checks from the success of the first movie fattened his bank account. His books were all holding tight to spots on the bestseller list. And Helen was on his arm.

Brooks met Helen at her audition to play Chester McCombs' love interest. He was smack in the middle of a honeymoon phase with Southern California, one hundred and ten percent star struck by Hollywood and all its glamorous trappings, including Helen. He was starry eyed, bowled over by her classic California good looks, mile-long legs, and a smile that could charm a drowning man out of a perfectly good life raft.

When production began, Brooks spent more and more time on set. He was not an active or necessary participant in the movie's production, but he held the honorary title of consultant and took the position seriously. He would pop up on set offering unsolicited, and mostly unhelpful, advice. Despite this, his good old Southern boy charm made him generally well liked. And after the blockbuster success of the first movie, he was considered a good luck charm of sorts. The crew set out a director's chair with Brooks' name on it. Of course, the name on the chair read Brooks Jagger, rather than his given name. His agent, Avery Jacobs, still maintained the opinion that Brooks Jagger could sell more books than Brooks Schmidt.

"My dear boy," he said in their first meeting, "far, far too many things rhyme with Schmidt." Considering his success, Brooks was really in no position to argue the point. Even Helen introduced him at cocktail parties as Brooks Jagger, the famous author, instead of by his given name. At first, he didn't mind too much. But then the first movie came out. He made the talk show circuits, and his picture was published next to Helen's in People magazine. He found grabbing a quick coffee to be nothing quick when the barista wanted to quiz him on plot lines. He missed Brooks Schmidt.

Two days before leaving the lights of Hollywood in his rearview mirror, Brooks ducked into a well-known Los Angeles jewelry shop. He chose quickly. "That one," he said, pointing to a platinum, diamond encrusted band set with a round solitaire that could double as a small skating rink. Leaving the shop, he could hardly feel the sidewalk under his feet. The sun was shining, and his future was bright. He was on track. And he was ready to settle down. Be Brooks Schmidt again. And Helen was the woman he wanted to do it with. He drove back toward the studio with the top down. He and Helen would set up house in a little bungalow on the beach, or maybe somewhere up in the hills. Somewhere small and private. They would have a little garden, maybe get a dog. It would have a quiet spot where he could get to work on the much overdue manuscript of the next Chester McCombs installment. He pointed the Thunderbird in the direction of the studio, humming along to the radio.

Helen had agreed to meet Brooks later that evening for a new restaurant opening, a night of rubbing elbows with the self-important and over-bronzed. Stuff like that was important for her career. Brooks got that, but for tonight, he had other plans. Perched on the backseat of the Thunderbird was a vintage picnic basket. Brooks had curated a scrumptious spread for a romantic sunset picnic on their favorite beach. Buttery Castellvetrano olives, nutty prosciutto sliced paper thin, plump figs, a soft Italian cheese, a small loaf of freshly baked ciabatta bread, a tin of caviar so pricey it would make you cry, and a tight bunch of black grapes so perfectly ripe they tasted of cotton candy. There was also a box of artisan chocolates for dessert. The chocolates were for Brooks. Helen never, ever ate dessert. Next to the basket, a bottle of French Champagne rested on ice in a cooler. He was downright giddy as he parked in the lot and made his way into the building to surprise his fiancé-to-be.

Brooks whistled to himself as he waltzed into Helen's dressing room. But when he opened the door, his hand stuck to the doorknob and his feet grew roots into the floor as all the oxygen left his body. A tale as old as time, his writer's brain said to itself. There was Helen, in all her movie star glory, turned away from him, blonde hair cascading down her back, silk blouse on the floor. She was wrapped in a passionate embrace around someone who while currently unidentifiable, was most certainly *not* her almost-fiancé. A hairy hand attached to the man was halfway up her back, unhooking a lace bra Brooks was certain he purchased. As Brooks pushed open the door, the bra snapped open, and the two illicit lovebirds sprang apart. The man playing Helen's love interest in this unsanctioned scene was none other than the movie's director, who in a sadly ironic twist, celebrated his own engagement a few short weeks before.

Brooks kneaded his eyes. His brain was playing tricks on him. His eyes refocused, and the scene was clearly the same. He was struck by a wave of nausea. He didn't wait to decipher the cacophony of words flying out of Helen's mouth. Her lips were moving, but the words were muffled as if she were speaking through a long tunnel. With great effort, he uprooted his feet from the floor and turned on his heel, ignoring Helen calling his name as she ran, half dressed, down the hallway after him. His long legs made purposeful strides down the hallway toward the exit. He ignored the small crowd gathering in the hallway. Helen was still in the pencil skirt and high heels she wore for her last scene. She clutched the lacy scraps of the bra to her chest with one hand while attempting to grab Brooks' arm with the other. He roughly brushed her hand away. She continued to spew words, and they started to reach his ears, piercing the bubble of dense fog around him. "Brooks, *STOP*! It's not what it looks like!"

"Wait! Brooks, *slow down*! You don't understand."

"Brooks, I love you! For goodness' sake, will you just *WAIT*?!"

"Brooks, people are *watching! Come back here!*"

"*Geez, this is exactly how I would write it,*" he thought. "*If I were a very unimaginative writer.*" He kept his long legs moving. One step at a time, one breath at time, until he was safely back in the parking lot ensconced in the driver seat of the Thunderbird. Helen, in her state of undress, stopped short of following him outside. Brooks peeled out of the lot but stomped hard on the brake at the exit. Without a word he reached into the backseat and handed the picnic basket with its wealth of gastronomic treasure to the parking lot attendant. "All yours, bud," he said gruffly. "Hope you're hungry." And he drove off.

The next morning, hungover and bleary eyed, Brooks re-entered the hushed quiet of the jewelry store he so buoyantly exited the day before. The old jeweler looked at him with kind, sympathetic eyes when Brooks set the velvet box on the counter. He spoke in a thick Greek accent. "I so sorry. It does happen, you know. Sometimes they no say yes." He shrugged his shoulders as he accepted the box back with wrinkled hands.

Brooks raised his gaze from his shoes and met the old man's eyes over the top of his aviators. "I didn't get around to asking," he said in a gravelly voice as he signed the return slip.

Brooks finished his story and sat quietly at the old farm table, staring at the floorboards. He rubbed his eyes, once again trying to erase the image of half-naked Helen in her dressing room.

GranNell got glittery eyed and sat up a little straighter when he mentioned the purchase of an engagement ring, but she didn't interrupt. By the time he finished, her expression changed to one of indignant anger.

"Oh, my sweet boy." She leaned forward and patted his hand again. "You should have led with the part about that blonde tart. I think this calls for something stronger than an Arnold Palmer." She pushed herself up slowly from the table and walked over to the mahogany and brass bar standing in the corner. She deftly poured a generous scotch for Brooks and a sherry for herself. She gestured to the glasses. "Carry these out to the porch, will you?"

Brooks obediently picked up the glasses and carried them out front. A breeze picked up off the water and he tried to let it carry away some of the gloom that had settled over him.

The sun hung low and heavy, casting glittering light over the small waves rolling in from the Gulf. An elderly man ambled along the beach. A terrier trotted alongside him, occasionally veering off course to chase the gulls as they skittered across the sand.

Nellie came out and sat down next to him in a rocking chair. "I could call your cousin Vinny, you know," she said with a sniff. "He still has questionable connections in Vegas. Shall we have someone drive out and pay this little Helen a visit?" GranNell pursed her lips and jutted her chin as turned to Brooks. Brooks just stared at her. "I'm only joking, darling. Sort of." She sipped her sherry. Brooks snorted.

"No, in truth I probably should thank Helen. Maybe I'll send a note in the mail," he joked. Then he remembered what Aggie said about being sad when Nellie left the island.

"Seriously, what was in your letter?"

"Well, quite a few things. And I am sorry to just drop this on you, but the fact is that I'm deeding you the house."

"What house? This house? I'm confused." Brooks wondered briefly if the scotch was going to his head.

"Yes, darling. Among other things, it has been called to my attention that I might not live forever."

"Oh, I'll argue that," laughed Brooks.

"No, dear, it seems there are a myriad of reasons a woman my age perhaps shouldn't live alone. I'm not saying I agree with all of them, mind you, but a few do have merit. The fact of the matter is that I'm deeding the beach house over to you, and I'm moving to Peach Tree House on the mainland."

Peach Tree House was a raucously expensive old folks home doing everything in its power not to resemble an old folk's home. Their success in this endeavor was impressive. Brooks visited once with Gran Nell years ago when she delivered a care package to a friend. He remembered it as a lush, green palace with expansive gardens and art classes.

Brooks' chair rocked forward hard and almost spit him out onto the deck.

"*What?!* Why? I mean, I just got here. You're moving?"

"Not to Brazil, child. Don't be dramatic. I did write to tell you, after all." Nellie eyeballed him pointedly, as she took another dainty sip of her sherry. "Anything that's left in the family coffers after I'm gone will go to charity. This way you won't have to deal with pesky attorneys to deal with the house."

"But I'm here now. I can swing by every day if you need me to." He realized in that moment that he had no intention of going back to California.

"You're a good boy, but I don't want a babysitter. And I don't want someone else living here with me, and yet it truly is just too big for one person. So that poses a quandary I have solved."

"What am I supposed to do with the house?"

"What most people do with houses, I suppose. You can live in it, or you could rent it out. You could turn it into a restaurant that will most likely fail in six months, although I wouldn't recommend that one. Or you can sell it."

"Sell it? It's been in our family for… since like…the beginning of time. You grew up here. Hell, I practically grew up here." Brooks heard himself and knew he sounded like a sullen teenager. "Wouldn't you be heartbroken if I sold it?" he asked in a quiet voice.

"Oh, my darling boy. You always were a softy." She laid her small, thin hand on his arm. "Let an old lady tell you something." She gestured at the house with her other hand. "These are just walls holding up a roof. Building materials well put together. Without people they have no value. Beautiful walls though they may be. They are simply a place to make memories with people you love. This house has given our family several lifetimes worth of those. But it is only a house." She pointed with an arthritic forefinger. "This place, it's too big for one person to rattle around in. And it reminds me that it's not full of people anymore. And that makes me sad. I'm moving to Peach Tree House to be around the few friends I still have that aren't dead. Even if they are little busybodies," she added, rolling her eyes.

"I've packed lightly for the move to Peach Tree. I'll have all I need. Except for someone to beat at cards," she added with a sideways glance. "So, you'll visit." It was a statement, not a question. "It's just across the causeway." She held up her glass as if to toast her move. After a few seconds, Brooks clinked it gently with his own.

"Well, yeah. Are you sure though? Really sure?"

"Yes, Brooks," she said, exasperated. And just as she had said to him as a small child refusing his request for a third lemon drop, "You have your answer, dear. Stop asking."

Chapter Three

Nellie sat in the rocker on the front porch of the beach house as the taillights of the Thunderbird grew small. She smiled to herself. He had come home. She did wish he had come back a long time ago when they could have lived on the island together. That would have been nice.

She lay her white head back to rest against the rocker. The sea breeze caressed her lined face. The gulls chatted with each other as they dipped into the waves in search of their supper. Her eyelids became heavy, as they often did these days, and she slipped into the familiar dreamland of long ago.

The summer of 1943 found seventeen-year-old Nellie Anne Francis pedaling her bicycle up Island Drive. The worn tires bumped over the cobblestone street running through the middle of town. Her father could have easily bought her new tires, or in fact a new bicycle, or a fleet of bicycles for that matter, if there were any to be had. But rubber and metal were rationed just like everything else that summer.

She flew past the tidy Island Drive Shops; the bakery, the hardware store, the barber shop with its red, white and blue pole turning round and round. Their brick and stone facades neatly lined up like little soldiers. Her curly blonde hair streamed out behind her as ribbons neatly tied that morning succumbed to the breeze and humidity.

Despite the war in Europe, ration cards and a shortage of basically everything, this had been the best summer of her young life. Nellie had quietly carried a torch for Billy Black since the day after her twelfth birthday when he pulled her pigtail and dared her to jump off the tool shed at the edge of the school play yard. She had done it, of course, spraining her ankle in the process. Billy had genuinely felt terrible and helped her back to class. That afternoon, she hobbled out the doorway of the schoolhouse, and there he was, waiting to offer her a ride home on the handlebars of his bicycle. He might as well have been a white knight riding a stallion.

The whole way home she alternated between fear she would fall off and make an even bigger fool of herself and wishing that the ride would last forever. She could feel his presence behind her, and his hot breath tickled the back of her neck when he stood up to pump the pedals, shooting goosebumps down her entire body and turning her insides to jelly. All too soon, they reached the big white house. She let him help her up the steps. At the door, he tugged one of her pigtails again, this time with affection. "See ya, kiddo. Next time someone dares you to do something dumb, tell 'em to go jump in the ocean."

She giggled and waved awkwardly as he rode off back towards town, her emotions a jumble of elation and misery. She was still giddy from the ride home, but Billy was fourteen and clearly still saw her as a little kid. This point was driven home to her daily in the weeks that followed as he rode off after school with Sally McPherson, (who was also fourteen and extremely developed for her age), on the handlebars of his bicycle.

But things were different now. Nellie was seventeen, practically a grown woman, and Billy was home from college for the summer working on his father's fishing boat.

He certainly noticed her when he strolled into The Blue Heron for a coffee early one June morning. Nellie and her two girlfriends, Gladys, and Emma Jean had commandeered a corner table to plan the planting of a Victory Garden. Nellie was asked to lead the project as her mother had the most coveted vegetable garden in town. Her family also happened to own plenty of land that would suit the purpose.

Billy's tall frame cast a long shadow in the doorway of the cafe, and Nellie looked up from her notebook with sketches of vegetable rows and lists of plants they needed to purchase. Of course, she knew he was back, but was determined to play it cool. As cool as Sally McPherson had been. Sally McPherson had been effortlessly cool. But Nellie was not cool. Not anything like it. She wore her emotions on her shirt sleeve in blinking neon. She couldn't fool anyone. Certainly not Emma Jean and Gladys, her companions since toddlerhood.

"Look who it is," whispered Gladys, elbowing Nellie in the ribs.

"Stop it, Gladys." Nellie was blushing a bright red.

"Be nice," Emma Jean said to Gladys. "You're always teasing her."

"I am being nice," Gladys hissed. "She'll thank me later."

Nellie wished desperately for the floor to open up and swallow her whole when Gladys stood up and waved an arm at Billy. "*Yoohoo*! Look who came all the way back from Houston to visit our little old island. If it isn't Billy Black."

Billy walked up to their table. "Morning, ladies. What are we working on?"

"Oh, Nellie is planning a Victory Garden," Gladys volunteered. "Her family donated the land and we're getting a committee together. Isn't that just wonderful?"

"It really is wonderful," said Billy, with a warm smile for Nellie. "We should all be doing our part."

"Yes, we should," replied Gladys as she stood, picking up her handbag and tugging Emma Jean to her feet by the sleeve of her dress. "Now, Emma Jean and I have appointments at the beauty shop, so we need to scoot. We'll see y'all later. Bye now."

Nellie would decide later if she was mad at Gladys or not. But right now, Billy Black was sitting less than three feet from her asking questions about sweet potatoes and whether they should also be encouraging everyone to build a chicken coop. Nellie shared her plans for the garden. Then she asked him about school and living in Houston. He told her about his classes and his dream of becoming a teacher. Maybe even a college professor. He enjoyed his history classes the most.

Then he broke off mid-sentence and glanced up at the clock hanging behind the counter. "Gosh, I'm sorry! I've got to go. My pop's gonna snap his cap if I'm late." He stood abruptly, almost knocking his chair over in the process.

"It's all right," Nellie smiled politely, but her insides felt like a balloon someone poked with a straight pin.

"Um," Billy paused and looked her in the eye. "Can I take you to dinner tonight?"

She couldn't stop the giant smile spreading across her face. Being cool was overrated. "Yes, Billy Black. Yes, you can." Nellie decided she was definitely *not* angry with Gladys.

Their dinner that evening was the first of many. Every minute of that summer when Billy wasn't working and Nellie wasn't planning the Victory Garden or busy with other volunteer projects to help the war effort, they found a way to be together. They swam in the Gulf and picnicked on the beach. They walked the trails of the bird sanctuary hand in hand. They met at the youth dances in the local VFW hall and jitterbugged to Glenn Miller. Sometimes they would sneak out of the hall and meet up in the dark alley behind, kissing until they were breathless, as if they would consume one another, and Nellie had to put a stop to it before they went too far. A war was raging, and newspaper headlines were grim, but the harsh realities of the world at large did not pierce their private bubble of joy. They made plans. He would have to go back to college in Houston at the beginning of September, and Nellie had one more year to finish high school. They settled that he would come back and speak to her father at Christmas, and they could have a June wedding after her graduation. Nellie had never been so happy.

That second Saturday in August was the annual Francis Island Sandcastle Building Contest and Nellie and Billy planned to win.

Nellie stood in Gladys' room and twirled in the yellow two piece bathing suit that had taken all her ration cards. "What do you think?"

Gladys was lounging on the bed flipping through an old magazine and didn't look up. "I think it's a thousand degrees outside. Why can't we hold this dumb contest in May?"

"Gladys! Seriously. What do you think of the swimsuit?."

Gladys looked up. "I think your parents are going to shoot you if they see it." But then her expression softened. "You look stunning."

"Thank you. I just know we're going to win. We'll win the twenty-five dollar cash prize, and our picture will be in the newspaper."

"Nell, I hate to be the one to tell you, but I don't think a prize winning sandcastle is going to make your father stop objecting to his daughter dating a fisherman's son."

Nellie's face fell. But then she brightened. "Maybe it won't, and maybe it will. But he can't stop us from being together. I love him, Gladys."

Gladys got up off the bed and hugged her. "I know you do. Have fun. Maybe I'll come down later."

Nellie's bicycle practically flew over the streets and down the boardwalk to the little patch of beach where she and Billy agreed to meet. She could see his tall, handsome figure as she approached. But what on earth was he wearing? That was the strangest beach costume she had ever seen. As she got closer, the bicycle suddenly weighed a thousand pounds and her heart fell into her stomach like a rock. The reason Billy looked odd was what he wasn't wearing. No swim trunks, no bag of tools swiped from his father's shed slung over his shoulder. He was wearing army fatigues, completely incongruous with the sand and surf.

Nellie slowed the bicycle to a stop before she reached him. She let it fall as she swung a leaden leg down to the ground. She walked across the soft sand as if through a fog, thinking no, no, no, no, no. As she got closer to him, her no's were audible, but still so soft they were tossed away by the ocean breeze.

Billy took off his sunglasses and stared at her, taking in her fetching daisy yellow swimming costume. It physically hurt him to do this to her. Like this. So sudden. So painfully abrupt to sever himself from her after this glorious summer. "I'm so sorry," he said as he took her in his arms, damned who saw them.

"You got called up," Nellie said, her voice thick with tears.

"No, Nell. I volunteered."

"You what?" She stepped back, hurt. "How could you do that? To me? To us? Without even talking to me?"

"I know." He paused and looked away for a minute, staring somewhere out over the ocean. When he fixed his gaze back on her, his own eyes were watery. "Nell,

Jack Neal is gone. His parents got the telegram yesterday morning. I can't simply sit by here, continuing to live my life while my best friends are laying down theirs for our country. For our safety. For yours, for mine, for our families." He was quiet for another minute and then he said, more softly "I'm scared to death to go, but I just don't think I can live with myself if I don't."

"Yes, yes you can! Stay here with me. We can find more ways to help here at home. Where there are no bullets or grenades. Tell them you changed your mind." Tears were streaming down her face now.

"It's too late. I signed the papers yesterday afternoon. I've got to catch the ferry to the mainland in an hour."

Nellie was stunned. Her words and her breath felt congealed in her throat. More hot tears welled up from her chest. Everything they had talked about. Everything they spent this summer planning. All her dreams for their future dissipated in front of her eyes like a mirage as she looked from him out onto the shimmering water.

He pulled her back to him and held her tight. He spoke gently into her hair. "I'm so sorry, Nellie. I'm so, so sorry. He held her back from him. The morning sun lit her face, and the breeze off the Gulf swept her blonde curls back from her face.

He wiped the tears from her cheeks. "I will come back to you. And we will do all the things we've planned.

I will come back to you. I swear it. I love you, Nellie Anne Francis. I love you, and I will come back to you. We will have the wedding we planned. We'll move to Houston while I finish school. I'll find a job and we'll buy a little house. We can stay in Houston, or we can come back here, and I'll teach at the island school. You can choose. We'll have as many babies as you want, and they'll all be able to swim before they can walk. I swear to you, I will come back, and I will make all our dreams come true. But please, Nellie, please hear me when I say I'll be worthless to you and everyone else if I stay."

Chapter Four

At four o'clock on the dot, Aggie flipped the Open sign around to Closed. She rested her head briefly against the window, her conversation with Shane rushing out of its box and straight to the front of her brain. She distracted herself by prepping dough and making menus for the next day. Then she attacked the floors with her bucket and mop. Only when the shop was gleaming, and there was nothing left to do did she head upstairs to her little apartment.

While the insulation in the historic building left something to be desired come summer and for a short stint in February, the apartment had a few things going for it. The door at the top of the stairs opened into an open living and kitchen area. Afternoon light filtered through the white linen curtains covering the tall front windows overlooking Main Street, giving the space a dreamy glow. An overstuffed, cream-colored sofa invited naps that Aggie didn't have the time or inclination for. A soft rug in muted blues covered the hardwoods. And at the back, a window above the kitchen sink offered a distant view of the Gulf of Mexico.

The previous owner ran out of money during renovations, and the kitchen was missing appliances when she moved in. But when Mr. O'Henry at the hardware store overestimated the island's demand for retro-inspired stoves and refrigerators in pale turquoise, and subsequently marked them at seventy percent off to make room for a line of stainless Thermador, Aggie scooped them up. She even sweet-talked Mr. O'Henry into free delivery with the promise of a month of free chocolate chip scones and lattes delivered discreetly to the hardware store. Left to his own devices, Mr. O'Henry would be Aggie's best customer. His wife, however, held the opinion that sugar was poison for the body and brain. And she always seemed to know when her husband snuck a pastry.

Aggie bypassed the kitchen, peeling her clothes off as she went. She dropped them neatly into a wicker hamper tucked behind the bathroom door and turned the shower on full blast. Her bathroom was tiny, but charming, with its clawfoot tub, original black and white penny tile, and brass fittings. She stepped gingerly into the shower. While the water pressure was reliable, the temperature was an absolute crapshoot. The finicky plumbing had two settings - freezing cold or scalding hot. Finding a happy medium required skills comparable to that of an ace safe cracker, making minuscule adjustments to the taps. Almost unbearably hot water pelted down. She let it pound the top of her head, willing the water to wash away the anxiety simmering in her chest ever since Shane's phone call.

Aggie finished rinsing the conditioner from her hair and turned off the water. Her skin was lobster pink from the heat. She wrapped herself in a fluffy Egyptian cotton towel, a holdover from her life in Houston when the cost of such little luxuries was of small consequence. She pulled on leggings and an oversized Tulane sweatshirt, moved her laptop from the desk to the sofa, and filled a kettle with water for tea. When it whistled, she plopped a hibiscus tea bag into her favorite mug and filled it with water. She returned to the living room and set the mug on the coffee table.

Sitting cross legged on the sofa, she balanced the computer on her lap and opened her spreadsheets. But she already knew the story they told with painful accuracy. Her margins were too slim. Her volume was too low. She needed more time. No one could get a new small business in the black in four months! She had to find another income stream. Something more than stocking a corner with t-shirts and coffee mugs. She carried her tea out onto her Juliette balcony to watch the sun sinking over the horizon, a dripping golden ball slowly sinking behind the downtown buildings lined up across the cobblestones. Soon the gas lamps would flicker to life and a few regulars would trickle into the Twisted Cork next door for happy hour.

Across the street, Mrs. Hernandez was locking up The Painting Bunting, the dress and gift shop she'd owned for the last thirty years. Sadie had told Aggie that Mrs. Hernandez owned over half of Main Street and was a little hacked she hadn't managed to snap up Aggie's building before she bought it. Aggie wouldn't admit it, but she was a little afraid of Mrs. Hernandez. She glanced up, and Aggie gave a little wave. Mrs. Hernandez didn't wave, only nodded slightly and headed up the street.

Aggie imagined going back into the office in Houston. It hadn't been that bad, had it? If she had to, if her savings was going to wither away to nothing before the shop was profitable, she could cut her losses. She could slip back into her old life. Sell her beautiful building. She could go back to what was safe and steady. And lucrative. In Houston, she was a predictable dot on a city map, home, gym, office, home, gym office. Was it only six months ago that she dropped her bombshell on Shane? She sipped her tea, and her thoughts drifted back to Houston and her old office.

It had been a Monday morning in July, and she had just returned from her first vacation in six years. She had tapped a nervous staccato on her desk, one ear trained to the hallway, as she clicked methodically through her in-box. She had been back less than twenty-four hours, and clients and employees alike were already pelting her with problems and complaints.

Unable to sit still any longer, she rose and crossed the expanse of her corner office to the window. Her feet protested the movement. After three weeks of sandy, salty, freedom, the high heels felt foreign and constricting on her feet, and the familiar tightening in her chest had returned the minute she crossed the 620 Loop. Down the hall a door opened, and two male voices floated down the corridor. Aggie stood still. The voices volleyed cheerful goodbyes. Only when the elevator doors dinged closed did she make her way down the hall.

Leaning against the door jamb, she knocked softly on the open door. Shane's back was to her, his attention already returned to his beloved spreadsheets. An impeccably styled head swung around at her knock. His large brown eyes, framed by tortoiseshell glasses, lit up, and he broke into a grin as he rose to envelop her in a hug.

"You're home! I didn't think you'd be in until tomorrow." He squeezed her tight, and she hugged him back, genuinely glad to see him, even if she dreaded the conversation that was looming.

"Did you meet Gabriel?" Shane asked. His enthusiasm was almost catching. "He just left. You're going to *loo-ove* him. He owns *three* different seafood restaurant chains. You might say he's quite the big fish." Shane winked at his pun. "And he has just signed with McAvoy and Jeffries for all his certified public accounting needs. Did I do good while you were gone or what?" Aggie could swear Shane's eyes actually twinkled when he talked business.

Aggie laughed despite her nerves and nodded. "You did swimmingly. Nice work."

Shane grabbed Aggie by the hand and tugged her towards the cushy armchairs facing his desk. "Come, sit, sit. I missed you! How was the vacation? Where were you, exactly? Sandy something or another? It better have been wonderful. I have had *quite* the time wrangling everyone around here." He fluttered his fingers in a circle indicating the entire floor of the sixty-story high rise the firm now occupied as he leaned against the desk.

"Sandcastle Island. It's only a four-hour drive. You've really never heard of it?"

Shane shook his head. Aggie snapped her fingers. "Oh, right, no Michelin restaurants or five-star resorts. Not your thing."

"Bingo," Shane said with a grin.

"Was it really that bad? Running things on your own?"

"Nah," Shane chuckled. "Gregory made me promise to lay on a little guilt. He wants to be sure we cash in on the duck confit dinner you promised before you left." He paused and held up a finger for effect. "With the cheesy potato business, *and* the chocolate soufflé."

Aggie let out a breath and smiled. "Of course." She loved cooking for Shane and Gregory. But she was going to owe Shane a lot more than a home cooked meal.

"Shane, we need to talk." She rose and shut the door.

"Okay." Shane moved to sit down at his desk, and Aggie took the chair opposite him. She took a calming breath.

"You remember how I was before I left?"

"I do." Shane replied, his tone losing its lightness. He took a good look at his old friend. She certainly looked better. Her thick chestnut locks shone, framing a clear, tanned complexion. The dark circles she'd sported for years had disappeared, and she had put on a pound or two. She seemed softer somehow. He nodded in approval. "You look fabulous! I don't know what you did for three weeks, but it did the trick."

Aggie smiled and leaned forward in her chair, hands on her knees. "Thanks, it sort of did do the trick." She paused and then spoke slowly. She couldn't quite meet Shane's gaze, and her eyes focused somewhere over his right shoulder, out the window at the smoggy Houston skyline. It was only mid-morning, but the buildings already shimmered with heat and humidity. Her practiced speech abandoned her. "I'm not sure I have the words to explain it, but while I was there… on the island… I just…I just felt more like myself than I have in *years*. I felt calm, centered. The people there are lovely, and the town looks like a postcard. There are actual cobblestone streets."

Aggie took another deep breath. It was better to just rip off the band aid. She gathered herself and looked him in the eye. "Shane, I want to move there. I put a contract on a building downtown on Sandcastle Island, and I want to open a coffee shop and bakery." The words started to spill from her mouth, unchecked. "You'll understand when you see it. I walked into this building, and I just fell in love. You know how I feel about old buildings. It's a hundred years old with all the original windows and millwork. It needs a little work, but it just has a soul. You can feel it. There's a little apartment above it where I can live until the business takes off. I made a low-ball offer on a whim. I never thought it would fly. But it did, and… I could breathe there, Shane. I can't breathe here anymore." Aggie slumped back in her chair, spent, and waited for the worst.

Shane was quiet for a full minute after she finished. She could practically see the computer of his brain clicking away, processing this new information, sorting through it, forcing it to make sense. Finally, he leaned forward and spoke.

"Let me get this straight. You want to leave the business? Leave Houston? Everything we built? Ags, this has been our dream since sophomore year. I thought this was everything you wanted. We've worked so hard. We've made it. We're even finally out of debt. You want to just *quit*?"

He was right. It had been their dream. But while the CPA route was something Shane took to naturally; Aggie chose the path because it felt safe. She would always be able to get a job. And there wasn't anything else she was passionate about. Not anything she could make a living at anyway. So, she sort of followed Shane along his path. She let his dream become hers.

She cast about for the right words and finally broke the silence that was stretching tight.

"I'm sorry. I'm so sorry. I know it's not fair. But I have to do this. And I want you to buy me out."

Shane's eyes widened and his voice rose an octave. "You're serious. Are you really going to leave your friends, your life, everything, to go open a coffee shop slash bakery on an island no one has heard of? How many coffee shops slash bakeries have we had on the books over the years? You know good and well it has at best a seventy-five percent chance of failing in its first year!"

"Gee, thanks for the vote of confidence."

"Ags, I have all the confidence in the world in you. No one works harder than you do. But really, you're going to just up and leave your life here?"

Aggie threw up her hands in exasperation. "What life? My parents are in Phoenix, my brother is in London, Lillian is in Colorado, and all my friends here are living it up in the suburbs with two-point-five kids and a labradoodle. Other than you and Gregory, my most meaningful relationships here are with the front desk guy at the gym and the girl who comes by with the lunch cart. I don't think this is the way it's supposed to be." Aggie's voice cracked, and she slumped back in her chair.

Shane ran a hand through his dark hair. He would have been less shocked if Aggie walked in with her hair dyed pink, announcing she was joining a Cyndi Lauper cover band. He removed his glasses and pinched the bridge of his nose. The long silence was palpable.

"What if I give you a year?"

"What?"

"I'll buy you out. Sort of."

Aggie's phone pinged just as the orange rim of the sun slipped fully out of sight, drawing her thoughts back to the present. The text was from Lillian. She blew out a breath and instantly felt guilty. She hadn't called to check on her friend in weeks. Lillian James Locke had been Aggie's best friend since second grade, the closest thing she had to a sister. Their teacher sat them in alphabetical order at the beginning of the year. When she rearranged her students after Christmas, they both resolutely refused to move desks. Almost four months ago Lillian's husband, Ben, underestimated the curve of a windy mountain road near their home. That in itself might have been fine if an oversized dump truck hadn't been straddling the middle line of the road going in the opposite direction. There was no time or space on the road for correction and he tragically left her a widow at the ripe old age of thirty-two. She was left alone to raise their eight-year-old son, Jude. Aggie was heartbroken for her friend. After the funeral, she didn't want to leave her, but she had just opened the shop and she couldn't spend any more time away. She tried to call and check in at least once a week. Aggie opened the text.

Lillian: Hiya.

Aggie: Hi, you! I've been meaning to call you for days. How are you?

Lillian: OK. You know, one foot in front of the other, one step at a time. All that crap the therapists say. Cold though. It's freezing here.

Aggie sent a screenshot of the Sandcastle Island forecast which showed nothing but abundant sunshine and seventy-five-degree temps for the next seven days.

Aggie: Want to come visit??

Lillian: God bless Texas winters. Lucky you. Actually, thinking about going down to the Cabo house. I need sun. Want to come keep Jude and me company? We can stop and pick you up.

Lillian was referring to the private jet service she and Ben had used for the past several years.

Aggie: You know I would love to. I would even brave an airplane for you, but I can't leave the shop.

Lillian: K. Maybe I can get to you soon?

Aggie: I would love that so, so, so much. Hug Jude for Aunt Aggie, ok?

Lillian: Will do.

Aggie: Hug yourself from me too. Love you.

Lillian: Will do. Love you back.

Later that night, Aggie climbed into her four-poster bed with the fluffy duvet and sixteen throw pillows feeling guilty. Lillian had real problems. She should stop feeling sorry for herself. She would come up with something.

Chapter Five

Brooks woke early the next morning to a cool, overcast sky. Excellent writing weather, he thought. Today he would absolutely, positively make a start on the new Chester McCombs. But first, coffee. He padded around the dated kitchen with its olive-green laminate countertops. He opened one creaking, wonky cabinet door after another until he found the French press he left there on one of his few trips before the move to California. After washing out a few dead bugs and a layer of dust, he set it aside and ground the beans he bought from Aggie the day before and set water to boil.

While waiting on the kettle, he carried a side table and a dining chair out onto the porch to set up a makeshift office. The air here had a texture to it, he thought. Almost like you could physically grab a handful. Maybe the next Chester McCombs book should be set at the beach. He was pulled from his musings by the whistling of the kettle.

A few minutes later, he was settled on the porch, fresh coffee and laptop on the makeshift desk, ready to put words on paper. He sipped the steaming brew. Brooks preferred his coffee exactly one degree below scalding. He set the mug down next to the laptop and poised his fingertips on the keyboard. The cursor blinked in the top left corner of the page. Five minutes later the same blinking cursor was giving him the stink eye, practically scowling at him from the top of the blank screen. Just start, he told himself. It doesn't have to be any good. Just put something on paper. Anything. The cursor blinked. His coffee cooled. No words ventured forth. *Dammit,* he thought. He leaned back in his chair. This was not his first writer's block rodeo. He needed to move. Maybe he'd go for a run. It couldn't hurt.

He glanced into the living room through the open doorway. His gaze fell on the shag carpet and the dated kitchen and fake wood paneling. He remembered all the ideas he had when he bought the house. Maybe he should just start. If he couldn't start the book, he would start his remodel. His handyman skills were admittedly minimal, but he figured demolition was in his wheelhouse. He could do a few things to get the ball rolling.

Yes, he thought, standing up, this is just the ticket. Nothing like some good old fashioned physical labor to get the creative juices flowing. He walked inside and examined the carpet, contemplating the best plan of attack. The far back corner appeared to be loose. He wrinkled his nose as he thought of what he might find underneath. Mold? More dead bugs? Or perhaps pristinely preserved original hardwoods? Doubtful, but there was only one way to find out. He walked over to the corner and bending over at the waist grabbed the corner and gave it a good yank. It didn't budge. He needed tools. A quick trip to the shed yielded an ancient hammer and a dry rotted pair of work gloves. He decided to forgo the gloves but took the hammer back inside. He used the back of it to pry back a few carpet tacks. Bending over again he grasped the corner and pulled with all his considerable strength. The carpet gave a smidge. Brooks kept pulling. The green shag was older than Brooks, and it proved a worthy adversary, giving itself up inches at a time. Brooks sat back, wiping sweat from his brow. He bent down once more and yanked as hard as he could, biceps bulging. All at once, a giant section came loose, and Brooks fell backwards at an awkward angle. He yelped as carpet tacks raked his fingers and his back shrieked in pain and began to spasm. He let out a string of four-letter words that would make a sailor blush. He sat still then, squatting, elbows on his knees, while he caught his breath. The finger pads of his right hand were dripping blood on the old shag, but that paled in comparison to the spasm in his back. He tried to stand up and the pain concentrated in one spot that pulsated angrily. It took him twenty minutes of alternated stretching and resting to make it over to the chair.

He eventually limped to the bathroom and returned with the aspirin bottle and a heating pad. Rather than doing anything productive, he spent the day lying on his back in the living room on the heating pad, watching old baseball games on his iPhone. But not before he shot off a text to Ambrose asking him when he could get a crew over to start on the house.

When the sun hung low and the shadows lengthened, he rolled to one side and made a move to raise himself off the floor. The pain was dulled but still present. He slowly limped out onto the porch, grabbing the bourbon bottle and a glass with one hand on the way. He set the glass and the bottle on the table next to his laptop that still sat there, and slowly lowered himself into the old wooden chair.

He poured a tall bourbon and took a gulp. The liquid burned as it hit his empty gut, and it occurred to him he should eat something. But one more gulp and the bourbon started to also work on his back. He rolled his head around, easing the tension that had taken up residence in his neck and shoulders. The laptop was still open on the table, and he tapped the keyboard once with his index finger. The screen came to life, a stark white against the darkening backdrop of the sky and ocean. A blank page with that damn cursor still blinking in the upper left corner.

"Shit," Brooks cursed. Although it was unclear if the curse was directed at the laptop, himself, the green shag carpet inside, the disloyal Helen or possibly the fictional Chester McCombs who simply refused to do anything interesting. Maybe he was just done. Not that he was counting, but this was his thirty-fourth attempt at the latest installment of his bestselling series. Maybe he was finished. The words just wouldn't come. Maybe whatever creative literary gifts that had been bestowed upon him were all used up. He was a dry well.

He finished his bourbon and poured another. He thought of Helen and of how close he thought he had been to a happily ever after. But it was all bullshit, all a lie. All waves of a Hollywood magician's wand. And all gone in less time than it took to strike a set.

He glanced at his phone. Fourteen missed calls and messages. All from Helen. None from any of the so-called "friends" he made in California. He tapped the screen. Delete. Delete. Delete. He had no interest in whatever Helen had to say.

Brooks had been called a master of words, or at least he used to be, he thought wryly with another dirty look at the laptop. And there were no words in the English language that would erase the feeling of all the oxygen being suctioned from his body when he walked in on Helen and that old jackass director. Maybe the jackass came on to her, or maybe she was in love with the jackass. Or perhaps she really and truly loved Brooks but was manipulating the old dude for her own purpose. Brooks wasn't sure if that would make him feel better or worse. Whatever it was, it didn't matter. It was broken.

His life in California was enjoyable. Life's version of an endless dessert table. The parties, the celebrities, people happy to stroke his ego. Everything was easy, the weather was beautiful, money flowed in, he had a beautiful woman on his arm. But as it turns out, none of that mattered. It wasn't real.

Brooks squinted and peered down, surprised to find his glass empty. He poured another bourbon. Twilight slowly faded to darkness, and he listened to the sounds he hadn't realized he missed until that moment. He could make out the sweet melody of a whippoorwill call, and a barn owl's low, hushed, w*hooo*. Layered underneath the nightbirds' song was a symphony of crickets and the rhythm of breaking waves. The sounds and the ocean breeze washed over him. The glass slipped from his hand as his head nodded forward and he fell into a deep, booze-soaked sleep.

Chapter Six

The following morning, Aggie glanced up from the assortment of rainbow-colored cupcakes she was arranging in the display case as Brooks limped through her door.

"Good morning," she said, smiling.

Brooks leaned on the counter without removing his aviators. "Is it?" he asked in a rough voice.

"Tough night?" Aggie asked.

"You could say that."

She pointed to his bandaged hand. "Is this the part where you tell me if I think you look bad, I should see the other guy?"

This got a half smile from Brooks. "I wish."

"Are you limping?"

"Yeah. It seems I may need to find a new line of work. I took a shot at construction. Or, I suppose, demolition. But as it turns out, I am a hazard to my own safety, and I should not be allowed to own so much as a screwdriver. Could I get a coffee please?"

"Hmm. Yes." Aggie eyes ran over the stubble on this chin. He was pale and slightly green underneath his tan. "When was the last time you ate?"

"Um…. breakfast yesterday?"

Aggie passed him the coffee. "Give me five minutes. Then you can tell me about your adventures in demolition."

Brooks sipped the intense Sumatra coffee and the pounding in his head slowly began to subside. Aggie returned with a breakfast sandwich. Crispy applewood smoked bacon, melted cheddar cheese, and a hard fried egg, all sandwiched in a homemade biscuit studded with jalapeños and sharp cheddar cheese. Brooks' stomach made an embarrassing sound. He was ravenous.

"Hangover helper," she said with a wink as she slid it across the counter and then sat a can of ice-cold Coca Cola and a glass of ice next to it. Beads of condensation dripped down the side of the can as Brooks nodded and popped the top.

"Good thought." He ignored the glass and downed half the Coke straight from the can. Brooks ate in silence with his eyes closed for a few minutes. "You are my hero," he finally said around a large bite, opening his eyes. "And this," he pointed to the plate, "is your superpower."

"Would you like another?"

Brooks nodded. "Pretty please."

Aggie laughed as she went back to the griddle. After he finished the first sandwich and started the second Brooks could physically feel his blood sugar stabilizing. Aggie's combination of caffeine, sugar, carbs and fat was a more effective hangover cure than any weird bartender concoction with tomato juice and raw eggs.

Aggie left him to eat in peace for a few minutes while she rotated pans in the ovens. When she returned, she studied him, her head tipped to one side. "You look better," she said, nodding approval. "Less gray."

"Thanks," he couldn't help but grin. "I feel better. I think I'll live now."

Slightly embarrassed, he told the story of his carpet catastrophe and his poor choice in medication.

"I think I can understand the medicinal booze. Just maybe a good idea to also, you know, eat food."

"Fair point. Why don't you give me something to go so I don't miss lunch? I have a meeting in a couple hours with a legitimate contractor to take over since I am obviously under qualified. They are going to show that shag carpet who's boss."

Chapter Seven

When Brooks pulled back into his driveway, Ambrose was already sitting on the porch, hat tipped over his face, boots propped on the railing. He rose when Brooks shut the car door.

"Hey there, son. What's goin' on over here?"

Brooks told his sad tale for the second time that morning, which earned him a hearty chuckle from Ambrose. "Well, you're in luck. The crew just finished up a job. We've got another starting soon, but if you can make some quick decisions, we can squeeze you in."

Brooks had a sneaky suspicion Ambrose pulled some strings rather than the crew just magically being available, but he was grateful either way.

"You got it. Hang on just a minute." Brooks ducked into the house. He returned to the front porch waving a set of rolled up papers triumphantly. "Remember these?"

"Ah, I think I do. Let's have a look." Ambrose blew on the papers and a cloud of dust took off on the breeze. He unrolled the stack and studied the plans the two men drew up years before. Ambrose made some muttering noises as he flipped the pages, before giving a decisive nod.

"Yep. I think we can make this work. You're gonna have to get over to the hardware store and pick out all your stuff. Faucets, tile, flooring and such. You may have to go to the mainland for a few things."

"I can do that." Brooks said without hesitation. It wasn't like he was making any headway on the book, anyway. Might as well make progress on something.

Ambrose rolled the plans back up and stuck them in his back pocket. "All right, I'll send the boys over first thing in the morning. They'll start demo."

Brooks woke the next morning with a feeling of purpose. Armed with quick decision-making skills, and the benefit of the cabin renovation brewing in the back of his mind for years, he made all his selections in one day. His makeshift office was once again set up on the cabin's front porch, and he could feel an inkling of an idea brewing for the start of the new manuscript.

The crew arrived at seven thirty on the dot. Brooks had a four o'clock card date with Nellie, but he would chain himself to his laptop until then. Brooks let the crew in and made a quick trip to the Bean and Bun for a coffee and a to-go sandwich, so he wouldn't have to break for lunch.

Back at the house he settled himself down intent on getting to work, proud of his outdoor office setup. He poised his fingers over the keyboard and started to type. Chester McCombs had sprung into action. Brooks' coffee sat untouched and grew cold. Two hours flew by without him noticing. Until that is, the crew opened the window around the side of the house and started chunking large swaths of the green carpet out into the yard.

Brooks tried to ignore the music from the workmen's radio coming from the open window and the hammering that started up as they got to work on the kitchen demo. After a few minutes he stood and went in search of his backpack. He was pretty sure the noise canceling headphones he used for air travel were in the bottom compartment.

Ten minutes later, headphones in place, he settled back down and returned to firming up the setting for Chester's newest escapade. The headphones were top of the line, but they were not meant to stand up to the racket of five guys with power tools.

Brooks looked down at the empty beach. He changed tactics and carried a folding chair and his laptop down to the sand along with his lunch. He re-situated himself, balancing the computer on his knees and got back to work. The waves and the wind drowned out the racket coming from the house. Perfect, he thought and started to type. The words were coming now. He wasn't particularly proud of the words, but he hoped if he just kept typing, Chester would come up with some good ideas. The sun came out from behind a cloud and made it impossible for him to see the screen. Frustrated, he toggled with the computer brightness settings. He kept working, adjusting the brightness every so often as the coastal sun played peek-a-boo behind white puffballs chasing each other across the stark blue sky.

When he had two thousand words on the page, he took a break and pulled out the sandwich. His teeth sunk into the homemade sourdough focaccia. Damn that woman could bake, he thought. Unlike Helen who couldn't be persuaded to learn to make grilled cheese. Not that she would have ever eaten cheese. Far too caloric. And bread of any sort was illegal as far as she was concerned. His thoughts yet again went back to the day he walked in on Helen half naked in her dressing room. It still stung, but he was starting to think he ego was injured more than his heart.

Brooks finished his sandwich, the laptop closed but still balanced on his knees. He was mentally congratulating himself on getting a good start on the book when he set the sandwich bag on the sand. A sudden gust of wind caught the bag and tossed it down the beach. Brooks reached for it and upset the laptop. Before he could get hold of either the bag or the computer, the laptop fell off his knees and into the sand.

"Dammit," Brooks cursed out loud. He made a final grab for the bag before it blew out of reach, stuffed it in his pocket and retrieved the computer. He opened it up and examined the keyboard. Not too bad, he thought, but there was a decent sprinkling of sand in between the keys on one side. He blew on the keyboard but then a bigger gust of wind tossed a handful of sand on the computer and in his face. He was reminded of the saying from grade school about March, something about blowing in like a lion. He had been spoiled to the even-tempered California weather.

He carried the laptop back up to the house which ironically was silent. The crew had wandered off to rest on the beds of their pick-up trucks and enjoy their own lunches.

Brooks spent half an hour on the front porch doing clean up duty on the keyboard. A few paper towels and a dozen q-tips later, he closed it back up and thought about his writing options. The cabin and beach were obviously out. He took the sandwich bag out of his pocket and tossed the Bean and Bun bag into the dumpster Ambrose delivered that morning. He wondered if Aggie would mind him taking up a table at her shop. Only one way to find out. He grabbed the laptop and hopped in the car.

Ten minutes later, Aggie looked up as the bell tinkled and Brooks walked in. "Well, hello again," she said with a smile. "Need another sandwich?"

"No, but I could use a caffeine infusion and little peace and quiet." He explained the situation at the cabin. "You mind if I hang out here?"

"Be my guest. It's my understanding that coffee shops are pretty popular with writers. I'll get your coffee. Another double shot Americano? Extra hot?"

"Yes, thanks. Now, which table do you think has inspiration and creative literary genius lurking underneath?"

"Hmm," Aggie glanced around. "My money would be on the sunny one by the front window. *However*, if you don't want the good people of Sandcastle to chat you up every five minutes, you might want to opt for the back one in the corner."

"Yep," he agreed. "That one looks lucky."

"Am I allowed to ask what you're working on?" asked Aggie.

Brooks hesitated. "Have you heard of Chester McCombs?"

"Sort of." Aggie thought back to her conversation with Sadie. "I've heard of him, but I haven't read the books or seen the movie."

"Well," Brooks said, "he is a modern-day international man of intrigue and mystery who has had seven books and two movies worth of riveting adventures. However, he also may be completely washed up as he refuses to engage in any activity more interesting than getting a cup of coffee."

"Well, I happen to think getting coffee can be very interesting." said Aggie.

The back of Brooks' neck tingled ever so slightly after she spoke. He held her gaze a few seconds longer than was appropriate, noticing the attractive pink of her cheeks and the way her hair fell around her face. "You know what? I think you might be right."

Brooks sat down with his headphones in place. Two Americanos and three hours later, he felt like he had at least half of a solid outline. He scrapped what he wrote that morning. Chester was now in Columbia, ordering coffee in a local bar. The drug cartel, a corrupt coffee farmer, and a new love interest were at play. He tipped his hat to Aggie who was busy serving cookies and cupcakes to an energetic after school crowd and went off to keep his card date with GranNell.

Brooks took the steps up to the beach house two at a time feeling massively pleased with his morning's work. Nellie opened the door with a smile. "I'm feeling lucky today, GranNell. Today's the day I may just break your winning streak."

"Hah, doubtful my dear boy." Nellie waved a hand toward the kitchen table. "Also, we have some business to attend to first. Go sit down."

Brooks glanced at the old farm table. At one end was an official looking sheaf of papers. "What's all this?" Brooks asked.

"It's the papers to deed you the house. Mr. McQueen, my attorney, should be here any minute to notarize them for us."

"You were serious about this?"

"As a heart attack, my dear." Nellie took a small pitcher of lemonade out the fridge and started setting out glasses and a tray of cookies. Brooks noticed the cookies were store bought. She used to turn her nose up at store bought cookies. He should have brought her something from the Bean and Bun, he thought as someone knocked on the door.

"Answer that, will you please?"

Brooks, assuming the role of sullen teenager once again, slumped his shoulders and reluctantly went to do as he was told. Mr. Sullivan McQueen, Esquire was efficient and tidy. After the lemonade and cookies were politely consumed, the legal papers transferring ownership of the family home to Brooks were dealt with swiftly. Mr. McQueen took his leave, and Brooks looked at Nellie across the table.

"I believe it is cocktail hour," said Nellie. "Why don't you pour, and I'll find a deck of cards?"

Over drinks, Brooks quickly lost three rounds of gin rummy.

"You are an absolute card shark," he grumbled.

"Why thank you," said Nellie with a smile. "The ladies of Peach Tree House better watch out."

"Really?" Brooks asked, his voice softening. "Is this really, truly what you want?"

"Yes, Brooks. As a matter of fact, could you clear your schedule for the day after tomorrow? I could use a ride on moving day."

"Yes, but are you really, really sure?"

"For goodness' sake, child, yes. For the very last time, I am sure. I'm looking forward to it. Half my old bridge group is there now, and I know I can whip every one of them. Also, bridge is Monday and Wednesday afternoons, so if you'd like, you can come help me sharpen my gin rummy skills on Tuesdays or Thursdays. And the food there is superb believe it or not. But if you wanted to bring some of Aggie's scones when you come, I wouldn't be too broken up about it. But be sure and bring them in a grocery bag and take them straight to my suite, mind you," she instructed. "I'm not certain I'll want to share." Brooks laughed and relaxed.

"Okay. You got it."

Chapter Eight

Brooks dumped his laptop bag on the back corner table of the Bean and Bun. Aggie now referred to it as the writers table as he'd been camped out there for three weeks straight. Brooks had settled into a routine. Early every morning, he went for a long run on the beach. He found the practice helped his creative juices flow as well as burned off the extra calories he picked up at the Bean and Bun every day. He would spend the morning and part of the afternoon holed up at his back corner table grinding away on his manuscript. Two afternoons a week he would take the ferry over the mainland and visit Nellie, always with treats from the Bean and Bun in tow.

He was almost superstitious about writing anywhere else now. The new Chester McCombs was finally shaping up. He hadn't flushed out the entire story yet, but the blank page with the blinking cursor no longer taunted him. Whatever put a cork in his creativity was somehow loosened and words flowed easily onto the page.

"You know," Aggie said by way of greeting, "when this book is a bestseller, you're going to be required to include the shop name in all marketing materials. Maybe the Bean and Bun will be like that cafe in Paris where writers go to try to sit in Hemingway's seat to find inspiration."

"More likely they'll find alcoholism," was Brooks' response.

"Maybe, but it's still good press. Plus, I don't sell alcohol, so they're safe." Aggie started the espresso for his coffee. She didn't even ask anymore. Double shot Americano with a splash of cream. Extra hot. No sugar. She also started bacon for the breakfast sandwich he ordered every morning.

"Is Nellie settling in at Peach Tree House?" she asked over her shoulder.

Brooks grinned. "She is more than settled. She is the self-appointed director of that cruise ship."

Aggie laughed. "Why am I not surprised?" she said, and then turned back to flip the sizzling bacon. She had grown comfortable with his daily presence in the corner of the shop. Sometimes he would zone out for hours, fingers flying over the keyboard of his laptop. The comings and goings of customers and the general buzz of the shop existed around him almost as if he was in a separate, bubble-like universe in the corner. Other times he would wander in and pester her in the kitchen.

He had also become her resident guinea pig. He gave everything rave reviews, with the exception of her most recent experiment. Such rave reviews that Aggie suspected he wasn't offering honest feedback. So, the previous week she tested a recipe for a licorice scone and waited for his reaction. He took a bite and was quiet. Then he looked up and made an apologetic face. "Sorry," he said. "Not a fan. I'm gonna pass."

"Okay, confession time. I was about ninety-eight, ninety-nine percent certain these would be a flop. But I was curious to see your reaction. But now I know you're giving honest opinions. Sorry you had to taste that."

"Have you tasted these?" he asked.

"No way." Aggie shook her head. "I hate licorice. Yuck."

That was the week before, and she had a new experiment for him to try today. His bacon sizzled on the stove. "Here, try this while you're waiting."

"Does it involve licorice?" he asked suspiciously.

"No," she laughed. "No licorice."

She started to hand him a steaming latte mug. Then she stopped, pulling the mug back towards her in midair. "First, you have to close your eyes and imagine it's cold and drizzly outside. One of those damp days when the chill gets in your bones." Texas is infamous for its fickle weather patterns. On that morning, it was hard to imagine anything but continued abundant sunshine, but the week was forecasted to close out with a bang. A strong cold front was on its way down from Canada, and

Sandcastle Island was predicted to be in for a cold and wet few days.

Brooks obediently closed his eyes. "I have an excellent imagination," he said, and Aggie could have sworn he shivered., imagining a winter day on Sandcastle Island. Brooks had an excellent imagination. It didn't get terribly cold on the Texas coast for long, but it was always humid, and a damp chill could get in your bones. He almost shivered.

"Ok, I'm ready," he said. With his eyes still closed, he reached out both hands, and .

Aggie carefully placed the mug in his grasp. She couldn't help but notice how his rolled-up shirtsleeves showcased his muscular forearms. She also couldn't help her fingers brushing against his as she transferred the drink. The connection lasted only a fraction of a second, but she felt it down to her toes. *Stop it!* She scolded herself. She liked Brooks, truly liked him. But they were friends. Not to mention he was on the rebound, and she had zero time for dating distractions if she was going to keep her business afloat. Shane's words echoed in her head daily. As the calendar crept closer to summer and the official kick-off of tourist season, business steadily picked up. Things were improving, but she was still solidly in the red. The merchandise corner she set up had all but sold out, and she had placed an order for more. She was looking for a venue to teach cooking classes. She thought those could be a decent money maker if she could pack more people in. But so far, she hadn't come up with anywhere large enough with a kitchen. The island was small, and her options were limited. She forced all inappropriate thoughts related to Brooks to the back of her mind and waited for his reaction to her latest concoction.

Today's experiment smelled much more promising than the licorice scone debacle. A cloud of steam rose from the mug and Brooks inhaled deeply with his eyes still closed. He registered aromas of chocolate, cinnamon, espresso, and was that caramel? He took a sip of the hot liquid. By this point, Aggie was familiar with his affection for drinks that came with the danger of second-degree burns. The creamy liquid was smooth as silk on his tongue, the chocolate and the coffee harmonizing with the spices.

Brooks swallowed and slowly opened his eyes.

"That…" he said slowly "is the best thing that ever happened to a chocolate bar. What is it? It's like hot chocolate, but it's not."

"It's a spin on an old-fashioned Mexican Drinking Chocolate. I found an old book on Mexican chocolate at a bookshop on the mainland. I took some liberties with the recipe."

Brooks took another sip and closed his eyes again. "It's so good. Different. I got chocolate and espresso.

And cinnamon, and caramel, and a tiny hit of something spicy. Maybe a touch a cayenne?" He re-opened his eyes to find Aggie staring at him.

"Color me impressed," she said. "How did you do that?"

"Elementary, my dear Watson." Brooks quipped and tapped his nose.

"Ah. Sherlock Holmes fan?"

"Yes, isn't everyone? However, I am in fact more of an Agatha Christie man."

"Oooh, me too. Although not as much as my mother. My mom loves her, like really, really loves her. Aggie is short for Agatha. She sort of named me after her. Which, come to think of it, is kind of embarrassing and now I'm wondering why I told you. I never tell anyone that."

Aggie gathered the mug back up. "If you tell anyone you'll have to find a new place to write."

Brooks crossed his heart with his fingers while he laughed. "Secret's safe with me. The chocolate's a win, though. People will pay big bucks for that on a cold day. Beats the hell out of the licorice scone business."

"Why thank you." Aggie smiled.

The bell on the door dinged and the first customer ordered a coffee and croissant. Brooks got down to work and Aggie spent yet another day running between the ovens, the coffee maker and the cash register. She thought once more that she really, really needed to hire an assistant. But that wasn't in her budget.

Brooks found a stopping point somewhere around two o'clock and headed over to check on the beach house. He still hadn't figured out what he wanted to do with it. Selling seemed the logical option. Nellie had been right about it being too large for one person. Also, he loved his secluded spot on the North end of the island. And when Ambrose was done with it the cabin would suit him perfectly. He had no interest in becoming a landlord. He just didn't have a use for the place, but the thought of putting it on the market didn't feel right either. Not to mention the weeks it would take him to get it ready to go on the market and the hassle of showing it to potential buyers and contract negotiations. Just the thought of it stressed him out. He was finally back to work, making steady progress on the new manuscript. He had sent his editor a rough draft of the first few chapters along with a semi complete outline, and it seemed to pacify him for now. The bi-weekly emails had slowed down. But he couldn't afford to take on another project. And getting the beach house ready to sell would be one hell of a project. And then he circled back to the fact that he wasn't sure he was willing to sell it. But it didn't make sense to have to keep checking on it every few days either. So, he left the beach house right back where he started, deciding to simply table the decision for now. He would finish the book first. Then he could figure out what to do with the beach house.

Chapter Nine

At six o'clock on Sunday evening, Aggie walked into the Twisted Cork carrying a box of her Texas Sheet Cake brownies and went straight to the back corner table where Amelia was already camped out with an ice bucket and a bottle of bubbles. She was grateful for the distraction. After she closed for the day, an email from Shane was waiting for her. It was a forwarded message from Mark Myers. There was no text. Just a link to an office space for rent one block over from their Houston office. Aggie shelved this to deal with later.

This evening, Amelia chose a Cava, Spain's delightful answer to French champagne. The Twisted Cork reminded Aggie of an old speakeasy. The bar that ran along one wall was a burnished walnut that seemed to glow under its own power. Its sheen reflected the small lamps and sconces that gave the room a cozy glow. The antique mirror covering the wall behind the bar reflected even more of the soft, warm light into the room. Amelia's eclectic taste in music was reflected in the bar's playlist. The tunes wafting from discreetly placed speakers ranged from Frank Sinatra to the Beatles, back to classic rock and then would swing over to Texas country tunes punctuated by a few contemporary pop numbers. Near the front windows were banquets with long benches that everyone squished into together, locals and tourists alike. Stools lined the bar and scattered around the room were bistro tables with velvet armchairs that always made Aggie want to curl up with a good book.

Aggie, Amelia and Sadie met one evening a month at the Twisted Cork for what they called book club. As with any decent book club worth its salt, there was always good wine accompanied by indulgent treats, lots of laughter and a minimal amount of actual literary discussion. Amelia suggested dropping the book club facade at one point, but Sadie was insistent that they keep up the charade. She claimed her guilt over leaving her husband alone with two tiny mischief makers for several hours was lessened if she were going to 'book club' then just out for drinks. Amelia pointed out the end result was exactly the same, but Sadie asked her to please just humor her. And so, they had.

"Where's Sadie?" Aggie asked as she slung her handbag over the back of a chair and set the box on the table.

"She texted. Running late. Something to do with the twins." Amelia shrugged. She didn't dislike children per se, they were just slightly beyond her grasp.

"My best friend, Lillian, has an eight-year-old. I remember when he was the twins' age. She came to visit once on her own and I think the first night she slept for fourteen hours."

"Fourteen hours of sleep sounds divine. Where do I sign up?" said Sadie overhearing Aggie as she sat down. "Sorry I'm late," she said, collapsing into her seat. "I'll be on time ten years from now. Maybe."

"No worries. How are things?"

"Chaotic. Crazy. Nuts. Insane. What's another synonym for one Lego injury away from totally losing my marbles'?" Amelia passed her a champagne flute filled to the tippy top and Sadie accepted it gratefully and took a healthy swallow.

"And work is unbelievable," Sadie added.

"What exactly qualifies as unbelievable in the real estate world?" asked Aggie.

"Ha!" Sadie snorted. "Depends on who you ask. It can mean lots of things. Sold six houses in one week? That qualifies as unbelievable. Sold nothing in eight months? Also, unbelievable. It's a nice little catch-all word that makes you sound successful and busy regardless. But this week it means that my phone hasn't stopped ringing since that article came out in Texas Monthly touting Sandcastle Island as a hidden gem. Everyone in Texas and half of California wants a place here all of a sudden."

"Can you hire an assistant?" Aggie asked.

"Look who's talking," Sadie retorted. "The queen of 'I can do everything myself,' in the flesh. You're worse than the twins."

"Fair enough," Aggie conceded.

"You need a vacation," said Amelia.

"Don't I know it. Mark and I would love to go somewhere, but neither one of our parents are willing to watch both kids for any length of time. And honestly, I can't say I blame them."

"How about a girls' trip?" Aggie suggested. "Mark could wrangle the kids for a few days, couldn't he?"

"Yes, he could, and bless his heart, he's offered. I'm thinking about a solo trip. All I really want is a few days, all by myself, where it's quiet, where I don't fix anyone's snacks, track down anyone's shoes, or missing Candy Land pieces, and not step on a Lego, and maybe possibly finish a thought. Also not listen to Peppa Pig or Sesame Street for a whole twenty-four hours. And get a massage. And maybe a facial. And just be silent. All by myself."

"My cousin once went to one of those retreats in India where everyone is in silence." Amelia offered. "She said it was life changing. Very zen."

"That sort of sounds like heaven. However, the logistics of traveling to India and back in the amount of time I can abandon my husband with two tiny humans does pose a challenge."

"Fair point," Amelia replied.

"I have been eyeing these retreats on Instagram, though." Sadie pulled out her phone and opened the app. "Look at these. It's like a spa day on steroids. The food looks amazing. Booze is included. The locations are stunning." She scrolled through photos of well-dressed women clinking wine glasses over glorious platters of food on beaches and in farm meadows and in vineyards with sunsets in the background. "This feed is like porn for thirty-something women. Look, here's one in Sonoma, and you go on wine tours and have a private class with a sommelier. There's a cheese making one in Maine near the coast. And a cooking school in Sedona - conveniently located next to one of the best spas in North America. *This* is what I'm after." The girls scrolled through the Instagram feed passing Sadie's phone back and forth, oohing and ahh-ing over the beautifully styled photos.

"You know what? We should do this!" said Amelia pointing to the phone.

Sadie replied, "I would love to, and I might. It's so pricey though. If you click through to the site…" Sadie tapped her phone a few times. "Look, only twelve spots for each one and it costs *five thousand* dollars a person for a weekend. It's a little out of my budget."

"No," Amelia shook her head. "I mean *we* should do this. Host one. Well, maybe not me per se, I have enough to do. But someone could host one of these retreats here on the island." Amelia leaned back in her seat. "We live *on…the…beach*." she said, enunciating the words. "In what I would call a charming, touristy little town. That was recently featured in Texas Monthly as Sadie just pointed out. I know it's not Napa, or Nantucket, or Sedona, but look!" She gestured out the window at the Sandcastle Island downtown all dreamily aglow with gas lamps and fairy lights.

Amelia leaned forward and moved to top up her friends' glasses. Aggie swiftly put a hand over her glass and shot her a sideways look. "No ma'am."

Amelia smiled, pushing the bottle toward Aggie. "Okay, fine. You're in charge."

"Thank you." Aggie topped up her friends' champagne flutes, but not her own. "Okay, just for shits and giggles mind you, where would one host a retreat worthy of a thirty-something woman parting with five grand for a weekend?" asked Aggie.

"Well, you could rent a beach house, but the cost to rent a big enough house for the time you need would probably eat up a pretty big chunk," said Sadie. "And you'd have to haul stuff in and out every time. It honestly sounds like a pain. Personally, I am barely," Sadie held her thumb and forefinger up about an inch apart to emphasize her point, "barely keeping my work/mama/wife head above water. I can't add any more jobs to my plate. I'm out on this, but you could maybe make it work if you could find the right rental for the right price."

"I'm out as well," Amelia added. "I'm still working on opening another location on the mainland. "But," she said, gesturing at Aggie with her champagne flute, "If you did this, I could come in and do wine tastings for you. We could work something out. I might sell some wine out of the deal."

"Hmm, I did host a few cooking classes at the bakery." Aggie said this slowly as the wheels in her head went into motion. "It was fun. A lot of fun actually, but my space is too small. You can't fit more than about four people in there, and the classes just didn't make enough money to justify the trouble. This is interesting though," she continued. She took a long pause, twirling her champagne flute. "I have to figure out a way to increase profits," she admitted. "The idea of going back to spreadsheets in Houston makes my stomach turn." She grimaced.

"Is that a possibility?!" Sadie turned to look sharply at her. "Your shop is always so busy. And your real estate agent also got you a killer deal on that space! Also," she frowned, "I cannot go back to Omar being the only coffee game in town. You cannot do that to me."

Aggie laughed. "Don't worry. Your caffeine supply is safe for now. But the shop is high volume, low margins. I'm simply pointing out that it would be smart to brainstorm some additional revenue streams." Was she ready to tell her friends that there might be a very real possibility her island days were numbered? Sadie gave her another sharp look and Aggie slumped a little in her chair. She had finally found real friends. If she couldn't tell them, who could she tell? "You guys remember Shane, my friend in Houston? My old business partner?" The girls nodded. "Well, when he bought me out of our accounting firm, he didn't want me to leave. We sort of made a deal that if I wasn't profitable in a year, I would sell my building here and use that money to buy back into the partnership. At the time it sounded good, it gave me a safety net. And if I am brutally honest with myself, in the back of my mind I thought that maybe if I took a year vacation of sorts, I would want to go back. I mean, I worked so hard to build that firm. I think part of me was hoping that I would want to go back. That life would feel like enough."

Amelia spoke up as Aggie paused for a sip of her Cava. "And *do* you want to go back?"

Aggie waited a beat, taking another sip. "No." She shook her head, setting her glass on the table. "No, I don't. But if I don't figure out a way to make an actual living here, I won't have a choice. And one of our employees is pressuring Shane to make him a partner. So, if I wait too long, there's a possibility I'll be going back as an employee rather than as a partner at the business I built." Aggie's gaze landed on Sadie's phone sitting on the table.

Aggie sat up a little straighter in her seat and leaned forward as she placed her hands on the table. "Let's talk about these retreats," she said, tapping Sadie's phone. She got very business-like all of a sudden, kicking into CPA mode. "If this was a client at the firm, I would advise them to buy a property under a named limited liability company as there would be a flood of tax write offs associated with it if run as a business. You could live in a small portion of it and write off probably eighty percent of the carrying costs, utilities, even the mortgage. "

"Could you do that? Buy a house, I mean." Amelia asked.

"Well," Aggie said slowly, "I always thought if I stayed, and the bakery took off, I'd buy a little cottage near the beach and rent out the bakery apartment. I don't have a note on the bakery building, but I'd have to get a loan to buy anything else. I'm not sure I'd qualify for a mortgage anymore. And certainly not for something beachfront that has the bedrooms to host enough guests to make it worth it."

Sadie piped up. "I'll beat the bushes. See what I can come up with."

"Thanks," Aggie said. "It's probably a pipe dream, but I'll think on it."

"Uh, oh, don't look now." Amelia nodded towards the door.

"What?" Aggie asked her eyes following Amelia's gaze.

"It's our favorite neighbor from across the street," Amelia said.

Mrs. Hernandez was standing by the bar. She stood out from the crowd in one of the colorful kaftans she sold in her shop.

"I'm surprised she's here. The last time I saw her, she huffed out of here so mad she was purple when I wouldn't even look at her offer to buy my building."

"She came to you directly?" Sadie asked.

"Yeah, a few months ago. She heard I want to open a location on the mainland and thought I could use the cash. Which I could, but I don't want to rent. I watched my parents at the mercy of their landlord for too many years."

Changing the subject, Amelia tapped the cover of her copy of Mansfield Park that sat on the corner of the table. "Did anyone even read this?" she asked. "I like Jane Austen, but I couldn't get into it."

"Me either." Aggie pointed a finger at Sadie. "You are not allowed to choose the next one."

"Okay, fine. You pick," Sadie retorted, gesturing at Aggie with her champagne flute.

"We could do an Agatha Christie," Aggie suggested, thinking back to her earlier conversation with Brooks. "That's a little bit more of a page turner."

"What's a page turner?" A male voice interrupted.

The girls looked up to see Brooks' six-foot-three frame towering over their table.

"Agatha Christie," Aggie replied, shooting him a warning look.

"Oh, I thought you meant this," he said pointing to the book on the table.

"Not hardly. Sadie has just lost book choosing privileges." quipped Amelia.

"Well, if your literary talk has concluded for the evening, may I buy you ladies a drink?"

The girls nodded, and Brooks wandered over to the bar where Amelia's newest employee, Ernest, who while looking slightly frazzled, was holding his own managing the Sunday evening crowd. When Brooks was out of earshot, Amelia hissed at Aggie. "What is up with you two? He's at the coffee shop, like every single day."

"Shh," Aggie whispered back. "There is nothing up with us. We're friends. He just needs a quiet place to write his book is all."

"Book? What book?" asked Amelia

"He's a writer, that's his job. He writes this series about a guy named Chester McCombs." Aggie supplied.

"Wait. I've read those books. That is Brooks Jagger?"

"No. Yes. His name is Brooks Schmidt. And keep your voice down," Aggie shushed her.

"Same person," Sadie offered. "Jagger is a pen name. He came back here and bought a beach cabin a few years ago. But then his books started getting made into movies and rumor was he left for California. But he's back. And he seems to have taken a shine to our girl."

"He has not!" Aggie spat out. "And hush. Here he comes."

Brooks was heading back with a tray, balancing their drinks.

"Oh gosh," said Sadie suddenly, as Brooks approached. She faked a look at her dark phone. "Mark just texted. Sounds like the inmates are taking over the asylum at home. I better scoot. You guys have fun." She shot Amelia a pointed look as she gathered up her handbag and made for the door.

"Oh, yeah," said Amelia. "I'm sorry, but I need to get over to the bar. The new guy looks like he's drowning."

Brooks spun a chair around and lowered himself onto it, draping his muscular forearms over the top chair slat. His long legs stretched to either side in a way that seemed to take up all the space. Aggie could feel the warmth from his body and smell his soap, woodsy with some sort of spice. "Was it something I said?" he asked with a low laugh that made Aggie's stomach flip inside out.

"No, not at all. Sadie needed to get home to the twins, and Amelia is always up and down when we meet here."

"Well, looks like we have some drinking to do." He pointed to the tray with four glasses he'd just laid on the table.

Warning bells went off in Aggie's head. Danger, they said. Stay back, they said. Heartbreak ahead, they said. She finally, in that moment, admitted to herself that she was hopelessly crushing on Brooks, and there wasn't a damn thing she could do about it. There was just something about him that was different from any of the guys she'd dated in Houston. They'd always felt two dimensional somehow. And there was a depth to Brooks she wanted to dive into headfirst. But there were only two ways this could play out for her. One, he would end up with his America's Most Beautiful girlfriend, who Aggie was embarrassed to say she had Googled and had to admit, the title was accurately placed. When she compared her own petite frame and chestnut curls to Helen's long, tan legs and platinum locks she felt downright frumpy. Option two, Aggie would be financially belly up and back in Houston by Christmas and never see him again. She started to say, *I should really get back.* But the alcohol had made her brain pleasantly slack. Her insides were warm and fuzzy. And there wasn't any harm in talking. She shouldn't be rude to a guy who was quickly becoming one of her best customers. It was bad business.

So, she picked up a glass and said, "Lucky thing tomorrow's my day off." And just like that, her responsible two drink limit went out the window. Again.

Two glasses later, Brooks asked "Hey, do you ever go down to the beach at night?"

"No. Why?"

"I've been wanting to go look at something and tonight is perfect. You up for a field trip?"

By now her whole body was buzzing and she nodded enthusiastically. She blew a kiss to Amelia on her way out. Aggie and Brooks giggled like school children as they walked unsteadily down the block to the wooden walkway that led over the dunes and down to the beach.

"It's pitch black out here," said Aggie, her eyes struggling to adjust to the dark.

"I know, this is perfect. Come with me." His hand found hers, and he pulled her closer to the shore. "Okay, just stand here and watch." Aggie tried to ignore the heat rushing through her body from where his hand held hers.

"Watch what? I can't see a thing."

"There!" He exclaimed, squeezing her hand. "Look!" The waves glowed with a ghostly blue light along their wave line as they crested. "Do you see that?"

"Yes. It's glowing. What on Earth? Has there been some kind of chemical spill?"

"No, nothing like that."

"Then what is it?"

"Well, if you take Nellie's word for it, the mermaids are throwing one hell of a disco party. But if you must get all scientific, its technical name is bioluminescence. Sort of like a fleet of microscopic, underwater fireflies. When they're disturbed by the motion of the waves, they release a flash caused by a chemical reaction that's part of their defense mechanism."

Aggie was mesmerized. "I like Nellie's version better."

"Me too."

They stood side by side watching the dancing, unearthly glow as the waves rolled in one after another, breaking softly near their feet. Brooks backed away slightly from the water's edge to where the sand was dry and sat down. Aggie sat next to him, still entranced.

"So, what about you?" Brooks asked in the dark.

"What do you mean?"

"How did you become a baker?"

"Hah. I didn't. I became a CPA."

"I'm not sure I follow, but okay. Did you always want to be a CPA?" Brooks asked good-naturedly.

"No." The champagne was making her head buzzy and her words loose. "I didn't know what I wanted to be. I just knew what I didn't want to be."

"And what was that?"

"I'm not sure exactly how to explain it. But when I was thirteen, my dad lost his job. We weren't wealthy, but we were comfortable, and we were happy. My brother was already off at college. My dad was sure he would find a new job right away, and he and my mom did a very good job of not looking worried. At first it was like nothing changed, except my dad was home more. But then they started to fight. They got snippy and the mood in our house shifted. Everything felt tense, too quiet." Aggie paused and took a breath. She never shared this with anyone. Not even Shane knew the real reason she'd chosen finance as her major or the reason she always worked extra hours instead of investing in any sort of a personal life. Lillian knew, but only because she'd lived it, with Aggie spending a lot of that year at her house.

Brooks quietly waited, and Aggie finally continued, her eyes still focused somewhere out over the inky water while her fingers drew circles in the soft sand.

"My dad sunk into a pretty bad depression, and my mom started looking for a job when it became clear he stopped looking for one. She had never worked a day in her life. She was the cookie baking, PTO president type. But envelopes with these angry, red, "final notice" stamps started coming through the mail slot. One day, I was finishing my algebra homework at the dining room table when my mom came home from the department store. My dad was on the couch, watching Bob Barker tell people to *'come on down!'* I still can't watch that show. Anyway, my dad was furious when he saw her shopping bag. He asked her what exactly she bought that was so important. She started crying and told him she had a job interview, and she thought she needed to look the part. She had bought a skirt suit on clearance. It probably cost thirty bucks. It was lilac polyester. She pulled the suit out of the bag, and my dad just stared at it, dumbfounded. Finally, he apologized and started crying too. He told her to go try it on, and when she came back, he hugged her and told her she was beautiful. My mom got that job, a secretary in a law office, and it kept us afloat until my dad found work, which he did. And my mom loved the law office so much she went back to school and became a paralegal. They survived that rough patch, and maybe they're better off for it. But I just never, ever wanted to feel like that again. I know money isn't everything, but it keeps you safe and it allows you to take care of the people you love. So, I wanted to know how to make money and how to save money, and how to grow money. So, I majored in finance."

Brooks was quiet for a little while. "Thank you for telling me," he said softly. "I still don't know how you ended up here. Are you running an accounting firm in the back of The Bean and Bun? Laundering money, perhaps?"

"No, of course not," Aggie laughed.

"So, exactly how did you come to be the best baker on Sandcastle Island?"

Aggie shrugged "Simple enough. I came for a vacation. Original, I know. I was your garden variety burn out case and thought a couple weeks of sun and quiet would fix me up, and I would go back to work. But I fell in love with the island. I fell in love with who *I was* when I was on the island. And when I went back, it all felt foreign and forced and like I was missing out on something important."

"Like what?"

"Like life. Like people. Like friends. Like doing something with my days that brings me joy instead of just saving other people money. Some days I just felt like Ebenezer Scrooge in a pencil skirt. It felt so flat."

"So, what did you do?"

"I sold my half of the firm and sunk that and pretty much all my savings into The Bean and Bun."

"That had to be scary."

"Petrifying." Aggie glanced over at Brooks. Her eyes had adjusted to the dark and she could make out his profile with his strong jaw and full lips. She needed to not focus on those lips. "A lot of people think I'm nuts. I mean, I had it all, I'd made it, and I gave it up."

"I don't think you're nuts." He said softly as he turned to face her.

She turned and felt Brooks leaning toward her in the dark. Was he going to kiss her? Every fiber in her being wanted him to kiss her. But what if he wasn't? And what if he did? What would that do to their friendship? Aggie's body desperately wanted to feel his arms around her, but her brain was screaming that this was a terrible idea. He was on the rebound. And he was drunk. And she was drunk. And she really, really liked him. She liked him too much for a drunken romp on the beach he would regret in the morning. Friends was better than a one-night stand. There was no way this, if *this* was anything, could be more right now. Mere weeks ago, he planned a proposal to another woman, for crying out loud. Not to mention she had to stay laser focused on her business. Her brain reeled from confusion and cava. He leaned ever so slightly toward her. Was he about to kiss her? In the end, she ducked her head down just before she would have found out and gave him an awkward hug. Sobered up, she said, "Thank you, Brooks. This was beautiful." They walked back in silence.

"See you in the morning," said Brooks as she let herself into the Bean and Bun to go up to her apartment. For one reckless second she considered inviting him in. Instead, she just said, "I'm closed tomorrow, remember? But see you Tuesday?"

"Oh, right. See you Tuesday." Aggie slipped inside, but watched him walk back to his car in the flickering glow of the gas lamp posts, a sinking feeling in her gut.

Chapter Ten

Aggie wandered down to the beach the next morning with her coffee and a croissant. She looked to see if she could see any traces of the bioluminescence, but it was impossible during the day. It was as if the magic from last night simply faded away. She thought about Brooks. Had he been about to kiss her? Well, she'd never know now. And if he was, she had done the right thing. Hadn't she?

To take her mind off Brooks she pondered the evening's earlier events, specifically the discussion about beach cooking retreats. She picked up her coffee cup, tossed the last of the croissant to the birds and headed back to her apartment. She spent the rest of the day sitting on her balcony with a notebook and her laptop doing research and running numbers. By dinnertime, she had a business plan and financial projections. The idea really wasn't a bad one. If she could find a house she could afford, and someone willing to give her a mortgage, she could also live there and rent out the bakery apartment. She spent some time scrolling the sites for other retreats around the country, mind boggled at the prices people were paying for an "experience vacation".

Clearly, it would be a ton of work. She needed a website, a social media account, and a hundred other things, but she was inspired. She could absolutely do this. It could be the answer to everything. She just needed to find the right place.

She called to check in on Lillian. She told her all about the previous evening, including the slightly surreal bit about walking down to the beach in the pitch dark with a handsome man to watch magical, light dancing waves and dodging a possibly, but possibly not, imaginary kiss.

"You what?" said Lillian. "Well, that was dumb. Why wouldn't you let him kiss you?"

"Because I like him. A lot."

"Well, that makes boatloads of sense," replied Lillian, her voice dripping with sarcasm.

"I know, but…." Aggie gave her a bare bones version of Brooks' Helen story. "He's on the rebound. Whoever he hooks up with now will be like a rubber ball and bounce him back into the universe. Right?"

"Maybe. But also, maybe not. You said he's renovating his house? Sounds to me like he's not headed back to Hollywood anytime soon."

"It doesn't matter. If he was, I blew it. Anyway, I've also been working on something else. You run with a pretty fancy-pants crowd. What do you think of this?" Aggie proceeded to tell Lillian about the idea of the cooking retreats at the beach.

"Oh, I think that will absolutely work. A woman in my yoga class was just talking my ear off about one she went to in Florida. She paid out the nose for it and I don't think it offered half the amenities you just listed."

"Okay!" said Aggie. She was getting excited now. "Now I just have to find a beach house."

"Well, good luck. I think it's great." Then she added, "And Ags, next time a handsome man tries to kiss you on a deserted beach while watching a magical light show, for goodness' sake, please let him. You're allowed a little fun, you know. There is more to life than work."

"So, I've been told," said Aggie.

"Love you."

"Love you too. Hug Jude for Aunt Aggie."

"Will do. Bye."

"Bye."

Aggie hung up the phone and despite what she just said to Lillian, opened her laptop and started a new spreadsheet.

Chapter Eleven

On Tuesday morning Brooks walked in just as Aggie opened the shop, a big grin on his face. "You look like you're up to something," said Aggie.

"I brought you a present."

"A present?"

"Yep," he said, unzipping his backpack.

With the pride of a seven-year-old showing off a prize piece of artwork, he held up three copies of the first Chester McCombs book. "For your next book club. Now, I would never go so far as to compare my meager writing talent to that of a literary hero such as Ms. Austen. But I have been told this one is a page turner."

Aggie grinned. "Thank you! But," she said, a sheepish expression on her face as she pulled a copy from under the counter and held it up. "I ordered one last week."

"I'm flattered," said Brooks seriously.

"Don't be," she joked. "I haven't read it yet. But I'll give these to the girls. It'll be our next book club book. I promise."

"I'll be anxiously awaiting the reviews." Brooks was joking, but somehow, it mattered to him what Aggie thought. He had dozens of glowing reviews from well-respected figures within the literary universe. But he realized he couldn't wait to hear what she thought.

A little after three o'clock, Brooks switched off the noise canceling headphones. It had been a frustrating day. For over three weeks now, the words flowed out of brain and through his fingertips onto the keyboard. Working from the Bean and Bun somehow made him forget to worry about anything. He was excited to go in every morning. He was calm and inspired there. The shop was the perfect spot to write. It was always spotless, and it smelled amazing. He should probably add a mile or two to his daily run to make up for all the treats Aggie dropped at his table. Anytime she tried anything new. Or when she made something that was one of her favorites and said he just had to try it. The writing was pouring out of him. But today he was stuck.

As he packed away his laptop Sadie walked in for her daily caffeine fix prior to pre-school pick up. Sadie's order was always a large, iced Americano. Three shots, splash of cream, a shot of agave, and one pump of vanilla. Even Brooks knew this after almost a month of observing the shop's daily rhythms. Sadie claimed if she missed the afternoon caffeine infusion, she wouldn't make it through the evening with the twins. Caffeine was her survival tactic when it came to mothering her high energy children. Today though, Sadie was brandishing her iPad, clearly excited. "Aggie, you have to see this!" she cried, holding out the tablet.

"What's that?" said Aggie, starting the espresso machine.

"Remember the retreats we talked about the other night?"

"You mean two days ago? Yes, I remember two days ago. Did you find one to book?"

"No, not yet. I meant us talking about *you* hosting cooking retreats. A beach house popped up for sale literally ten minutes ago that would be absolute perfection!" Sadie started tapping on the iPad. "It's right smack on the beach," she gushed as she tapped the screen to flip through the pictures for Aggie to see. "It has six bedrooms, and they all have their own bath. The kitchen is huge, and it's completely updated. I, personally, would pay big bucks to be your first guest." Sadie was practically jumping up and down like an excited puppy.

"Wow this *is* stunning." Aggie scrolled through the rest of the photos. The whole place was white on white with high ceilings and pale wood planked floors with tall windows offering panoramic views of the dunes, sand, and the ocean. Aggie kept scrolling until she found the property details. Her face fell. "Oof, the price. There's no way. Sorry, sister," she said, handing the iPad back to Sadie.

"What are we studying so intently over here?" Brooks asked, sidling alongside the two women.

"Oh, nothing," said Aggie. "Just dreaming."

"My favorite topic," said Brooks. "What about?"

Aggie put her hands on her hips. "Did anyone ever tell you that you are awfully nosy?"

"Oh, yes," quipped Brooks right back. "It's one of my better qualities. Also known as curiosity. Being curious leads to many things, among them ideas for books." He tapped the backpack that held his laptop. "When I'm stuck sometimes, I'll go find a seat in some crowded place and just very *nosily* listen to all the conversations going on around me. It's amazing inspiration. Speaking of that, I should go try it this afternoon."

Aggie and Sadie laughed. But when Aggie still didn't answer his question, Sadie answered for her.

"We think Aggie should start a new business teaching cooking retreats. She certainly has the skill set, but we need a location." She tapped the iPad. "Which this property would be perfect for, but it seems it won't work."

"Wait, whoa, what do you mean new business? What about the Bean and Bun?" Brooks asked anxiously.

"Don't worry, your favorite writing spot isn't going anywhere. This would be in addition to running the

Bean the Bun," Aggie replied. Sadie showed Brooks the Instagram feed the girls pored over at the bar two nights ago.

"Which brings us to the additional problem that there is only one of me." Aggie added. "I would need to find an assistant to help out a few hours a day and also run the shop while I'm busy hosting retreats. Which costs more money up front. It's a bit of a chicken and egg scenario. I'm working on it." She looked at Sadie. "I did think about it A lot. I even ran some numbers. I think it could work, but not with that property," she said, pointing to the iPad. "And I need to find out if I could even qualify for a mortgage these days. Banks don't typically love self-employed people. Sorry Sadie, the house is lovely. But it's too far out of the budget."

"Okay, okay. I get it." She accepted the coffee Aggie passed across the counter. "I'll keep an eye out. Maybe we can find a fixer upper." She slipped her iPad into her handbag between a pack of baby wipes and a box of crayons. "I'm off to pick up the tiny humans. I'll make some calls tomorrow and see if I can come up with something. I'll also send you the number of a mortgage guy. You can see what he says."

Sadie took off with a backward wave, and Aggie shifted her gaze to Brooks. "I think she might be even more excited about this idea than I am."

"Are you excited about it?" Brooks asked.

"I am," she nodded. "I really, really am. The Bean and Bun is doing well, but if I want to make a career out of this and not go back to Houston with my tail between my legs, I need additional income streams." She pulled out the spreadsheet she created the night before. It felt good to talk her business ideas over with someone. "Anyway," she concluded, after she ran through her projections, "I think it can work. And I think it would also be so much fun." She smiled. "But we'll see."

"Well, if anyone can make it work, it's you," said Brooks. "I don't think I've ever met anyone as hardworking as you. I've been here almost a month and aside from the other night at the bar, I've never even seen you sit down."

Aggie felt her face get warm at the mention of the other night, but she just laughed.

"Ha!" she said. "That is the definition of a workaholic. And I've been told that is not one of my best traits."

"There are worse traits. Well, good luck. I'm off to meet GranNell for dinner and to let her beat me at cards."

"I don't think anyone will believe that you *let* her win."

"Don't tell anyone, but I think in my entire life I've won maybe six games."

"Not surprising at all. Tell her I said hi. See you tomorrow."

"Yeah, see you tomorrow. Bye."

Brooks left, and Aggie closed up the shop soon after and went upstairs to make dinner. One couldn't live on baked goods alone. She pulled chanterelle mushrooms from the farmers market from the fridge. She set a skillet on the stove, plopped a generous pat of local salted butter in the middle and waited for it to sizzle. Just as the butter started to foam, she added the golden mushrooms in the pan. Once the butter and heat turned them an even more golden brown, she added garlic and fresh ginger along with curry powder, a splash of soy sauce and coconut milk. The mushrooms would cook perfectly well unattended, but it soothed her to stand there, nudging them gently with her spatula as the fragrant steam rose and dissipated into the air.

She eventually left them to simmer on their own and sat down at her laptop and pulled up a search for nearby beach houses for sale. She sorted them by price. There had to be something she could afford. She scrolled through several listings of homes that had already been redone and were therefore commanding top dollar. She re-sorted her list, moving the least expensive homes to the top of the page. The pickings were slim. The only ones she thought she could afford were several rows back from the beach. She couldn't imagine anyone parting with the kind of money she would need to charge if they weren't waking up to an ocean view. Depressed, she closed the laptop and went back to the stove. She nudged the mushrooms once more and dipped a finger in the sauce. The coconut milk concentrated down with the aromatics to a silky, sensual sauce that clung to the chanterelles like a blanket. Aggie turned off the heat and poured the decadent mushrooms onto a plate. This was the beauty of living alone, she thought. One could prepare one single, gorgeous dish and call it dinner. She ate at the small bistro table on her balcony, watching as the town rolled up the sidewalks for the day. She waved to Mr. O'Henry as he locked up the hardware store. He gave a wave and headed for his pick-up truck. Aggie felt a sudden pang at how much she would miss all of this if she had to go back to Houston. Shane would give her a job, no questions asked, even if she didn't make his deadline to step back in as a partner. But the thought of going back to that life, to high heels, and smog, and grumpy clients, of leaving this little island, her friends and her beloved Bean and Bun, made her throat burn with unshed tears.

She finished her dinner, washed the plate and pan and tidied her already clean kitchen. Then she opened the laptop once more. There had to be something, she thought. But there wasn't. Nothing had magically appeared within her budget in the list of beach homes for sale in the last hour. Aggie went to bed early, and even though her belly was full, she had a hollow feeling in her gut.

Chapter Twelve

Brooks left the Bean and Bun, his mind occupied with Chester McCombs. Before heading to meet Nellie, he swung by to make his weekly inspection of the beach house. He let himself in through the back door. The house felt weird without Nellie. Empty and sort of sad. He really needed to think about selling it. The part of him wanting to hang on to it was losing to the part of him that needed to finish a manuscript. He went through the house, mentally cataloging all the tasks that needed to be completed before he could put the old girl on the market. He would have to clean out all the drawers and cabinets, double check with Nellie to make sure nothing she left behind was a treasure. Even though she insisted she didn't want any of this stuff, he still had a hard time believing she would be fine just passing their family heirlooms on to the next owner or letting strangers rifle through them at an estate sale. He needed to get the house off his plate, but when was he going to have time to go through a hundred years' worth of stuff? He stood in the living room wondering where the best place was to start. If he worked on this for say, an hour a day, how long would it take him to have the house ready to sell? And could he sell?

Brooks was pulled from his mental tug of war when a fat drop of water plunked on his head. He started and yelped. "*What the…?*" He swiped water from his hair just as another heavy drop smacked him on the forehead. He looked up to see there was in fact water dripping down from the living room ceiling. What was directly above him? It had to be the bath attached to the front upstairs bedroom. Brooks took the stairs two at a time. There, he found a pool of water on the floor. Closer inspection revealed the culprit, a leaking pipe leading to the toilet. Brooks reached over the puddle to turn the water off at the wall and then started sopping up the mess with bath towels. As he was carrying an armful of wet towels downstairs to the laundry his phone buzzed in his pocket. It was still buzzing when he deposited the sopping mess into the washing machine and fished into his pocket. It was Avery, his agent. Brooks groaned audibly before reluctantly answering the call.

"Hello, Avery," he grunted.

"Hello, old boy." Even though he and Avery were roughly the same age, Avery spoke like someone's grandfather. Or possibly someone's great-grandfather. Brooks always imagined him chomping on an unlit cigar with his feet on his desk.

"What can I do for you, Avery?" Brooks held the phone to his shoulder with his chin as he poured detergent in the ancient washing machine.

"Just calling to check in. The movie folks are anxious to see the new manuscript before we ink the contract for the rest of the series. Where are we?"

"*We're* working on it." Brooks tried not to growl into the phone.

"Fine, fine. When can I see pages?"

"I sent you an outline two weeks ago."

"I know, I know, but I want to see something a little more concrete before I send it over to the studio."

"I'm working on it, Avery."

"Right-o, right-o, just send me what you have. I have a meeting with them in a couple weeks."

"Fine. I'll send you something by the end of the week."

"That'll do, my boy. When are you coming back to civilization?"

Brooks cocked his head. He thought he made it clear he wasn't coming back. Perhaps he never verbalized it.

"I'm not. I mean, I'll have to come back eventually for the rest of my stuff before my lease is up. But I'm staying."

"You're *staying* on that tiny island?" Avery said this as if Brooks announced he was going to live in a hut in Nepal. "I've never even heard of it."

"Good," Brooks said tightly, slamming the lid on the washing machine and turning the dial.

Avery brushed off the comment. "Alright, old boy, fine, fine. I'll look forward to reading pages over the weekend." And with that, he signed off, leaving Brooks standing in the laundry room with his phone in his hand. Dammit. He had to finish the book. What was he going to do about the house? He didn't have time for this. Not in the least. "Dammit!" He cursed out loud. Then he texted Ambrose and asked him to send over a plumber. He sat on the kitchen counter and dialed Nellie.

"Brooks! Hello darling. Are you on your way?"

"No. I'm sorry. Can we move our plans to tomorrow? We've got a bit of a problem at the beach house."

"Of course, dear. Gladys can stand to take another beating at gin rummy." Brooks thought he heard Gladys say something in the background.

"What was that?" he asked.

"Oh, nothing. Gladys is just grumpy. She's fine. And I'll see you tomorrow. What's wrong at the house?"

"Oh, nothing too terrible. Leaky pipe. I'm waiting on Ambrose."

"All right, darling. I'm sorry. I'll see you tomorrow."

"Okay, I've got to go - Ambrose just pulled up."

"Okay, bye, bye, sweetheart."

Brooks ended the call and went to let Ambrose in. The older man surveyed the damage. He opened a tool bag and went to work.

"Sorry, Ambrose, I didn't mean for you to rush over."

"No trouble. I was just down at the O'Henrys. Clara was trying to thank me for fixing her sink with a gluten free, dairy free, sugar free cookie. Thing tasted like old cardboard. I appreciate the escape." He laughed and went to work on the pipe. Twenty minutes later, he was packing up his tools. "You know, Brooks, if you're not going to live here, you probably need to sell it. These old houses, they need people in them to head off stuff like this. If this leak had gone on much longer, you could have had a much bigger issue.

"I know. It's hard."

"I know, kiddo." Ambrose looked him in the eye and put a hand on his shoulder. "You'll figure it out. I'll see you later. I'm gonna go see if the Bean and Bun is still open. I need a real cookie."

Chapter Thirteen

The next morning, Brooks tapped on the door of the Bean and Bun before it was open. A perturbed Aggie opened the door.

"I'm not open yet," she said with her hands on her hips. She started walking back towards the kitchen, talking over her shoulder. "You can come in, but unless you want to make it yourself, you're going to have to wait for coffee."

"That's okay, I think you may be very happy I'm here early." He sat down at the counter and put his backpack on the floor.

"Oh yeah? Why's that?" Aggie turned from the kitchen door. Damn, he looked good, she thought.

"Well," Brooks began slowly. "GranNell deeded our family beach house to me when she moved to Peach Tree House. I don't want to live in it. I much prefer the North End and my cabin renovation is almost complete - at least that is what Ambrose keeps promising. I planned on selling it at some point. What if I sell it to you?" Aggie just stared at him, dumbfounded.

"What? Are you kidding? You're not serious."

"I am totally serious." Brooks held up three fingers. "Scout's honor."

"Were you truly a Boy Scout?"

"Yes. Pack 284. You would be doing me a favor. If I put it on the market, I'm going to have to go through every nook, cranny and drawer of that house, empty it out, spruce it up and deal with showings, etcetera, etcetera. My editor is pestering me for more pages of the new book. And I currently have no clue what Chester's next move is. So, I would really appreciate it if I could sell it, quick, simple and clean. I can only do that if I sell it to someone I trust, just in case you find pirate gold in the walls or something. If you take it as is, and I don't have to do any work, I could make you a very, very good deal."

"Brooks, I can't do that. I can't take advantage of you like that. Also, what would Nellie say?"

"She'd be thrilled. She was fine with me selling to a stranger, so it stands to reason she would be more than happy selling to a friend. That way she could visit. And if you baked her your blueberry lemon scones in her old kitchen, odds are she would not only be thrilled for you, she would probably bring a very extravagant housewarming gift."

Aggie just stood at the counter, speechless. A pair of young tourists walked in, startling her out of her stupor. They ordered a cappuccino and a latte, and

Brooks sat politely waiting as she brewed the drinks on auto pilot, her mind reeling. After the couple walked back out onto the street, she turned slowly back to Brooks. "Let's just say this is an actual possibility. I don't even know if I can qualify for a loan. I used up almost all my cash reserves on this place."

"Well," said Brooks, the wheels in his brain turning quickly. "What if I financed it? This is not a bad idea. Hear me out." His thoughts were spinning faster than he could spit them out at Aggie. "How about this? We set up a rent to own scenario. You pay me monthly, and I apply it toward a note. I'm no loan shark, the rate will be comparable to what you would get at a bank. We both avoid closing costs. If for some reason it doesn't work out, it will be as if you were renting it, and I'll keep the house. If it does work, at some point you finance with a bank. Simple enough. Although, you showed me, in great detail, what I would consider a pretty solid business plan. I have a suspicion that this *will* work. I think this will be a success that exceeds even the projections on this little spreadsheet of yours." He tapped the paper that was still sitting on the counter.

"Brooks." Aggie looked up at him. "I don't know what to say. You're amazing. Really?"

"I very much enjoy being amazing. Thank you. And I think we just solved each other's problems. Really."

"And you are sure Nellie won't mind?"

"I am one thousand and fifty percent positive, but if you don't believe me, why don't you come with me to Peach Tree House tomorrow afternoon, and she can tell you herself?"

"Um, yes." Aggie stammered. "Okay. Oh my gosh, I have so much to do. This is crazy."

"Would you like to go see your new house? You might want to look over the whole thing before you agree to this. To the best of my knowledge, Ambrose has kept everything in good shape, but the old girl is over a hundred years old."

"You have a point." Then she flipped her spreadsheet over and in heavy black marker, hastily wrote "BACK IN AN HOUR" and taped it to the front door.

Brooks laughed and held the door for her. He walked around to the passenger side of the Thunderbird and opened her door while she locked up.

"Thanks," said Aggie. "I don't remember the last time someone opened a car door for me."

"Really?" said Brooks. "GranNell would have my hide if I let a woman open her own door."

"Some women would say that is a very sexist comment."

"Would you happen to be one of those women?"

Aggie thought for a second and shook her head. "As a matter of fact, no, I don't think I am. Thank you, Brooks."

Aggie walked through the front door of the beach house almost as if in a trance. She saw the house with fresh eyes. There was a large front room with sliding doors that led into a dining room and another set of sliding doors leading to the kitchen beyond that.

"Do you think we could take down these walls and open up this whole space?" Aggie wondered out loud.

"I would think so, but we can get Ambrose over here to take a look before you sign anything if you want."

"Okay, that's a good idea. And I do need to talk to the bank. I would still need to get a loan for any work on the place."

"Alrighty," said Brooks. At that moment Aggie's phone pinged with a text from Sadie with a link to another house option, quickly followed by text with the info for her mortgage guy. Aggie slipped the phone back in her pocket, and she and Brooks continued the tour. Behind the kitchen was a large pantry.

"Wow, this is huge," said Aggie.

"Remember when the house was built, getting supplies was a huge pain, so they stored a lot of stuff in here."

"I think it's big enough for everything I would need, and I could also make a little office space along that wall," said Aggie, pointing. Off the pantry was a small, screened in back porch.

"I used to sleep on this porch when I was little," said Brooks.

"Really? What an amazing place this must have been to grow up."

"It really was. I mostly only spent the summers here, but all my favorite childhood memories take place about a stone's throw from this spot."

"Lucky you." Aggie glanced around. "There are still a lot of family mementos here. Surely Nellie wants some of these."

"She packed up everything she said she wanted when she moved to Peach Tree. But you can certainly double check with her. That's sort of the part I don't have time for. You'd have to deal with all the stuff."

"I can do that," said Aggie. She could tell it would be boatloads of work. But if Brooks was really and truly willing to sell to her for the well below market price he was quoting, she was willing to do just about anything. They walked back out into the front room. There was yet another set of beautiful wooden sliding double doors with aged brass hardware leading into another room off the living area. Aggie pushed them apart. She hadn't seen this part of the downstairs before. The doors slid easily on their tracks. "Oh. Wow," she said. "Just wow."

"It's my favorite room too."

Opposite where they stood was a stone fireplace. The front wall had a huge bay window that flooded the space with light and offered expansive views of the ocean. But the other two walls are what rendered Aggie speechless. Every inch of wall space that wasn't taken up by the fireplace, windows, or doors held floor to ceiling bookcases stuffed with books. The polished wood gleamed in the sunlight and more of the aged brass hardware attached a rolling ladder to the wall for access to the higher shelves. Which was necessary as the first floor ceilings had to be sixteen feet tall.

"Oh. My. Goodness," said Aggie, slowly turning in the middle of the room, taking in every detail. "An honest to goodness, actual library. I've always wanted one. Is there also a secret passageway somewhere?" she joked, turning to Brooks.

He just laughed. "Not exactly."

"What? You mean, there's sort of a secret passageway?"

"No, not really. But this is kind of cool." Brooks moved a set of books about midway down a shelf. Hidden there was a recessed area with a lever on the side. He pulled the lever down and a section of the wall popped forward. Aggie jumped. Behind the wall was a space about four foot wide and six foot deep. "This always creeped me out as a kid. But my great- great-grandfather was a little paranoid. In his defense, they did host a lot of different folks over the years. Some friends, some strangers. This library functioned as his office, and he used this space to hide valuables or important papers. Or so I was told. But I digress, shall we continue?"

Aggie had no words. She just nodded and stood motionless while Brooks re-assembled the wall. They exited the library and on their right was a wide staircase with a gorgeous hand carved rail with a wooden dolphin as the finial.

"I can't believe I didn't notice the dolphin before," she said. "The details, the craftsmanship here, it's just… it's just, I don't know. I have no words." She gazed up at the intricately carved moldings on the ceiling.

He grinned at her. "Good thing we already agreed to a price. You're not playing your cards very close to the vest." She smiled but said nothing as she started up the wide wooden staircase, running her hand along the banister. The wood was worn smooth as silk. Upstairs there were five bedrooms. They weren't huge as bedrooms weren't back then. They did, however, each have an attached bath. Great, Great Grandpa Francis had spared no expense in the construction of his family's vacation retreat and wanted his guests to not only be comfortable, but also impressed by his wealth. All the bedrooms had doors out to a second story deck that wrapped all the way around the house, the same as the deck on the main level. At the end of the hall was a smaller door.

"Where does that go?" asked Aggie.

"Oh, this is cool. It was my favorite rainy day play place as a kid."

Aggie tugged the door open. It was tight in its frame as if no one had opened it in a long time. It revealed a dark and narrow staircase leading up to a third level.

"Really? This was your favorite? Looks a little creepy to me."

"It's fine," said Brooks. "And I have an idea for it for you. Go on, to the best of my knowledge there are no ghosts." He held up two fingers.

"Yeah, yeah, Scout's honor," Aggie grumbled. "Okay." She took a breath and ventured upward in the darkness. She reached for a handrail but missed it. Her foot caught on the step, and she fell backwards on the steep stairs. Luckily Brooks was right behind her and broke her fall. She forced herself to ignore the jolt of electricity that went through her entire body as they made contact. If he was going to be holding her mortgage, she was going to have to get a grip on her hormones.

"Is there a light?" she asked.

"Somewhere, yes." His long arm reached over her head and felt around in the dark until he found a string hanging from the ceiling. Harsh light from a bare bulb now illuminated what Aggie could now see was a very dusty staircase with spiderwebs clinging to the ceiling overhead.

"Okay, so it could do with a cleaning." He shrugged his shoulders. "Go on, I promise it's worth it."

"Have I ever mentioned that I really, really don't like spiders?"

"You happen to be in the company of a very competent spider killer." He pointed to his shoes. "Size twelve spider stompers at your service. Go on," he said for the third time. "It's better at the top. Trust me." Aggie pushed on, forcing herself to concentrate on the square of light at the top of the stairs and not look down at what might be lurking in the corners of the staircase. As she emerged from the steep staircase and stepped out onto the floored attic space, she let out a sigh.

"Ah. I see," she sighed. Each of the four walls boasted a dormer window, and the sunlight streamed in. Unfinished oak planks covered the floor. The space was filled with old trunks and wardrobes and boxes and odd pieces of furniture. She felt very much like one of the March sisters from *Little Women*.

Brooks pointed to the window with a view of the ocean. From their vantage point three floors up, the view was exquisite. You could see for miles. "I wrote my first short story right over there," he said, pointing to a small window seat. "I was about ten. It was all about pirates. On rainy days my brothers and I would play up here. We'd make forts and play hide and seek. If we were super good and promised to leave no crumbs, GranNell would bring up a picnic."

Aggie smiled. "That's so cool." She looked at Brooks. The air felt slightly electric as the dust motes floated in the air and they held each other's gaze. *No, no, no*. Aggie thought. She broke their gaze and peered out the window. "My nephew is super into pirates. And also, dinosaurs."

"All boys are into dinosaurs," laughed Brooks.

"So, what was your idea for up here?"

"Well, I thought if you are going to rent out all the rooms downstairs, this would make a great little apartment for you. After we evict all the spiders, of course." Aggie shivered involuntarily. Brooks continued as he crossed to the corner of the attic. "I'm almost certain there is a bathroom directly underneath here, so you could tap into the plumbing to add a bath. I figure you wouldn't need a kitchen up here, but there's plenty of room to make a little bedroom and sitting area. What do you think?"

Aggie felt the same way she did the first time she walked into the dusty, dirty bakery building. As she stood there listening to Brooks, she could see the project unfold in her mind's eye. Yes, a very, very thorough cleaning. A coat of paint. Some furniture. She had a view on all sides. Now that her wheels were turning, she could see the downstairs coming to life too. She would keep all the original details she could. She would have to gut the kitchen and open up the walls. She would paint most everything white but keep the gorgeous original wood floors. Some brightly colored rugs and throw pillows. Some of the furniture she would be able to use, but she would mix in a few more modern pieces. But it would all feel comfy, a place to relax and recharge. A place you would want to return to again and again. And a place that hopefully people would be willing to pay a pretty penny for their stay.

"Oh my gosh. I can't believe it," she said, breaking out into a grin. Brooks laughed at her when she hopped up and down twice in glee.

"So, you like my idea?"

"So much. So, so much."

Chapter Fourteen

The following afternoon, Brooks and Aggie left as soon as Aggie closed up shop to pay Nellie a visit at Peach Tree House. Aggie brought a box of scones and a bag of her homemade granola as well as a bag of freshly ground coffee beans as a gift. She and Brooks arrived at Peach Tree House a little before five o'clock.

"Wow" said Aggie as they came up the palm lined drive. "This looks nicer than a lot of hotels I've stayed in."

"It is," said Brooks, parking the car. They walked up the crushed shell drive past the brightly colored hibiscus, and bougainvillea, and potted plumeria plants that framed the big picture windows. Inside, Aggie noticed there were none of the unpleasant odors that are common to assisted living facilities. It smelled fresh and floral with a hint of savory baking wafting in from somewhere. There was soft music playing and tables set up around the room. There was a couple playing chess and a few people involved in what appeared to be an energetic round of spades. "*I keep telling you not to count your queens!*" One old man yelled to the woman across the table as he threw his cards down.

"Sometimes the volume does get a little loud. Half these folks forget to turn their hearing aids on," Brooks said. They continued down a hallway to a door at the back of the building. The door led out into a walled courtyard filled to bursting with more flowering plants. There was a bocce ball court and shuffleboard along one of the bougainvillea covered walls. In the far corner of the courtyard underneath a massive magnolia tree sat two women with artist easels intent on their work. A smartly dressed nurse was making her way around the yard inquiring if anyone needed anything.

"This is fantastic," said Aggie. "Forget the beach house. Can I just stay here?"

"You could, but it will cost you a pretty penny." Aggie almost fainted when Brooks discreetly shared the monthly expense of Peach Tree House.

"Well, nothing but the best for Nellie."

"Indeed. And speaking of my favorite Peach Tree resident." They approached a foursome gathered around a table in the shade drinking lemonade and working on various forms of fiber art. "Hey, I didn't know you could knit?"

"Well, I can't. Not very well anyway." She held up a lopsided bright purple project. "But it keeps the fingers nimble. Never stop moving, they say."

"Well, in that spirit, how about a little exercise?" He held his hand out for her. "Hello ladies," he said, addressing her companions. "We've brought some treats. Can I leave these in your care while I steal my Gran for a little walk about?" His request was met with a chorus of coquettish yeses.

"Ladies!" Nellie admonished the group. "One would think you'd never seen a handsome young man before. Good grief." She tried to look irritated, but she was proud to show off her handsome young grandson who visited her twice a week, usually with a box of goodies. "Well," said Nellie. "This is a lovely surprise." She rose nimbly from the table. She hugged Aggie and then Brooks. As soon as they were out of earshot she said to Brooks, "I think I'm a bit cross with you. Aggie clearly brought those lovely treats for me, and those biddies will make short work of them. There best be a blueberry lemon when I get back."

Aggie giggled. "I'll be happy to bring more."

"You are a love, my dear." And Nellie linked arms with Aggie. The threesome walked the little path that led out of the courtyard and down through the meticulously groomed grounds of the Peach Tree estate. Brooks stopped at a bench underneath another majestic magnolia. "Why don't we sit here?"

"Lovely, my dear," said Nellie and primly took a seat at one end, forcing Aggie and Brooks to sit next to each other. Aggie tried hard to ignore the way her knee tingled where it brushed against Brooks' thigh while

Brooks explained their plan for the beach house to Nellie.

"I told Aggie I knew you would be fine with it, but she insisted on hearing it from the horse's mouth."

"I'm not sure I like being compared to a horse, but I think it's a wonderful idea. So innovative. And if you are sharing baking secrets, Aggie dear, then I may be one of your first guests."

"Oh, I would love that so much," said Aggie and she squeezed the old lady's hand.

"Now, let's go see if those old biddies left us any scones."

Chapter Fifteen

Now that Aggie had a plan, she sprang into action with her typical efficiency. Not having to jump through the eight hundred hoops required to obtain a mortgage as a self-employed individual saved her weeks of valuable time. She did meet with Sadie's banker and was able to secure a line of credit against the bakery building that would cover renovations, furnishings and setting up the business. Which she reminded herself would all be fully tax deductible as she got this fledgling business off the ground. She refused to think about what would happen if she defaulted.

She met with Ambrose the following week an hour after she and Brooks signed all the paperwork transferring the beach house officially into her name. She had been thrilled when Ambrose said the walls dividing the front living space could certainly come down, opening up the small front room, the dining room, and the kitchen into one large airy space. The kitchen would be a full remodel as would her upstairs apartment. Each of the upstairs bedrooms needed various amounts of work, as did the bathrooms. Three of the bathrooms still had the original tile work and clawfoot tubs. In an unfortunate decision sometime in the nineteen sixties, it seemed someone tackled a renovation of their own in the two other baths, swapping the lovely black and white penny tiles for avocado green in one and salmon pink in the other. Those would need to be gutted and re-fitted. She would also add a small built-in desk in the pantry area which would function as her office, tucked away from guests.

Ambrose suggested starting on the upstairs apartment first so she could go ahead and move in, allowing her to rent out the bakery apartment to generate some income. Aggie liked this plan, even though it meant she would be living in a dust bowl and without a kitchen for a period of time. She could live with that. She spent most of her time and ate most of her meals at the Bean and Bun anyway. She was also thrilled to learn that the long-promised completion of Brooks' beach cabin was finally imminent, and Ambrose and his crew could start sometime the following week.

That evening Aggie, Brooks, Amelia, and Sadie popped a celebratory bottle of Champagne at the Twisted Cork. "To new adventures!" said Brooks. Aggie held out her phone and snapped a photo of the four of them.

Chapter Sixteen

While Aggie was busy celebrating and planning her next steps, in Colorado, her best friend was still struggling to put one foot in front of the other. The morning after Aggie officially bought the beach house, Lillian Locke stared into the flames dancing in the massive fireplace of her living room. The coffee mug she held with both hands was more for warmth than caffeine. Nothing could keep her warm these days. Granted, early April in the Colorado mountains is not known as a warm weather destination. The thick, chunky knit sweater layered over the workout gear she lived in, hung on her tall frame. Her athletic body, normally toned by daily yoga and long hikes in the mountains, had grown bony. Since Ben's accident, food just didn't sound appealing. Lately, everything pretty much tasted the same to her. Like sawdust. Chewing was a chore.

She met Ben when he gave a presentation to an entrepreneurship class she signed up for on a whim in college. Later, he turned up at the goofy karaoke bar in the French Quarter where she and Aggie hung out with Shane on Thursday nights. He was eight years her senior, but once they met, they were inseparable. They were married as soon as Lillian finished her English Lit degree, and their only son, Jude, came along a few years later. Life with Ben was never dull. Benjamin Locke did nothing by halves. Everything he did, he went big. Houses, cars, vacations, gifts, charitable contributions. Grand gestures were his signature style. Ben dropped out of college to move to San Francisco at the age of twenty-one. When he and Lillian met, he already owned a successful software company. Shortly after their marriage, he developed a program that he eventually sold for a hefty sum to a Fortune 500 financial corporation. That sale set them up for life, and they purchased the Colorado house to be near Ben's hometown. He continued to take on occasional projects when something came along that interested him, but mostly his time was his own, which meant he got bored. Ben was a loving husband and devoted father, but he also had an impulsive streak. Once, on their way back to a hotel in Denver, they drove by a car dealership and left with a spanking new Ferrari. Lillian never liked fast cars and taking turns on windy mountain roads terrified her. She herself drove a tank of a Land Rover with four-wheel drive. Two summers prior, on a trip to Cabo San Lucas, Ben bought a beach house as a surprise gift for Lillian. "For anytime you can't get warm," he said when he presented her with the keys. That was also about the time they started using the private jet service.

She looked back into the fire and then out the big picture window that framed the snow-capped mountains in the distance. Her eyes felt hot as they unwillingly misted, and the mountain shimmered in the distance. The tears didn't come full force anymore. Not the deep, wrenching, body racking sobs that would overtake her when she suddenly remembered she was, in fact, a widow. What in the hell was she supposed to do with the rest of her life? The accident plunged their family's sunny, carefree existence into a black abyss. For Jude's sake, she forced herself to get out of bed every morning, to make sure he ate breakfast and did his homework and drove him to the fancy private school Ben had chosen.

She did the things people told her she needed to do. She kept regular appointments with a therapist for herself, and also for Jude. She took the antidepressants faithfully. She even went back to yoga. The flow of movement and breath eased the tension in her chest just enough that she could breathe for a little while. The studio felt like a safe space. She did her best to slip in right as class started and leave before anyone could ask how she was or what her plans were. The answers *"pretty shitty"* and *"I have no fucking clue,"* didn't change and weren't exactly suitable for casual chit chat in the serene little Zen Studio. So, until she had better answers, she thought it best to keep to herself.

She flicked her gaze to the gold Cartier watch on her left wrist, a gift from Ben on their first wedding anniversary. Their wedding date was engraved on the back, and she never took it off. She also still had not taken off her wedding rings. One step at time, her therapist, Margaret, kept saying. One step at a time. She had exactly seven minutes to get in the car if she was going to make her ten o'clock yoga class. With what felt like monumental effort, she pushed aside the afghan draped across her lap and clicked off the gas logs in the fireplace with a remote. She padded across the heated floors to the kitchen, rinsed her coffee cup and placed it in the dishwasher. She picked up her bag from the bench by the back door, walked into the heated garage and slid into the leather seat of her Land Rover. As she turned into the studio parking lot her phone buzzed. Aggie. Bless Aggie, always checking in to make sure she was at least limping along at life. A hint of a smile crossed her face. She picked up the iPhone and tapped the text icon.

A message from Aggie popped up on the screen.

Aggie: Guess what I did!

There was a picture of Aggie with a handsome looking guy and a girl she didn't know. There was also a photo of Aggie on the beach with a huge, historic looking beach house in the background.

Lillian: Bought a herd of flamingos? Holy smokes, I made a joke, she congratulated herself.

Fair guess. Aggie shot back. *Want another?*

Lillian: I do, but I'm pulling into the yoga studio and if I miss this class, I may lose the very, very loose grasp I have on my faculties. Can I call you later?

Aggie: You better, we have about eleven overdue conversations, but the big news is I bought a gorgeous old beach house that I probably can't afford, it needs a lot of work, but a few rooms are habitable, and I can't wait for you to see it. Glad you're at yoga - good for you! Big hugs! Talk soon.

Lillian put the phone down and got out of the car. She wished Aggie didn't live so far away. When Aggie decamped from Houston, Lillian campaigned hard for her to join her in Colorado, but Aggie said her blood was far too thin and the only direction she was moving was South. Only Aggie and her therapist, Margaret, knew exactly how much effort it took her to get out of the house these days. Lillian slipped into the dim studio and rolled out her mat seconds before class started. Everyone was already sitting quietly in mediation with their eyes closed. Perfect timing.

Chapter Seventeen

Construction on the beach house started with a bang. One crew started ripping out the kitchen and another started on the little third floor crows' nest apartment. Aggie chose a lovely pale gray paint for the walls that would change with the light throughout the day. She was adding spray foam insulation in the ceiling that Ambrose claimed would pay for itself in her utility bill savings. The windows were, thankfully, all in good shape and could be kept. The plumber was able to tap into the plumbing from the floor below with minimal fuss. The bathroom would be similar to the one in her old apartment. She found a penny tile for the floors that was a close match to her old bathroom above the Bean and Bun and beautiful curved brass fixtures for the shower and sink. The only difference in this bathroom from the one above the Bean and Bun would be the dependability of the water temperature. No more dancing between hot and cold showers for her.

Aggie was thrilled with how fast the construction project was moving. A mere four weeks after she signed the papers, her attic apartment was ready. Sadie found a renter for the bakery apartment within hours. While

Aggie wasn't excited about living in a construction zone, the rental income was vital. Between moving and running the bakery, Aggie barely slept, and she was exhausted as she sat on the balcony of the little apartment above the Bean and Bun for the last time.

She had been on the phone with Lillian, and she was worried. Obviously, it was understandable for Lillian to be sad, but she just sounded so low. She picked the phone back up and shot a text to Lillian.

Aggie: Hey, why don't you and Jude fly that fancy plane down here for a visit? The house isn't done, but there is a room you could stay in. I know it's not Cabo, but we do have a beach here."

Lillian texted back almost immediately: *Jude is staying with my parents for a couple weeks. He's on a school break.*

Aggie: "He's staying with your parents at the old folks home?"

Lillian: "Oh, yeah. He's having a blast. He's like their new mascot. And also, the reigning ping-pong champ."

Aggie: "So? That means you're free?"

Lillian: "I could do with some sunshine. It's still winter here. It's almost always winter here."

Aggie sent a screenshot of the Sandcastle Island ten-day forecast. Sunny and highs in the mid-eighties.

Lillian: "I'll think about it. Thanks, love."

Aggie: "Ok, think hard. About all the buckets and buckets of sunshine. Night, night."

Lillian sat as close to the fireplace as she could without catching on fire after texting with Aggie. People kept asking what her plans were. She should probably make some. Lately, she considered the day a success if she managed a shower and waited until five o'clock in the evening to pour the Chardonnay. She needed to get out of this house, where everything was a memory and reminder that she was alone. So alone. She had never made any true friends here. She had plenty of acquaintances. Yoga friends, shopping friends. She met with a few ladies for book club once a month, but they only ever talked about the book which Lillian thought was weird. She and Ben had a few couple friends that they would go out with occasionally. Mostly his business associates and their wives who seemed uncomfortable around her now. She never made any real friends after college. She was close to her family, but they had their own lives. Her sister was a big shot publisher in New York City, and her parents were kicking up their heels in an over fifty-five South Florida community with fierce games of bridge and badminton and four o'clock cocktail hours.

Her only true, real friend lived a thousand miles away. She gazed around her office and out into the open living room and kitchen. The giant fireplace, the floor to ceiling windows with their leaded glass. The sliding doors that opened onto the vast patio and the pool which was once again covered in snow. The tall, rustic wood paneled walls and ceilings, the crystal and iron chandeliers, the hand woven Navajo rugs in muted colors. She had chosen all of it. The simple, graceful furnishings, the perfectly plumped velvet covered, down throw pillows. All of it luxe, yet comfortable. She worked hard to make a home that felt like it hugged you when you walked in the door despite towering, twenty-foot-tall ceilings. She loved this house. But it was starting to feel like a beautifully appointed prison, the walls closing in a tiny bit every day.

She sat down at her desk and reviewed her to-do list. It was so damn long. There were still thank you notes to write, correspondence to respond to, and she had put off meeting with Harvey Oliver, their financial advisor for weeks now. She had to do it, but the thought of driving into downtown Denver was just so exhausting. It was a long drive and even the thought of that much effort rooted her to the spot. The one time she actually committed to an appointment a snowstorm rolled in and kept her home. She was familiar with their financial situation; the meeting was routine. There was a medium sized trust set up for Jude as well as accounts set aside for his schooling. And various investment accounts, which she supposed she really did need to get up to speed on. Ben always handled that stuff, and now it fell to her. It just felt so hard.

Alternatively, popping down to see Aggie's new beach house, thawing her freezing bones in the Texas spring sunshine for a few days. Now that didn't sound so bad. The meeting could wait another week or two, right? She made a quick phone call and arranged for a plane to meet her the following day at 10am and for a car to be waiting for her at the Houston airport. She left a message for Mr. Harvey's secretary's secretary to reschedule her meeting once more. Then she shot a text off to Aggie and went to pack her bag.

Chapter Eighteen

"I cannot believe you are really and truly here! When I said I couldn't wait for you to see it, I really meant like, later, when it was done and wasn't covered in sawdust, and I could greet you properly with chilled rosé and fancy canapés. But I love that you actually came!" she squealed and wrapped Lillian in a hug. It was like hugging a blonde skeleton.

"Well, I needed to see it for myself. You know if I can't picture where you're sitting while talking to me on the phone, I just feel unsettled."

"I know, I get it. Here, come into the library. It's the only room downstairs that's finished. I can at least rustle up some bubbles and pretzels if nothing else." Aggie led Lillian into the library. Lillian walked into the middle of the room and dropped her Louis Vuitton handbag into a chair and slowly made a complete three-sixty-degree turn, taking in everything. It was a room out of a Jane Austen novel, of which there was a collection on the shelf to the right of the fireplace. There was an extensive collection of classics, along with more contemporary literature, fiction and nonfiction. There were also some interesting volumes on the history of the island and the

Texas Coast. And a healthy selection of paperback chick lit, perfect for devouring on the beach. Aggie had added her own collection of books to the extensive one that Nellie left behind.

"Isn't it amazing?" Aggie broke the silence. "I love this room. All we did in here was sand the floors and clean it up."

"You know how I feel about a good library. This is amazing. Show me the rest." Lillian felt a glimmer of excitement for the first time in months. She was ecstatic for her friend. This house was a treasure, and she couldn't wait to see the rest of it.

"In a minute. First things first. Follow me." Aggie led her into the kitchen and pulled a bottle of her favorite French champagne from the back of the fridge. She was saving it, but she couldn't imagine a better opportunity to crack it open. She unboxed two of the new champagne flutes from the boxes stacked in the pantry and poured.

"To my first guest!"

"And to you, brave girl. This was a hard leap. I'm proud of you." She raised her glass to Aggie. Aggie toured Lillian through the rest of the house, dodging the workmen and the nails that littered the floor.

Later that evening, after Lillian's monogrammed luggage was settled in one of the intact bedrooms, the girls relaxed on the front deck, enjoying the rest of the

Champagne and a dinner of random leftovers Aggie cobbled together. There was a hunk of Manchego cheese, some prosciutto, a jar of homemade hummus with seeded crackers and a bowl of perfectly ripe, bright red strawberries Aggie picked up at the farmers market the day before. Lillian bit into one of the strawberries. It was like sunshine in her mouth. She chewed and reached for a wedge of Manchego. The salty nuttiness of the Spanish cheese was divine, and she realized this was maybe the first time her taste buds registered anything in months.

The next morning, Aggie was long gone when Lillian woke up. Lillian took a quick shower and drove her rented Porsche convertible into town to check out The Bean and Bun. Aggie delivered her coffee along with a plate heavily laden with a freshly baked croissant, poached eggs and fruit. "You need to eat," she said simply.

Lillian bit into the still warm croissant spread with local butter and Aggie's raspberry preserves and sighed. What had she been eating? Mainly granola bars and bananas, she admitted to herself. She surprised even herself by cleaning her plate. Aggie just smiled as she removed the empty dishes.

"That was excellent. I think I forgot what real food tastes like," Lillian said.

"Want a cupcake? Dessert with breakfast is legal on vacation." said Aggie as she ran back into the kitchen to rescue a pan of scones. The timer had been dinging while she rang up the last two customers.

"You need to get some help in here," Lillian observed.

"I know, I know. I'm working on it."

The girls made plans to meet up later and Lillian headed back to the beach house feeling full and nourished. That afternoon after a long walk down the beach, Lillian lay on a towel in the sand like a lizard, soaking up as much of the sun's rays as possible. She closed her eyes and let the sunshine and the warm, salty breeze wash over her. She breathed in deep. Mountain air was wonderful, but this was delicious. There was no other way to describe it. Every muscle in her body felt relaxed. She wasn't huddled under or into anything to keep warm. The tension that had taken up residence in her shoulders the day she received that awful, life changing phone call dissipated slightly and only now did she realize she had been wearing her shoulders around her ears for months.

Lillian spent most of the next week soaking up as much Texas sunshine as possible. She wanted to store it up in her bones, build up a reserve for when she had to return to the mountains in a few days. In the evenings, the girls drank chilled rosé on the porch and ate more of

Aggie's glorious cooking. After only a week, Lillian could see her face was filling out and there was color in her cheeks. She was sleeping better, and her bones felt more like they were holding her up, rather than trying to poke out of her skin. Seven days with her friend, the sun, the sea, and beautiful food had done her more good than months of therapy. The jagged crack in her insides was starting to slowly soften in a way that indicated it might one day stitch itself back together.

The morning before Lillian's flight back to Colorado, she and Aggie were enjoying a second cup of coffee on the porch. It was Monday, Aggie's day off, and the girls were contemplating how to spend their last day when Lillian's phone buzzed. She frowned at the phone. It was Mr. Oliver's office. She was tempted to send it to voicemail, but she answered the call.

"Mrs. Locke?"

"Yes, this is she."

A nasally voice came over the line. "This is Henrietta Brown, from Crane, Oliver and McCartney. I have Mr. Oliver on the line for you."

Lillian was irritated. It was a glorious morning, and she was anxious to get out and soak up her last bit of sunshine for a while. "I have an appointment with Mr. Oliver on Wednesday. Can't this wait?"

"I'm sorry, Mrs. Locke. He said it was most urgent that he speak to you."

"Alright." She smiled apologetically at Aggie. "Sorry," she mouthed. "I have to take this."

Aggie just nodded and carried their breakfast dishes into the kitchen.

"Hello, Mr. Oliver," Lillian said somewhat tersely when the financial advisor came on the line. "I thought I rescheduled our appointment for later this week."

"Yes, ma'am, you did. But that is the fourth time you rescheduled, and I urgently need to speak with you."

Lillian walked inside and sat down at the small desk in the library. "Okay, Mr. Oliver, what is so urgent it can't wait two more days?"

"Well, Mrs. Locke, I really did want to be able to discuss this with you in person, but you absolutely must be made aware of the financial situation your husband left you in."

"What do you mean, left me in?"

"Well, there are some matters that need your immediate attention."

"Such as?" The hard-won softening in Lillian's chest clamped up again, and her shoulders immediately hunched back up around her ears.

"As you well know, your husband made many sound business investments over the years that have performed extremely well. Six months before the accident, Ben sunk a considerable sum into a new tech company. The projections were highly enticing, and your husband was excited about the venture. Unfortunately, Knox Jones, the bright young man behind the company seems to have a substance abuse problem. He landed himself in jail for a year. In his defense, he has been trying to run the business remotely, but his team has been floundering for months now and the whole project just went belly up."

"What, exactly are you saying?"

"Roughly a month before your husband passed, we started hearing rumors about Knox's problems. Ben was concerned about a possible —make that probable— very substantial loss. He was in talks with a large Northeast financial firm to re-write some of their software. It was quite a lucrative contract and would have made up a portion of your recent losses. Unfortunately, he did not have a chance to do the work."

"Recent losses?" Lillian felt as if she had been plunged into an alternate universe. Ben had never mentioned this. Or did he? She racked her brain, trying to remember. She really didn't bother to keep up to date on their financial status. Lillian took a deep breath. Just like yoga she thought. Just breathe. "Mr. Oliver, once more, in very small words, please tell me exactly what you are saying."

"Well, I'm not saying you're destitute, but we need to make some swift moves to keep you afloat. And your lifestyle I would say will probably need some, um, tweaking."

Keep her afloat? The last time she sat down with Ben to review their investment portfolio, the bottom-line number had a hell of a lot of zeros. "Lifestyle tweaking?" she repeated dumbly.

"Yes ma'am. Jude's trust and school funds are intact. Your homes in Colorado and Cabo are paid for, your vehicles are paid for. The silver lining is you have no debt."

"The silver lining of what?" Lillian's infuriation at his dancing around was cutting through her fog of confusion. He finally cut to the chase.

"Your investment accounts are roughly ten percent of what they were a year ago." Ten percent, she thought. How was this possible? Math was never her strong suit, but ten percent wasn't a difficult calculation.

Mr. Oliver plunged ahead. "While you have no debt right now, the maintenance and carrying costs of your primary residence and the Cabo house are considerable. If you choose to sell both properties now while the market is strong in both places, you could recoup a substantial amount. If you keep them as it is, you will eat through your current holdings. If you want to be able to continue to live off the interest of your investments, you will need to sell both properties. Immediately. And even then, it might be a good idea to look into some form of employment. You should be fine, but certain um, extravagances will need to be curbed. I would certainly say no more private air travel and the like."

Curbed? Employment? Lillian wasn't afraid of work, but aside from a part time gig selling clothes in a boutique in college, and a truly horrible waitressing job she was fired from because she was a massive klutz, she had never held an actual job. She had thousands of hours of volunteer work but no actual employment history. Who would hire her? Her therapist's voice echoed in her head. *Deep breaths, one thing at a time.* Okay, but what was first?

After hanging up with Mr. Oliver, Lillian looked out the window at the cute Porsche convertible she rented in Houston. It seemed like a good idea at the time. She's barely driven it since she set foot on the island. So silly. She should have gone with the Ford. Or perhaps a bicycle. What the hell was she supposed to do now?

Chapter Nineteen

Lillian slowly made her way back into the kitchen.

"You look like you've seen a ghost," Aggie said, turning away from unloading the dishwasher.

"Well, I have sort of. That was Ben's - well, our - financial manager. Apparently, Ben made some less than stable investments right before the crash and well…" Lillian stumbled over her words. "I'm not broke exactly, but I need to make some um, "lifestyle changes" as he put it." She started ticking items off on her fingers. "I need to sell the Cabo house and the Colorado house. Downsize. Economize. Possibly find a job. Definitely return that Porsche out front ASAP. What the hell? How could he risk everything without telling me?" Lillian slumped into a chair and lay head down on the old farm table. Aggie moved to sit next to her and simply lay her hand on her head.

Aggie had been a big Ben fan from day one. His heart was huge and everything he did was over the top. His generosity was matched only by his impulsiveness. He had just never been caught holding the bag. Until now. And he wasn't around to cobble things back together. Lillian was. But Aggie did not say any of these things. Instead, she said, "I'm sure he had a plan. He just didn't get to see it through. I know he was impulsive, but he wasn't careless or stupid."

"No. He was brilliant, but yes, very impulsive. He clearly didn't quite think this one through." Instead of spending the day sunning and shopping, Lillian spent most of it sitting on the same patch of sand, staring at the waves and the clouds. She was numb. Again. But there were no more tears. It was like her insides were all dried up. It was just money, wasn't it? She enjoyed their lifestyle, who wouldn't? The private jets, the clothes, the vacations to five-star resorts in exotic locales. She loved to travel, but to be honest she wasn't sure she enjoyed the exotic luxury trips all that much more than the backpacking adventures she and Aggie had in Europe during college when they stayed in the cheapest hostels they could find and ate street food three meals a day.

The Cabo house could go, the private plane could go. The idea of selling the Colorado house pained her. So many memories. That house was meant to be their forever home. How could she uproot Jude from the only home he had ever known just as he was starting to adjust to his father being so abruptly and painfully ripped from his life? She could keep the house, she supposed, but the taxes, insurance and carrying costs would put too costly a strain on what was left. Even she could see that.

She was going to have to sell it. Find something smaller. More manageable. Dammit, how was she going to tell Jude? She picked up her phone and sent an email to the pilot to change the flight plan. This was going to be her last private flight. One extra stop wouldn't change her circumstances too much. She would stop in Florida, pick up Jude early, and they would go home together to spend however much time they could saying goodbye to their home. But then where would they go?

Aggie sensed Lillian needed some time to process so she left her to herself most of the day. She spent her time in the kitchen perfecting a few recipes and going over final plans for finishing the house and her first retreat. She felt a little guilty feeling giddy at the prospect while her best friend seemed to be drifting about untethered.

When Lillian came downstairs after showering, she was dressed to go out. Their original plan was to go out to a final dinner before her departure the next morning. But the smells coming from the kitchen indicated otherwise. The aroma of onions, garlic and tomatoes wafted through the house and made her stomach audibly rumble.

"Hey," said Aggie as Lillian entered the kitchen. "I know we said we'd go out, but I was in the mood to cook. To my knowledge, there is no meal that goes better with '*I've had really shitty news*' than Ravioli Alla Lastra." Lillian sniffed at the aroma wafting around the kitchen like a puppy identifying a scent.

"Is this the Italy dish?" She had begged Aggie to make this for her on numerous occasions over the years. On that college backpacking trip, they stopped at a small hillside Tuscan village. It was raining, they were soaked and cold. The bus let them off near their hostel, and as they looked around, they realized the sidewalks were rolled up for the night. They had resigned themselves to a dinner of granola bars and bottled water when they turned a corner and saw at the end of the block, a solitary restaurant, clearly still open for business. A golden pool of light spilled out the door and glistened on the wet cobblestone street. Inside, the lively chatter of Italian families filled the room. The waitress sat them down next to the fireplace and plunked a bottle of Chianti on the red and white checkered tablecloth. There was no menu, but what followed, which included the pasta dish currently on the stove was the stuff dreams are made of. Aggie's twist on it was hand-made ravioli stuffed with pancetta, ricotta and spinach. They were lightly simmering in a savory tomato sauce made with garlic, sage, celery, carrots, and onions.

Lillian knew full well this was not simply an urge to cook on Aggie's part, and her eyes welled up. Aggie was cooking in a construction zone. The kitchen was still half ripped apart. The workspace was limited to the island. At Aggie's request, the crew left the old appliances until the last minute and were scheduled to be replaced the following week. But this, this business of feeding people, this was Aggie's love language. She knew exactly what people needed according to any crisis. For example, love troubles called for carbs filled with chocolate. Death needed something warm and light. Tonight, Lillian needed this pasta. They ate out on the front porch listening to the waves. Lillian took her first bite. "Oh, man, you made the pasta today, didn't you?"

"You bet I did! You're having an existential crisis. Did you think I would serve you boxed pasta?"

"You are a very, very good friend and I do not deserve you. I can't thank you enough for this week, this meal, all of it. I really wish I could jet us off to Cabo as a thank you. But I think you're going to have to settle for a bottle of cheap Prosecco and a hug."

"No thanks needed, lady. You know I would go crazy if I didn't have people to feed."

Lillian nodded, her mouth full of pasta.

Chapter Twenty

Early the next afternoon, Sadie walked into the Bean and Bun and collapsed onto a stool at the counter. Her curly hair, usually shiny and full of bounce despite the Gulf's raging humidity, was frizzy and her mascara was smudged like she'd been rubbing her eyes.

"What's up?" Aggie asked. "You look like you might need wine more than coffee. Sure, you shouldn't go next door?"

"Oh, I most certainly need wine, but that will have to wait a few hours. I've got a big deal scheduled to close tomorrow, but the buyer is threatening to back out if I can't get all the furniture out by closing. I've called all the moving companies, and no one can get there until next week at the earliest."

Aggie moved over to the coffee machine to start an espresso. "You think they'll truly back out over furniture? Isn't there a contract?"

"Of course, there is a contract." Sadie rolled her eyes. "But the guy is an attorney, and if nothing else, he will make my life miserable for a week or two just for fun." She paused, catching a glimpse of herself in the mirror. She rooted around in her handbag for a ponytail band to pull her hair back and wiped at the mascara smudges underneath her eyes. Then she continued. "I think he'll eventually calm down. My gut says he's putting on a show for his new, *very young,* wife who wants to renovate the whole thing into something out of a sci-fi movie. Chrome-Glam she calls it. It's so stupid. The place was refurnished two years ago, and it's *to-die-for* gorgeous. All Restoration Hardware and Serena and Lily. The owner wanted to sell the house furnished and they've already left town. It's a waste really." Aggie's hands were frozen on the controls of the coffee machine. She realized her mouth was hanging open, and she snapped it shut. She was stressing about how to finish furnishing the beach house. Her line of credit was close to maxed out. Nellie's furniture that came with the house was functional, some of it quite beautiful in fact. The old farmhouse table was a perfect example. And the rest were all lovely pieces of the highest quality. But they were obviously dated, and didn't quite jive with the beach bohemian aesthetic she was counting on to create an Instagram wonderland worthy of persuading women of a certain age to part with large chunks of cash in exchange for a few days of her cooking and a restful weekend in a beautiful space.

"How much do they want for the furniture?" she asked tentatively.

"They just want it gone. The buyer is some big shot attorney from Houston. He doesn't seem to care. And the seller has already left for Florida. The house they're buying is already furnished. They don't want the stuff either."

Aggie managed to finish the Americano without burning herself and passed it across the counter. "So, are you saying that this houseful of gorgeous furniture is up for grabs if someone can get it out of there?" Her hand was already reaching into her pocket for her cell phone.

"Well, yes. I hadn't really thought of that. Do you know someone who would come get it?"

"Yep, me. What's the address?"

"412 Oceanside, right down the beach from you. But what are you going to do? Strap the sofa to the roof of your Mini Cooper?"

"If it comes to that, yes." Aggie was already scrolling through the photos of the online listing on her phone, drooling over the furniture. This was exactly what she needed to make the beach house pop. She tapped the screen again. "I'm calling Brooks to see if we can borrow his muscles for the afternoon."

Brooks was writing from home and was at that moment struggling with another case of writers' block. He was only too happy to come be Aggie's hero. He said he would borrow a truck from Ambrose and meet her right after she closed up the shop. The rest of the afternoon seemed to drag, but the little hand on the clock finally reached the four. Aggie turned the sign on the door around to Closed, and practically skipped out the door to go meet Sadie and Brooks. As they walked into the house, Aggie couldn't believe her luck. They loaded up armchairs, side tables and the exact Serena and Lily barstools Aggie had been eyeing for months, knowing she couldn't afford them. She couldn't help but feel she was robbing the place. When someone walked in from the front porch, she dropped the lamp she was carrying, which thankfully did not break, and looked up feeling guilty.

"Excuse me, may I help you?" a very thin, very blonde woman with too much collagen in her lips demanded in a nasally, Northern accent. Aggie also noticed her forehead didn't move, even though she couldn't be old enough to need Botox. Aggie stammered about for a bit, but managed to introduce herself as Sadie walked back in with Brooks.

"Oh hello, Angelica. I wasn't planning to see you until closing tomorrow," said Sadie smoothly.

"I need to get some measurements for the new countertops. The contractor needed them like, yesterday," the blonde ice queen snipped.

Aggie looked at her in disbelief and glanced back at the kitchen. The current countertops were a pristine

Carrara marble. "You're ripping these OUT?" She was horrified.

"First thing after we leave the closing table. We're starting in the kitchen." Angelica's nasally voice trilled.

Aggie couldn't imagine someone like her cooking so she wondered why she would start in the kitchen, but she guessed the gorgeous marble didn't go with her Chrome Glam aesthetic.

"That's fine," said Sadie. "Feel free to get all the measurements you need. We'll finish up here first thing in the morning. It will be empty by one o'clock when you and your husband sign the papers."

"Good thing. I don't want one more thing delaying this project."

Sadie internally rolled her eyes, but put on a bright, professional smile. "Wonderful. I can't wait to see what you do with the place," she lied through her teeth. Aggie did her best to cover a guffaw with a cough.

Angelica snapped her fingers and motioned a sad puppy of a young man through the door. He quickly took half a dozen measurements and made notations in a notebook. With an apologetic smile, he took his leave with Angelica who tottered back to a black Lincoln Navigator on impossibly high heels. Aggie caught sight of the signature red soles. Beautiful shoes, but she couldn't imagine anything more impractical for a day at the beach. "Nice to meet you, Angelica." Aggie called after her.

Angelica turned and lowered her oversized, black designer sunglasses. "It's pronounced An-*HELL*-ica," she tossed back over her shoulder. It came out like a hiss. "But it's nice to meet you too. I have to go now." She slammed the door of the Navigator.

This time, Aggie didn't even try to cover her laugh, but she did have the decency to turn back toward the kitchen so An-hell-ica couldn't see her. But she stopped abruptly and groaned when she realized this woman was going to be her neighbor. The houses were spaced pretty far apart on this section of the beach, but she was only two doors down. Maybe she wouldn't come down from Houston often. She looked up to see Brooks and Sadie were laughing too. Sadie abandoned her professional demeanor and rolled her eyes. "I've had some wack clients, but she absolutely takes the cake."

"She might possibly take the lemon water, but I assure you that woman has never eaten cake." Aggie giggled.

Brooks quipped "Oh, I like her. She just snagged herself a spot as a character in the new Chester McCombs. As a matter of fact, I think my writer's block is cured." He grabbed Aggie and twirled her around the now almost empty room.

"Stupendous," she replied. "I won't even charge you to be your muse. Now let's load up these gorgeous Chesterfields before she meets someone with any taste, and I lose this goldmine of stuff." They finished up and dropped everything in a jumbled pile in the beach house living room. Aggie would be climbing over furniture for a while, but Sadie and Brooks both promised to come help place it when the sawdust cleared.

Chapter Twenty-One

Angelica returned to Houston tired. She should have just stayed in a hotel on the island and met her husband, Jim, in the morning. It had been ridiculous for her to drive all the way back to Houston tonight just to turn around and go back in the morning for the signing of the papers to close on the beach house. But the three-hour drive from Houston to Sandcastle would be more time than she had spent with her new husband in one stretch since their wedding six months ago.

She swapped her high heels and designer jeans for workout clothes and faithfully clocked a full hour on the elliptical machine in their home gym. After a quick shower, she pulled on a brightly colored kaftan, dabbed on perfume and headed into the kitchen to make dinner. She checked the clock. Jim should be home any minute.

She turned on music and lit the candles in the kitchen. She was going to make the most of this rare evening at home, and then they would spend the whole day together tomorrow. She was humming along with the music, pulling out fish and vegetables from the fridge when her phone buzzed. She picked it up, read the message and slammed the phone down on the counter. Jim was skipping dinner at home in favor of meeting a potential new client at a steakhouse downtown. Last night it was drinks with a current client that stretched long past the dinner hour, and she didn't even remember what the reason was the night before. His work ethic was admirable, but this was not what she signed up for. And she was pissed. She wanted to scream, to throw things, to take a baseball bat to the giant plate glass wall that overlooked the Houston skyline.

Jim asked two things of her when he proposed. First, there was the prenup. Second, he didn't exactly tell her she *had* to quit her job as a travel and lifestyle writer, but he pointed out again and again that her travel schedule would be hard on their new marriage, and he hinted at starting a family. But a family wasn't possible when he was never home, and she doubted he would have noticed if she were currently in Vancouver, or Kyoto or St. Tropez. What in the hell was she supposed to do if she wasn't working, and he was never around? She took deep calming breaths, just like her therapist taught her. It took her awhile to calm down, but eventually, she put the food away and made herself a protein shake and settled herself on the sofa. Most women would have tried to warm the place up when they moved into an apartment like Jim's. But Angelica loved it. She grew up in a very traditional house stuffed to the brim with chintz and throw pillows and knick-knacks covering every single surface. Even though she was generally left alone with a nanny in the big house, it had always felt suffocating. She loved the clean lines of Jim's, well, now *their* apartment. The glass and stainless-steel motif suited her. She could breathe in a space like this. Thank goodness they were buying this beach house. She was absolutely bored to tears with nothing to do. She had plans for a full, modernizing renovation. She might be there by herself most of the time, but at least it would keep her busy for a few months. She sat for a minute and then texted Jim back. This would not do. He had promised her a proper honeymoon for months now but kept pushing it off. She was taking matters into her own hands. She used to travel for a living, for crying out loud. In response to his text, she just sent a photo of a coastal hotel in the South of France she visited last year. She added. "Booking this for two weeks next month. You pick the weeks. You owe me a honeymoon, mister." A few minutes went by until she received his response. No doubt he was busy trying to add this new client to his stable.

Her phone buzzed again. "You pick the weeks, I may have to work a little while we're there, but we'll make it happen. Love you. Xoxo." Well, that was better than nothing. She booked the hotel and flights with a few clicks of her keyboard and sent the details to Jim and to the secretary that kept his calendar. Tomorrow, she was closing on her very own beach house. And in a few short weeks she would jet off to the South of France with her new, handsome, successful husband. So why did she still feel like she wanted to rip someone's head off?

Chapter Twenty-Two

The next few weeks were a racing merry-go-round for Aggie. Bakery, beach house, retreat prep, marketing for the retreats, perfecting recipes, ordering linens and tableware, pillows and bedding, planning, planning. She slept like the dead in her crow's nest apartment, crawling under her fluffy duvet well after midnight only to drag herself out of bed at five in the morning to get to the bakery. The crew was making steady progress on the beach house, and it was inching closer to completion. Reservations for her first retreat were filling up. She ran an Instagram ad and placed an ad in the Houston Chronicle, figuring that covered her bases. Did people still read newspapers? She didn't really know. But lo and behold, both proved a worthwhile investment. With each reservation email that came through, her heart soared. Despite her utter exhaustion, she felt vindicated. This was going to work. It had to.

Aggie locked the door to the Bean and Bun late on Sunday afternoon. It still felt a little strange to not just head upstairs after work. She settled into the driver seat, and let her head lay back for a moment. She was so tired. Even her bones were tired. Her phone pinged with a text. It was Ambrose asking her to meet at eight o'clock tomorrow morning to discuss a few things. She groaned as she started the engine. The last few weeks taught her that anytime Ambrose asked to discuss anything in person, it was generally not good news. Typically, it was expensive news, and her budget was stretched thinner than her croissant dough.

That evening, she carried a glass of rose and her notebooks out onto the front porch. The weather was glorious, the evening light soft and pink. She went over her plans for her first retreat one more time. The contractors should finish just in time for her to get in and prepped for her first group of guests. She chose a French theme. She would greet her guests on the porch with champagne and gougers, those glorious little puff ball French pastries. For dinner she would serve a French feast of duck confit, potatoes Anna, and a bright acidic green salad with a shallot vinaigrette. They would finish with a chocolate mousse the ladies would help prepare. The following morning, she would have freshly baked croissants, fruit, and coffee. After breakfast they would have their first cooking demo where the ladies would learn to make croissants. A light lunch would be served on the porch. Then she would send them off for an afternoon at the beach where she would set up loungers with umbrellas. At four o'clock they would regroup in the kitchen for a wine tasting session with Amelia.

Boxes upon boxes of linens and wine glasses and kitchen goods were sitting in the pantry waiting to be stacked in the beautiful glass front cabinets in the big open kitchen. The kitchen, and in fact all of the downstairs, was completely finished and tomorrow she would spend her day off unpacking. Bedding, blankets, and throw pillows galore were ready and waiting to be fluffed and placed.

She went back inside and sat down at the tiny office desk in the pantry and opened her laptop. She reviewed her spreadsheets again, even though they were practically printed on her brain. She was skating a thin line with her finances, but everything worked on paper. The Bean and Bun itself was trending towards profitability, but was still solidly in the red. These retreats could keep her afloat and give her the second substantial income steam she so desperately needed to stay on the island. She was going to have to deliver a heck of an experience to this first group and hope for some rave reviews. The second retreat was half filled up, which was excellent news. She needed to stay fully booked to make this work. She would host groups of ten. Couples or friends, two to a room. As soon as the crew stopped generating dust and paint fumes she would go in and add the finishing touches.

Aggie woke early the next morning, anxious to hear what Ambrose needed to discuss. It would be a bit before she found out. The sun had only just fully extended itself over the horizon as she let herself back into the house after a walk on the beach. She looked around, assessing how close they were to the finish line. The living room, kitchen and library and her little third floor suite were complete. Three of the five guest suites were finished and the fourth should be just about done.

She still needed to hire someone to handle the bakery on the days she would have retreat guests. She had been putting it off as long as possible quite simply because paying someone would require coming very close to scraping the very bottom of her savings. The shop couldn't afford to close down on Saturday and Sunday, certainly not during high season. Someone had to be hired and trained. Pronto. The anxiety she felt at letting someone else into her business was outweighed by her inability to be in two places at once.

Standing in her gleaming, brand-new kitchen, she faced the big island and looked across the kitchen through the living room and out to the view of the sparkling ocean beyond the sand. The double stainless-steel refrigerators and walk-in pantry and office space were ready to be stocked with all her supplies for a weekend of luxury indulgences. The oversized kitchen island, topped in a gorgeous quartz was plenty large enough to gather ten guests around. The original wood floors gleamed like warm honey and the plate glass windows flooded the room with sunlight as the sun rose higher over the Gulf of Mexico.

She was startled as the back door opened and Ambrose strode into his construction site. "Morning, Aggie girl!" he boomed. Years of power tools and a lackluster respect for ear coverings left him with maybe sixty percent hearing. Aggie was always a little tired after their conversions. But today, after his initial greeting, he spoke softer than normal as he laid a spreadsheet out on the counter for her to examine. "Aggie, hon, you said time and time again funds were finite, and we absolutely could not go one penny over budget."

"Yes, you absolutely heard that right," she said as her thoughts went back to the ledger sitting on her desk. There had been a laundry list of overages she hadn't accounted for in her initial budget for the project. There had been plumbing issues with the second bath, a small electrical disaster on the second floor, and the wood rot in the attic. Not to mention the other half dozen issues they ran into that shouldn't have been a surprise when renovating a home that sat next to an ocean for the last century. The house had seemed so solid, and the renovations all appeared cosmetic. But then she needed to move a wall and the projects piled up.

"Aggie, I'm sorry, but you're out of cash. The boys finished up the fourth bedroom, but the fifth one still needs work. The floors in there need refinishing. There's a little bit of wood rot, and that bathroom hasn't been touched yet. It's not a huge project, but I think you may need to wait on finishing that one."

Aggie absorbed all of this, doing the simple math in her head. One bedroom less was two guests fewer she could accommodate and that was a twenty percent decrease in revenue. She felt a panic rise in her chest. She supposed she could put people in the little third floor suite, but where would she live? She already signed the paperwork to lease out the bakery apartment. And even if she hadn't, she really needed the rental income. Was she going to sleep on the couch? She closed her eyes and sighed. And then, glimpsing a glimmer of a silver lining, Aggie opened her eyes. "Does that mean we're done?"

"Yes Aggie, hon. I think we're done. You're 'bout ready as you're gonna be for a while. I'm sorry. I really wanted to finish this for you. So did the boys. We know how excited you are. I hope you'll let us take it to the finish line for you when you're ready."

"Thanks, Ambrose," responded Aggie with a little catch in her throat.

"Alrighty then. Bye now." He patted her awkwardly on the shoulder, sat his key on the island, turned to go, and let himself out the back door.

She had imagined this day much differently, popping champagne with the crew, cooking a giant, sumptuous thank you dinner, celebrating the completion of a job well done and the launch of her new venture. Aggie looked around once more at the gorgeous job they did for her. She walked upstairs to examine the finished work and access the unfinished space. She sighed again as she walked up the wide staircase with the smooth original railing the boys painstakingly sanded down and refinished. Her hand glided over the smooth railing thinking how many hands had done the same in the last hundred years. She reached the second-floor landing and walked into the newly finished fourth bedroom suite. The same gleaming honey oak floors as downstairs and the same oversized windows with French doors opening onto the second story deck with massive views of the ocean glittering in the morning sun. This was one heck of a bedroom, she thought. The attached bath had been original, and she opted to keep the black and white penny tile. How hard it must have been to get that grout clean she thought, noticing it looked brand new. Her smile fell as she crossed the hallway to the unfinished fifth suite. It was the bathroom that had suffered the unfortunate avocado green tile renovation, and it was very, very grimy. But she turned the tap, and the water ran clear and hot, and nothing appeared to leak. The aforementioned wood rot in the bedroom appeared to be limited to a corner. It certainly wasn't her darling suite on the third floor. It would be a pain to move out of her rooms during retreat weekends, but she could make it work. The bathroom was functional, even covered in grime. With a good scrub, it would do. She would clean it up and put a bed in here. She could maybe even start finishing the work in here herself. If she could find any spare time lurking about, that is. She couldn't fit two people in the third-floor attic suite unless it was a couple, but at worst it was a ten percent decrease in revenue rather than twenty. She made her way back downstairs. As she walked back into the kitchen her spirits lifted. Despite everything she realized she couldn't wait to cook here. She took another look around at the gleaming floors and sparkling windows. She pulled out her phone and dialed Ambrose.

"Aggie, hon! Hi there, what is it? You come into a windfall in the last hour?" He was laughing and his voice was booming again. He was on another job site. She could hear the power tools in the background.

"Ha! Not quite. Ambrose, when you and the boys finish up today, head back over to the beach house. They deserve a party." She spent the rest of that Monday, her one day off, in party prep mode. This wouldn't be the sumptuous gourmet meal she had envisioned, but even if it was just pizza and beer, she needed the boys and Ambrose to know how much she appreciated their craftsmanship. She also wanted to let them show it off to her friends. She quickly whipped up a quadruple batch of her pizza dough and left it to rise on the counter. She made a dash to the store for pizza toppings and fresh buffalo mozzarella. She called Amelia with an invitation and a request to pretty, pretty, please bring the booze. Aggie deftly chopped sweet yellow onions and fresh garden tomatoes for the pizza sauce. She left them to simmer with fresh herbs and lots of garlic. Quick calls to Sadie, Brooks and Mr. O'Henry from the hardware store, who lived next door with his wife, rounded out her guest list, and she got ready for her first celebration. Amelia showed up early with wine and beer and helped assemble the pizzas. With stacks of disposable plates and cups, it still was nowhere near the fancy dinner party she had envisioned, but she was ready, and the house felt alive. Sadie arrived with a bluetooth speaker and Willie Nelson's Whisky River filled the house. Then she toured herself around the house with a glass of champagne, exclaiming over how well it had all come together. Brooks arrived with Nellie in tow. "Brooks, you brought Nellie!" Aggie exclaimed.

"Brooks was in danger of being skunked at cards when you called so he was thrilled for an excuse to head back. I insisted upon inviting myself along."

"I'm so glad you did!" She settled Nellie in one of the cushy chairs and found her a glass of champagne. The crew arrived in one giant crowd, lumbering through the door, and Aggie spent the next hour playing hostess. She hugged them all and handed out beers. A few surprised her by forgoing the craft beer selection and daintily sipping from champagne flutes. The O'Henrys showed up, Mr. O'Henry heading straight for the food. Mrs. O'Henry declined champagne and asked for a sparkling water.

Aggie popped pizzas in and out of the ovens and was pleased to see the new appliances turning them out perfectly. The pizzas disappeared into hungry mouths, and the whole place hummed with music and laughter. One of the younger guys from the crew appointed himself as tour guide and took Brooks, Sadie and Nellie through every room.

After his tour, Brooks found Aggie in the library by herself. "What are you doing?" he asked. "I may be wrong, but I think the party's out there." He pointed a thumb over his shoulder towards the living room. Aggie turned, tears running down her flushed cheeks.

"I'm sorry. I just needed a minute." She sniffed and swiped at her cheeks with her palms.

"What on earth is wrong?" he asked, closing the pace between them in two long strides.

"Nothing. Nothing at all. I'm being silly." Aggie shook her head and took a deep breath. "I'm just a little overwhelmed. It's everything I've worked so hard for, and it's all finally come together. It's not perfect, but it's done. I'm just really happy."

"Women have an awfully funny way of showing joy." Brooks was teasing her, but he took her hand.

"I have you to thank, you know," said Aggie, staring up at him.

"Oh no," said Brooks as he looked around the library. "I may have moved the ball down the field a few yards, but this is all you." He moved his hand to the side of her face, and Aggie turned into it. Then the library door opened, and Brooks dropped his hand and Aggie stepped back. Ambrose stuck his head in.

"You two havin' a private party?" he asked with a wink.

"Of course not," said Aggie, as she flushed a deeper shade of pink.

"I just came to tell you I'm headed home," Ambrose said. Gesturing around to the house, he added. "I think all in all, the old gal looks pretty good." Aggie left Brooks' side and walked over to hug Ambrose.

"Thank you so much. For everything," she said as she wrapped her arms around the old man. And her eyes welled up all over again. Eventually, the guys all left after squeezing Aggie one more time and promising to come back as soon as she was ready for them to properly finish the job. Sadie took off as well to get home in time to tuck in the twins. Aggie, Nellie, and Brooks sat on the front porch in the twilight, Brooks with a beer and Aggie and Nellie finishing off a bottle of the champagne. Aggie was a little nervous when she turned to Nellie and quietly asked, "So, what do you think?"

"It's absolute perfection, my dear. This house was meant for parties. For music, for crowds, for dancing, for laughter. And for excellent food. I never really enjoyed it here after the children left and it was just me. It's too big a house for one person. It needs a big family to fill it up. Or," she said with a wink, "lots of housewives who need to learn to cook. You've given the old girl a nice facelift. I love it."

"Thank you." She squeezed Nellie's papery soft hand. "That means so much. How is Peach Tree House treating you?" Aggie asked, somewhat afraid Nellie might want her house back.

"It's just like high school," Nellie giggled. "It's funny how people never change. You have the cool kids table, and you still have the mean girls, and you have a few girls running after the same man. It's like watching a very juvenile, yet fairly entertaining soap opera." Nellie took a small sip of champagne. Aggie laughed, and as she looked up, caught Brooks staring at her over the top of Nellie's head. Nellie sat her glass down on the table.

"Brooks, I think I need to ask you to take me back now. I'm getting tired, and I have a mean girl to whip at the bridge tournament in the morning."

"Well, you certainly need to be well rested for that," Brooks agreed. "Besides, it looks like we're about to get some weather." Off in the distance a bank of dark clouds was putting on an impressive light show. "Let's go ahead and go before that gets any closer." They said their good-byes. Brooks put the top up on the Thunderbird and helped Nellie into the passenger seat. Aggie stood on the porch after they left. Lightning flashed across the darkening sky, and the wind grew stronger. A storm was definitely brewing.

As Brooks drove off the ferry after safely depositing Nellie at Peach Tree House, he was thinking about Aggie. Specifically, what might have transpired if Ambrose hadn't broken the spell in the library earlier. He started towards the North End of the island and his cabin. Lighting flashed again illuminating everything bright as day for a nanosecond. Almost immediately a massive clap of thunder made him jump in his seat. It was too early in the year for a hurricane, but this storm wasn't messing around. It occurred to him he never showed Aggie how to work the storm shutters. He made a u-turn and headed back for the beach house.

Chapter Twenty-Three

Aggie was curled up in the rocking chair on the porch when headlights pulled into the drive. She loved a storm, but this one worried her. Rain was pelting down hard, bouncing off the roof, and she prayed it wasn't hail. The last thing she needed was hail damage the day the remodel was complete. Who could it be out in this mess, she wondered as the headlights slowed to a stop. Brooks bolted from the car and ran for the porch, the rain now coming down in wild sheets. Thunder boomed, shaking the porch. Brooks clomped up the steps and started for the door but stopped short as Aggie rose from the chair. His cotton shirt was soaked through, clinging to his broad chest and shoulders.

"What are you doing here?"

"I wasn't sure if you knew how to work the storm shutters."

Aggie gestured towards the front bay windows. They were covered with sturdy metal sheets that would protect the old glass from anything thrown about by the wind.

"Oh," Brooks said. "I should have known." He stood there with water dripping from his hair and Aggie fought an urge to wipe the raindrops from his face. "Okay, then, good night." And he turned to head back down the stairs.

Aggie shook her stupor. "Are you crazy? It's insane out there. You can't drive home in this."

"Okay." They stood opposite each other, neither confident enough to take a step toward the other. She was his best friend on the island. He held her mortgage. It was inappropriate and foolhardy in so many ways. But he did it anyway. He crossed the porch in two steps and before he could think of any more reasons that he shouldn't, he did. He took her in his arms and gazed down into her face. Her heavy chestnut hair that was always pulled back in a ponytail flew wild around her face as it danced in the wind. Aggie was shocked into stillness for a mere second. Then she reached up and wiped his face with both hands before wrapping her arms behind his neck and pulling him down to her. They stood on the porch lost in that kiss for longer than either of them knew. The storm raged at sea and the wind tossed driftwood down the beach. The rain continued to come down by the bucketful, but all they knew was each other as they each cast aside every single one of their reservations. Without breaking contact, Brooks lifted Aggie up with one arm and opened the front door with the other. He carried her right through the living room. He paused at the foot of the stairs and looked at Aggie with the question in his eyes. She nodded almost imperceptibly, and he carried her all the way up to her third floor bedroom that right now felt as if it sat at the very top of the world. The lightning illuminated the room as they slowly undressed each other. Everything Aggie had felt from the first tingle up her arm when they shook hands came raging forth. All the emotion and desire she had tamped down for months was fanned into flame.

Chapter Twenty-Four

The next morning Aggie woke long before the sun despite the fact that very little sleeping took place in her attic bedroom the night before. She could sense Brooks' presence in her bed rather than see him. She thought about waking him, but in the end decided against it. They had things to talk about, and she had to get to work. She left him a note that there was coffee downstairs and to come by the Bean and Bun later.

Aggie floated through her morning and was quite literally singing to herself while she assembled chai spice cinnamon rolls, homemade giant pretzels and three flavors of scones. She popped the last pan into the oven just as the sun broke the horizon. There was a tap, tap, tap on the front door, and she jumped. She looked out. There was a Brooks shaped outline on the other side of the door. She quickly opened the door, feeling silly.

"So, love 'em and leave 'em, huh?" said Brooks, one corner of his mouth turning up. Brooks held up a coffee mug. "I tried the coffee. It's not bad, but somehow it tastes better here. Also, you're out of cream."

Aggie took the cup, and he followed her into the bakery. She handed him a steaming mug of a Oaxacan blend she was testing out. "Tell me what you think of that."

"Hmmm," Brooks made approving sounds as he slowly sipped the brew with his eyes closed in appreciation. "I vote yes."

"Wait here, I'll get you something to go with that."

But Brooks followed her into the kitchen and came up behind her dropping kisses on her neck. She turned around and let herself get lost until the oven timer dinged. "Get out of here," she laughed, disentangling herself as she swatted him playfully with an oven mitt. "Before I burn all the day's stock." Brooks reluctantly returned to the counter. She brought him one of the chai spiced cinnamon rolls. "Here you go." In response, Brooks reached for her hand and just held it while he looked in her eyes without speaking. Then the oven timer dinged again, breaking the spell. By the time Aggie finished transferring all her baked goodies to the display cases up front, it was time to flip the *Closed* sign to *Open*.

"Are you writing today?" she asked with a glance toward his usual table.

"Actually, I have errands to run on the mainland. If you promise not to make fun of my cooking, I'd like to feed you dinner. Want to come over later?"

"I would really, really like to, but Lillian and Jude get in this evening. I've been so busy, I don't think I told you, but they're moving to the island. At least temporarily, while they figure out where they want to be. They're staying with me for a few days while they find a place to rent."

"Okay, well I have a date to lose at cards at Peach Tree House tomorrow afternoon. Tomorrow night?"

Aggie nodded, smiling. "It's a date."

Chapter Twenty-Five

The sorting of the house in Colorado took less time than Lillian expected. She was a speed ball of energy. She had spent months walking around in a fog of loneliness and grief. It was as if all that sunshine burned off the fog, and now she couldn't seem to sit still. She met with the real estate agent and was pleased to find that the house, along with what she would net from the sale in Cabo, would easily set her and Jude up comfortably. That is, if she invested the proceeds well and was careful, and stuck to what Mr. Oliver described as "her new circumstances." No more private planes, no more designer clothes, no more expensive jewelry. But somehow, this didn't bother her. Ben had constantly surprised her with expensive gifts, new clothes, shoes, handbags, jewelry. He had been the one to want the giant house in Colorado. He was always the instigator for a nicer car, a bigger boat. She enjoyed these things, of course she did, who wouldn't? But the thing she loved most was just seeing him happy. It brought him joy to spoil her, and so she went along with all of it. She owned more jewelry than she could ever wear. All her jewelry, except her wedding rings and her watch, were now safely tucked away in a safety deposit box. If worse came to worst, Jude could probably buy a nice little house with the contents of that box one day. She would sell the house furnished. The large-scale furniture simply wouldn't fit in whatever place she found in Sandcastle and most of the decor simply wouldn't work at the beach. She would have to re-furnish, which she could afford as the place would be tiny. The movers came and packed off their personal belongings. She had selected a few pieces of art and furniture that were treasures simply due to that fact that she and Ben found them together in some remote corner of the globe.

She allowed Jude to take whatever he wanted. He had lost his father and now was losing his home. If he wanted to take every single last one of his one gazillion toys, books, and stuffed animals, so be it. She was surprised at the small amount of resistance she received from him when she proposed the idea of a move to Sandcastle. The week with his grandparents in Florida had been a revelation to him that he could wear shorts and play soccer outside in March. She had underestimated how appealing beach life might be to an eight-year-old boy who hated to be cooped up indoors.

She packed the suitcase she would travel with on her road trip to Texas. She was looking forward to stashing her parka and snow boots at the far back of a closet. Most of her winter clothes were in Salvation

Army boxes. She didn't see herself ever returning to Colorado full time. Or any cold weather climate for that matter. She had loved every minute of the life she and Ben built here with Jude, despite her downright hatred of the cold and snow. These would always be her good old days. Her eyes misted up a bit as she indulged herself in a small trip down memory lane as she walked through the house. Family dinners, homework assignments, indoor soccer games, nerf gun fights, movie nights, snowy days with the three of them sitting around their fireplace, planning warm weather vacations. But what she would miss about this life wasn't coming back and could never be again. She took a deep breath. She had to be done with the tears. She had to stop falling apart. She pushed away at the fog that tried to creep back with an almost physical gesture.

The next morning, she took one final look around the house. It was a showplace, a stunning home that had been filled with love. It would be a beautiful refuge for someone else now. She hoped it would house another family, maybe one with lots of children and extended family and friends that would fill it up and scratch the wood and ding the cabinets by riding tricycles inside. Even though it was full on Spring in most of the Northern hemisphere, snow clouds were building in the distance over the ridge. She and Jude climbed into the Land Rover. She smiled at Jude and reached over to squeeze

his shoulder. Then she put the SUV in gear. She had
seen her last snowstorm.

Chapter Twenty-Six

After Brooks' pre-dawn visit to the Bean and Bun, Aggie was a whirling dervish of activity. Despite the flashbacks from last night interrupting her every other thought. There was so much to do to get ready for Lillian and Jude's arrival that evening and also for her first retreat which was fast approaching and fully booked by a group of women from Houston. She spent the day dashing between the ovens and the cash register and the espresso machine. She filled the few quiet minutes checking and rechecking her to-do lists for the retreat.

Sadie breezed in around two o'clock to find a red faced and frazzled Aggie sitting on a stool behind the counter.

"Hey, hey!" She called.

"Hey, yourself," Aggie looked up from her lists.

"So, did I miss anything exciting after I left the party last night? The house looks so great!"

"Thanks," said Aggie brightening and also flushing bright pink at the thought of last night.

"What's up with you?" Sadie asked.

"Oh, nothing. Just tired" Aggie said.

"Really, are you okay?" she asked. "I just realized I don't think I've ever seen you sit down."

"Oh, I'm fine. Just trying to solve the time space continuum in order to be in two places at once."

"Huh?" said Sadie sitting down at the counter.

"Oh, nothing. The first retreat is in a week, and I haven't found anyone to help out here while I'm there."

"Ah, I follow now," said Sadie. And then she smiled. "I may have a solution."

"You are an expert in quantum physics?" Aggie raised her eyebrows. She also pointed at the coffee machine. "Usual?"

Sadie nodded. "Yes please. Three shots."

"Long day?"

"Very, but I think life is about to get easier."

"Oh?"

"Yes, and maybe for you too. My niece, Emma, is moving back to the island. She was almost done with college. I think she has about a year left. But last semester she did something super dumb, and she's suspended for a whole year."

"A year? What did she do?"

"She's a computer whiz and someone dared her to hack the school's grading system. She claims she was only seeing if she could do it and had no intention of changing anyone's grades. But long story short, she now has an unexpected gap year. My sister is so pissed."

"I bet she is. But how does this help you?" Aggie's brain was tired.

"Well, she's going to stay in our garage apartment. Free room and board in exchange for helping out with the twins. But I was thinking she needs a job during the day while the twins are at preschool. Bakery hours might work for her?"

"So, I'm to hire a juvenile delinquent to run my currently stable business while I attempt to start my new one?"

"At least meet her. She's a good kid. She made a bonehead move, but she's never been in trouble before. Plus, I'm inclined to believe her story. The kid has a 4.0 grade point average. She has no reason to change her grades."

"Hmm. Does she bake?" Aggie handed Sadie her coffee.

"She's twenty-one." Sadie rolled her eyes. "What do you think? Aggie didn't think it was pertinent to share the amount of baking she herself was doing at age twenty-one.

"Plus," Sadie added, "word on the street is you teach people how to bake."

"Touché. Honestly, she wouldn't have to do much actual baking. And she'd only be here on her own on the retreat days. Also, I don't exactly have a lot of other applicants. If she promises to not mess with my computer system, she's hired. Bring her by after closing."

"Ok, I'll do that."

"Oh, hey." Aggie stopped her as Sadie gathered up her bag. "What time are you picking up Lillian and Jude tomorrow?" Aggie had arranged for Sadie to tour Lillian and Jude around the island and show them some rentals.

"I think around nine in the morning. Will that work?"

"I'm sure that's fine."

"And there's a new little cabin that just came up for rent. It's darling, up on the North End near Brooks' place."

At the mention of Brooks Aggie felt herself flush. "Oh really?" She said, trying to play it cool. She avoided Sadie's gaze and started polishing the already spotless espresso machine with her dishtowel.

"Yes. Why are you being weird?"

"What do you mean? I'm fine." Aggie risked a look back at Sadie after she composed her face. She wasn't trying to keep a secret, but she wasn't ready to share her news about Brooks just yet. It was like a brightly polished gem radiating with warmth in her pocket. Like she could take it out to look at it anytime she wanted, and she wasn't ready to share it yet. As if sharing it might diminish its value somehow. Also, she wasn't sure how Brooks felt about sharing their news. If there was any news. It had only been one night after all. Well, practically one and a half if you counted their dawn shenanigans in the Bean and Bun kitchen that morning. But anyway, for now, she was going to keep it to herself.

"Are you sure you're okay? Your face looks like a cartoon character."

"I'm totally sure." Aggie shook her head. "I'm just excited is all. The first retreat is this weekend. And I'm tired," she admitted, sniffling a yawn. "But bring Emma by later. This would check a big to-do box." She waved her yellow pad covered in lists at her friend.

"Will do. Be back soon."

"Okay. Bye." Aggie waved as Sadie headed off to pick up the twins.

An hour later, Sadie walked back into the shop, the twins in tow. Adelaide and Alexander were holding hands, wearing matching smiles. They loved nothing more than a special trip to what they called Miss Aggie's Magic Shop. This delighted Aggie, and she made a fuss over them. Today she presented a little plate with an assortment of pastel colored meringue cookies, piped out in little swirls. The plate resembled the inside of an Easter basket, and the twins' eyes widened. Aggie set the plate down on a table and asked what they wanted to drink. "Miss Aggie's Lemonade!" they chorused.

"Um, I think water will do. Unless you want to deal with the fallout from the sugar crash," said Sadie sternly, pointing at the plate.

"Okay, okay," said Aggie, as she poured the waters into the little colored cups she kept for children and carried them over to the table. "Now," she said, turning back to Sadie and the young woman standing beside her. "You must be Emma. I'm Aggie." She held out her hand, and the young girl shook it.

"Yes, it's nice to meet you." She was obviously young, but she looked Aggie in the eye and her smile was warm and genuine. Aggie liked her immediately. The three spent the next hour discussing the job requirements and how it could dovetail with Emma's responsibilities helping out with the twins. By the time the twins finished the plate of cookies, they had hammered out a schedule that would work for everyone. After she was trained, Emma would help out while the twins were at school, and she would run the shop solo on the weekends when Aggie was running retreats. Paying Emma's wages was a hit to Aggie's bottom line, but there was no alternative. They agreed to a trial run, and Aggie crossed her fingers that this would work. She liked Emma and had a good feeling about her. The older Aggie got, the more she learned to trust her gut. And today it was telling her that even though Emma had clearly messed up big time at school, she was basically a good egg. And Aggie admitted to herself, she had zero time to look for someone else. Aggie walked out with Sadie, Emma and the twins and locked up.

As she pulled into the beach house drive, Lillian's Land Rover was parked in the driveway. Aggie jumped out of her car, wishing she hadn't waited to meet with Emma. She should have been here to meet them. But where were they? Aggie hadn't left a key out, and Lillian and Jude were nowhere to be seen. A child's laughter wafted down the beach. Aggie started up the walkway that led up over the dunes and down to the sand. Lillian was there, standing halfway between the walkway and the surf, yoga pants pulled up around her knees, shoes dangling from one hand. Her other hand was busy snapping photos of Jude running back and forth, splashing in the shallow waves.

Aggie called out, but the wind carried her voice back toward the house. She sidled up alongside her old friend unnoticed. By way of greeting she just said, "Jude looks like he's having fun."

"Hi!" Lillian jumped when Aggie spoke. "Hi, hi!" The two hugged and then stood watching Jude.

"He is having fun. He's been cooped up in the car for two days. You should have seen the look on his face when we pulled in. I was so worried I was making the wrong choice. Selling the house, moving him away from his friends and everything he knows. But he seems to be thrilled."

"Kids are so adjustable," Aggie responded. "I mean, I don't have any, but that seems to be a common opinion."

"They are. Jude! Jude!" Lillian called. She waved him over, and he ran towards them.

"Say hi to Aunt Aggie, then you can get back out there."

"Hi!" he said with a wet hug.

"Hi yourself, kiddo." Aggie ruffled his mop of blonde hair. "How are you?"

"I'm great!" he exclaimed. "This is way better than Cabo. Did you know you can't even get in the water in Cabo? The ocean will suck you right in, and you have to go live with an octopus underwater."

"Is that so?" said Aggie, with a glance at Lillian. Lillian just shrugged.

"Mom, can I play for a few more minutes? Puuhleeease???"

"Ok, but come in soon, and help me unload the car."

"Deal," he said and took off for the surf.

"He's going to love it here," said Aggie. "You'll see. The school is really sweet and small. He'll make friends quickly."

"Gosh, I hope so," said Lillian, watching her son. "Whoever said having children was like letting your heart walk around outside your body was dead on the money." She turned back to Aggie. "And who knew the Texas Coast could beat Cabo? What have I been doing dragging him to Mexico all these years?" The two women laughed and headed for the house. Inside, Lillian stopped short. "Wow," she said, taking in all the details Aggie had painstakingly put together. The living room, which had a construction zone the last time Lillian visited, was now a bright, inviting space, furnished with the cream colored linen chesterfields and cushy armchairs, littered with brightly colored throw pillows and a few beach-y boho accents that kept it from feeling like you were in a magazine spread. "Is Nancy Meyers filming a movie here?" She asked with a straight face as she moved toward the dining area and kitchen.

Aggie looked at her and laughed. "Not hardly, but I don't think you could have possibly paid me a higher compliment."

"Well, if I could, I would. It's just gorgeous." She clapped her hands lightly in applause. "And thank you for having us. I swear we'll be out of your hair by the end of the week. Sadie emailed me some listings, and there are some good rental options. I'm sure we'll find something tomorrow."

"Of course, silly. You're welcome to stay as long as you need to. Although, if you're still here Friday, we're all camping out in the unfinished bedroom."

"However, I think Jude will be on board if you find something on the beach," Aggie added, pointing through the big front window. From inside the living room, they could see him still running back and forth on the beach. Lillian called to him to come in, and a reluctant and wet Jude came loping up the porch steps.

"Are you hungry?" Aggie asked.

Jude threw his head back and said with much drama, "I'm ALWAYS hungry."

"Why don't we get you something to eat?" Aggie heated up a lasagna and tossed a giant Caesar salad, and they all had second helpings of both. It had been a while since Lillian and Jude had a home cooked meal. Ben had been the one to do most of the cooking. Since he passed, Lillian tried to make an effort, but her heart was never in it. She took a bite of the lasagna. The combination of Aggie's herbaceous, garlicky homemade tomato sauce and gooey melted fontina and mozzarella made her swoon. "Ags, you are a wizard. I'm thinking I need to take one of your classes."

"Yeah, Mom, you might," piped up Jude, and they all laughed.

"I may not be able to afford your classes anymore," Lillian said wryly.

"I think we can work out a friends and family rate for my oldest and dearest."

"That's kind of you."

"Sort of selfish, actually. If you learn, you can help me teach!"

"That's an ambitious idea," Lillian scoffed. "Maybe I can be your resident dishwasher."

"Also not opposed to that idea."

Jude was ecstatic when Aggie brought in a plate of brownies after dinner. "Mom hardly EVER lets me have dessert," he said around a giant mouthful of brownie.

"Child abuse!" Aggie admonished, and Jude nodded. Lillian sent Jude off to take a shower, and the two women cleaned up the kitchen. "So, how are you two doing? Really?" Aggie asked as she passed Lillian a plate to put in the dishwasher.

"We're…. okay. We're not great, but we're making it. I need to get Jude settled in a house and school, the sooner the better, I think. There is a soccer league here, right?"

"Hmmm. I think so," said Aggie. "I mean, there are kids that come in on Saturday afternoons in some sort of jerseys. It could be soccer."

"Okay, I'll find out."

Jude reappeared in the kitchen, his thick blonde hair still wet from the shower and sticking straight up.

He was wearing a shirt with the words *Soccer Is Life* emblazoned across the front.

"Are you guys talking about soccer?" he asked sleepily, rubbing his eyes.

"Yep. You like soccer, bud?" Aggie asked.

Jude stopped rubbing his eyes and looked at her with all the solemnity an eight-year-old can muster. "Oh yes, Aunt Aggie. Soccer is my life sport."

"Well, then. We'll just have to get some info on that. Shouldn't be too hard to figure out."

"No, it shouldn't," said Lillian "Now, it's time for you to get to bed, mister man."

"Okay. Will you come tuck me in?"

"Sure, sweetheart, I'll be up in just a minute. You go ahead." Before Lillian headed upstairs, she hugged Aggie again with tears in her eyes and a whispered "thank you."

"Don't be silly. Go get some rest. I'll finish up down here."

Jude and Lillian, their bellies full and exhausted from their road trip both slept soundly in the beach house's beautifully appointed guest rooms, but Aggie tossed and turned. Almost as if she was too tired to sleep. Her mind kept racing between anxious thoughts about the retreat plans to a completely different set of thoughts about Brooks. He had sent a text earlier confirming their dinner plans for tomorrow night. He said he was excited to break in his new kitchen and cook for her for a change. She smiled to herself in the dark, wondering what it would be like to be with him on his turf. They were only ever together at the bakery or the beach house. She wondered what it looked like. Would it be all man cave decor with stainless steel and leather everything? What would it be like to wake up there? What would it be like to brush their teeth together? Then her thoughts turned back toward her retreat plans. Should she furnish toothbrushes? How much was too much? She tossed and turned and sometime far too late, she finally fell into a fitful slumber.

Chapter Twenty-Seven

Far too few hours later, Aggie's alarm jolted her awake. She rubbed her eyes looking at the clock. Her 5am wake up calls were getting harder and harder. She realized the last time she had seen the clock last night the numbers said 2:13am. She had clocked a grand total of perhaps five hours of sleep in the last two nights. No wonder she was exhausted. As she stepped into the shower, she remembered Emma was starting today. Well, that was something.

It was a busy morning, training Emma along with keeping up with the steady rhythm of the ovens, the coffee machine and the cash register. Emma however, proved a quick study and by lunch time, felt comfortable enough with the espresso machine and the cash register that Aggie went back to the kitchen, leaving her to handle the front of the shop.

It had been less than a full day, but Emma was already proving herself an asset, friendly and helpful with the customers. Not only that, but when there had been a lull, she took it upon herself to straighten the display cases and the merchandise kiosk near the front window that held t-shirts, aprons, mugs and bagged coffee. She even wiped the counters and swept the floors. Aggie was a little bit in awe of her. She was like a very efficient and helpful little fairy. Aggie walked back up to the front carrying a tray of fresh sourdough focaccia loaves when Sadie came in with Lillian and Jude.

"Hey, team!" Aggie said with a big smile. She deposited the loaves and put a hand on Jude's shoulder. "So," she asked him "Did you and your mom pick out a house?"

"Yep!" he grinned. "And guess what, Aunt Aggie? It's on the beach! Like, right on the beach. Mom says I get to play on the beach every single day. I can even play soccer out there." Aggie gave him a high five and smiled at Lillian. She was smiling back.

"We just signed the lease. I feel good about this."

"Me too!" Jude punched the air for emphasis.

"And it's ready to move in. I'll change some pieces out later, some of the pieces in there are pretty worn and dated. But it's completely furnished down to the forks and spoons. We're going to grab our suitcases and stay there tonight. Jude is excited. His room has a view of the beach."

"Are you sure?" Aggie said. "You know you are welcome to stay with me."

"I know, and I love you for it. But I think Jude and I need to start making this a home as soon as possible."

"Okay," said Aggie. "I think I get it. Alright, now who's hungry?" Jude made the same silly face from yesterday. "Aunt Aggie, I am ALWAYS HUNGRY."

"Indoor voices, Jude," Lillian admonished her son. "Why don't you go find us a table?" Aggie made them all sandwiches on the still warm focaccia and put a giant monster cookie on Jude's plate. Jude's eyes got big at the sight of the cookie half the size of his head loaded with chocolate chips and M&Ms. "Thank you!" He almost yelled when she walked over with their food.

"I have a feeling Jude's sugar intake is going to spike living here," Lillian said.

"Hey," said Aggie "there's like ten grams of protein in that cookie. And fiber from the oatmeal. It's practically health food."

"Sure," said Lillian. But she was smiling. If sandy beaches and sugary cookies were the recipe to seeing her son animated and smiling again, you wouldn't catch her putting up a fight.

"So," Aggie asked Lillian and Sadie "where is the house?"

Sadie answered her. "It's up on the North End. Just a couple houses down from Brooks' cabin." At the mention of Brooks, Aggie felt her face flush hot again. Sadie shot her a look, raising her eyebrows in question. But Aggie quickly changed the subject, asking Sadie what she knew about kids' sports programs on the island. As she had hoped, that sent Sadie back into realtor mode, spouting off information. She was a walking tourism board. She, Lillian, and Jude went off shortly thereafter, Sadie volunteering to take them by the Parks and Recreation office to get Jude registered for the local pee wee soccer league. It was a little late in the season, but the director was a friend, and she thought they would bend the rules.

At the end of the day, Aggie showed Emma how to cash out the register. The cleaning up and prep took half the time as usual. Aggie could get used to this, she thought. Emma headed off to go meet Sadie with the twins and Aggie headed for home. Despite being achingly bone tired, every fiber of her being was buzzing at the prospect of dinner with Brooks. She let herself into the beach house and went upstairs. She took a long, hot shower, washed her hair, and shaved her legs. She selected a pretty sundress that still had the tags on it and a pair of sandals. She dug around and found her perfume in the back of a drawer. She eyed herself critically in the mirror. Not bad, she thought. The dress complimented her curves nicely, even if it was more snug than when she bought it. In Houston, she had kept to a strict daily workout regime. She was curvier now, even though her days of constant activity seemed to balance out most the extra carbs. She decided she liked her new curves and left it at that. She left her hair to dry naturally in loose waves. The constant humidity rendered her hair straightener useless so there was no point in trying for anything else. She applied a dab of concealer to the dark circles under her eyes. She stifled a yawn. She really should have tried to find time for a nap. A swipe of mascara and a dap of lip gloss finished her makeup routine and she headed downstairs. She had half an hour before she needed to leave. The drive to the North End would take less than ten minutes, even with the island's thirty-five mile per hour speed limit. She picked up her handbag and went out onto the porch. She sat in the rocker, checking her watch every few minutes. Maybe she should just go ahead and go, she thought, but she worried she might look too eager. She lay her head back against the rocker, thinking about how lucky she was. This was really her house. Well, it was hers until she couldn't make the payments. But it was hers for now. Was she turning into one of those glass half full people? And she might, just maybe be starting her first relationship with someone she could see herself with. She smiled to herself.

***

Brooks looked around his new kitchen. He wasn't much of a cook, but he was apt at curating. There was a simple salad of fresh, local greens and deep red garden tomatoes. Scattered over the salad were knobs of tangy herbed goat cheese, and the whole business was

217

drizzled with a bright, fruity Italian olive oil and a reduced balsamic glaze. There were two Wagyu strip steaks ready to go on the grill and a loaf of fresh ciabatta bread from the farmers market ready to sop up more of the fruity green olive oil. He had deliberated on the bread choice. On one hand, he felt a twinge of guilt purchasing bread somewhere other than The Bean and Bun. But was it weird to serve Aggie something from her shop? In the end he didn't have time to get by The Bean and Bun anyway. He was proud of his menu, and he was excited to show off the house to Aggie. A bottle of Argentinian Malbec was breathing on the sideboard, and he went ahead and poured two glasses. He carried the glasses out onto the porch thinking maybe they would take them down for a walk on the beach before dinner. Aggie would like that, he thought, and he thought she would appreciate the food too. He loved how she unashamedly adored food. He also loved that he always knew what she was thinking. So unlike Helen with her calculations of her calories and her affections. He thought yet again how lucky he was to be away from her, away from Los Angeles. He took a deep breath of sea air and pushed all thoughts of Helen from his mind. He sat down to wait for Aggie.

Twenty minutes later he was still sitting, checking his watch. She wasn't the type to keep him waiting. And she also wasn't the type to not call. He started to get worried. And then he started to wonder if she regretted the other night after the party. She didn't seem to regret anything in the bakery the next morning when they almost had a repeat of the night before. Her text response yesterday was brief, but she was entertaining her friend, so that was understandable. He dialed her number. When there was no answer, he sent a text. No response. Brooks drained his glass and started on the one he'd poured for Aggie. The sky darkened, and so did his mood. He checked his phone yet again. Still nothing from Aggie. He went inside, put one of the steaks in the refrigerator and set the other on the grill. The sizzle and smoke of heat reacting with the well marbled beef gave off a mouthwatering aroma, but it was lost on Brooks. He carried the salad and the bread out onto the porch and ate his dinner in a sad silence. At one point a set of headlights could be seen coming up the road. He got up from his seat but sat back down when the headlights turned in two houses down the beach. Brooks finished his meal and the bottle of wine and went to bed in a boozy, melancholy haze.

***

Around midnight, Aggie woke up with a start in a state of complete confusion. What was she doing outside? Then she looked down at her dress and realized her mistake. How could she have fallen asleep? No, no, no, no. She fumbled in her bag for her phone.

What time was it? The numbers 12:14 glowed in the dark. Dammit, dammit, dammit, she thought. She tapped the screen and saw two missed calls from Brooks and a text. Shit. He must think she was the world's biggest jerk. She sat back in the rocking chair. There was no way she could go over there now. And it was way too late to call. What would he think? In the end she sent a text.

Brooks I am so, so, so sorry. I know this sounds incredibly lame, but I fell asleep. Come by the bakery in the morning, please? I'll make you breakfast.

She went in the house and up to bed feeling horrible.

Chapter Twenty-Eight

The next morning, Aggie was in The Bean and Bun early. In between serving customers, she was showing Emma how to roll dough for her chai spice cinnamon buns. Emma had no baking experience, but she was a willing student, and Aggie had high hopes. Every time the little bell attached to the front door tinkled Aggie's heart beat a little faster, and she peeked out of the kitchen hoping to see Brooks. As soon as she got these buns in the oven, she would text him. Better yet, maybe she should take him some breakfast over to the cabin. Yes, that was better. She popped the tray in the oven and gave Emma instructions to let them cool completely before adding the chai spice glaze. Then she started assembling an apology basket of goodies for Brooks. As if a delivery of carbohydrates might make this better. It was ridiculous, but she didn't know what else to do. He still hadn't answered her midnight text. Or the one she sent this morning.

She made him one of the breakfast sandwiches he liked and wrapped it in wax paper. She added a loaf of the sourdough focaccia and bag of her homemade granola. And for added measure a small white bakery box with a brownie. Then she ground beans for an extra hot Americano, just the way he liked it. She poured the coffee into a thermos. She even warmed the cream before adding it. Emma seemed to have everything well in hand, so Aggie told her she'd be back in an hour and took off for the North End. Her stomach was in knots as she drove the narrow road that led north. She passed Lillian and Jude's new house and felt a little guilty not stopping. But she wasn't in the mood to share the events of the last twenty-four hours. She hadn't even told Lillian about the night after the party. She hadn't told anyone. Her palms were clammy as she parked her car and carried the basket up the walk. The Thunderbird was parked behind the house, so he was home. She took a deep breath and walked up the steps to knock on the door. There was no answer. She stood there feeling more and more like a fool as a full five minutes ticked by. She finally set the basket down by the door and turned to leave, but then she heard a rustling inside. Brooks answered the door barefoot, wearing a pair of rumpled jeans, obviously tugged on mere moments before, and heaven help her, no shirt. His face was creased with sleep and his thatch of sandy hair stood up at odd angles.

"Hi," said Aggie meekly. "Um, did you get my text?"

"No. No I didn't," said Brooks hoarsely. He leaned against the door frame, not moving aside or inviting her in.

"Brooks, I am so, so sorry," The speech she rehearsed on the way over deserted her and she started babbling. "I was just so tired. I hadn't slept in days, and I only sat down for a minute. I was all ready to drive over here and, I…I sort of passed out. I woke up at midnight. I'm so, truly sorry." She clapped her hand over her mouth to stall the cascade of words.

Brooks was silent for a few seconds. Then he eyed the basket. "What's all this?"

"An 'I'm sorry' basket? And an, I'm really, really, sorry coffee? Just the way you like it. Careful. It's so hot I wouldn't serve it to anyone but you. I'd worry about being sued." She risked the joke and was rewarded with something like a snort. Brooks accepted the proffered thermos. He still didn't invite her in but moved out onto the porch. He sat down and gestured for her to sit with him. "Do you by chance have one of those magic sandwiches in that basket?" he drawled, his voice husky from sleep and too much wine.

Aggie smiled, brightening. "I do," she said, handing over the wax paper package. Brooks chewed silently for a minute. "I don't suppose you also brought an ice-cold coke?" Aggie shook her head.

"Too bad. This chick stood me up last night, and I had to drink a whole bottle of Malbec by myself. I feel like hell."

"Man, she sounds like a real asshole." Aggie said.

"Hey now, don't talk about my girl like that. I kind of liked her."

"Do you still kind of like her today?"

Brooks chewed thoughtfully. "I think I do."

"So, you forgive her?"

"Well, I think I'm going to have to. She has the only decent coffee in town."

Aggie laughed. "I'm so glad to hear that. I do have to get back to the shop. Can I make you dinner tonight?"

"I leave for Houston in a couple hours. I have a flight to L.A. this afternoon to go meet with my agent and the movie people."

"Oh," said Aggie, suddenly deflated.

"We'll catch up when I get back." He stood, dusting crumbs from his lap. "Thanks for the food."

Aggie looked up at him from her chair. "Brooks, I really am so, so sorry."

"No worries. It's cool. Really. I'll call you when I get back. Probably just be a few days."

"Alright," she said. "Can I cook you dinner when you get back?"

"I'll call you."

"Okay." Aggie felt awkward. This is not how she hoped this would go.

"Well, I do have to get back to the bakery. See you in a few days?"

"You bet."

"Okay. Bye then." She walked down the steps and held it together until she made it to her car. But the whole drive back to the shop the road shimmered through the tears that kept filling her eyes.

Aggie made it back to the bakery and swallowing her tears, forced herself to concentrate on the task at hand. In a little over twenty-four hours, her first retreat guests were arriving. Aggie made it through the rest of the day in a fog. Why hadn't Brooks mentioned his L.A. plans before? Surely this wasn't a last-minute trip. Was he entertaining a move back to California? She closed the shop at 4pm but didn't feel like going home. Her to-do list for the retreat had been checked twice and everything was ready. So instead of heading for the beach house, she packed a box of blueberry lemon scones, along with a bag of orange cranberry granola and a brownie and decided she would pay Nellie a visit at Peach Tree house. She wasn't going to go whining to Nellie about her boy problems, specifically as they involved her grandson. But maybe Brooks had talked to her about any plans he had. She wouldn't ask her outright, but if the old lady happened to drop a crumb, it would make her feel better. Or would it? What if he had told her he was moving back to Los Angeles? Aggie's mind was reeling, and she forced herself to pull it together as she drove slowly down the manicured drive of Peach Tree House. She was always struck with the lush beauty of the place. She found Nellie at a card table set up in the courtyard. Her back was to Aggie as she walked up, but Aggie could hear her say "GIN!" triumphantly as she laid her cards down on the table.

"I swear you cheat," the woman across from her said grumpily.

Nellie laughed. "I can, but with you I don't have to."

"Of course she doesn't cheat!" Aggie defended Nellie by way of a greeting.

Nellie looked up from the card table. "Aggie, my dear! What a wonderful surprise. You will excuse me, won't you, Gladys? It seems I have a visitor."

Gladys grumbled something as Nellie got up, spry as ever. But she did take Aggie's arm for balance as they moved toward the path that led out of the courtyard out onto the expansive grounds. "Don't mind Gladys, she's been grumpy for decades," Nellie said, "Is Brooks with you, or do we get a little girl time?" asked Nellie looking over Aggie's shoulder.

"Just me," said Aggie. "Brooks is in Los Angeles. But I had some blueberry lemon leftover today. I thought you would enjoy them."

"Well, you are certainly correct in that. Thank you, my dear. Let's set the box on the bench, and you can help me get my steps in. Nellie held up her left wrist to reveal a new smart watch. The doctor says I need at least five thousand steps a day. Movement will keep me young apparently. I told him it must be working. I don't feel a day over eighty-five." The two women laughed and continued down the path. Nellie pointed out the different flora and fauna. The aroma was intoxicating.

"I didn't know you knew so much about botany," said Aggie.

"Well, I've always loved my garden, but I've started learning about what's here. Must give the old thinker something to chew on every now and again." She tapped her head.

"Ah, so that's your secret. Learn new skills and get your steps in."

"Well, that, and plenty of chocolate. And good wine." Said Nellie thoughtfully. "Tell me child, what's wrong. You look like someone ran over your dog."

"I'm fine, Nellie. I'm just tired." And she prattled on telling Nellie all about the retreats. The two women spent a pleasant evening in the garden listening to the birds and chatting. Aggie made to leave when it was time for Nellie to go in for dinner.

"Would you like to stay for dinner?" Nellie asked. "The food is excellent."

"No, thank you," Aggie said as she gave her a hug. "I have a very early morning."

"I know you do." Nellie put her hand on Aggie's arm, stopping her as she turned to go. "My dear, I've lived a very long time. Please don't take offense when I tell you that whatever it is that is eating at you, go fix it. You are too joyful of a being to walk around with a sour face. Whatever it is you need to do, go do it. Life is too short for regrets."

"Yes," said Aggie. "You're right." She hugged the old lady one more time and took her leave.

Chapter Twenty-Nine

Aggie spent the morning before her retreat guests arrived in the shop, making sure Emma had everything she needed to run the place on her own for two days. Emma was proving herself invaluable and tireless, as only a twenty-one-year-old can be. Not only would she run the shop, but after closing, she would high tail it over to the beach house to help in the kitchen. Sadie didn't need her on the weekends, so she was free.

The morning rush was about over when the doorbell tinkled, and Aggie looked up. She thought she recognized the woman walking in out of the bright sunshine but couldn't place her. She was impossibly thin and perfectly tanned with mile long legs and a large bosom that couldn't possibly be real. She was a real-life Barbie doll.

"Hello," Aggie greeted her brightly. "What can we get you?"

The woman didn't remove her dark Chanel sunglasses. And she didn't try to make eye contact when she spoke but kept her gaze on the menu. "Do you have any green juices?"

"Oh, nope, sorry. Lemonade is probably the closest we get to that," Aggie said with a smile. "Can I get you one?"

"No, no that's okay." She continued to scrutinize the menu. "I'll take a decaf iced Americano, black. No sugar. And please make sure I get a straw with that."

"Coming right up." Aggie turned to start the espresso machine.

"Can I ask you a question?" asked the woman. "I'm looking for a friend of mine who I think lives on the island."

"Certainly," Aggie said, but a pinprick of intuition started to tingle up her spine.

"Do you happen to know where Brooks Jagger lives?"

Aggie froze as all the pieces clicked into place. Luckily, she had her back to the woman as she was turned around filling her to-go cup with ice. With great effort, Aggie took a breath and composed her face before turning around to face her. "Do you mean Brooks Schmidt?" she asked slowly.

"Yes, yes," the woman replied, waving her hand as if it was all the same to her.

"I do." Aggie could hear herself talking. Her voice sounded like she was hearing someone else speak. She heard herself say, "He does live here. But he's out of town. He had to go to Los Angeles for a meeting." Aggie screamed at herself inside her head. Why was she offering all this information up to this woman? *Maybe because you just want her to leave*, she thought to herself.

"You have *got* to be kidding me," said the blonde, finally removing her sunglasses to reveal crystal blue eyes with lashes so long and thick they had to be fake. I just came *all* the way *from L.A.* to talk to the man." She rolled her eyes dramatically. "Guess now I'm heading straight back. Just as well." She picked up the coffee from the counter and took a delicate sip through the straw. "Oh!" she exclaimed, raising her eyebrows in surprise. "This is actually good."

"Thank you," Aggie said through tight lips as she swiped the platinum credit card the woman held out and wished her a good day. She turned toward the kitchen as the woman left the shop to find Emma in the doorway staring after the woman open mouthed.

"Do you know who that is?" she said excitedly, gripping Aggie's forearm.

"If I had to venture a guess, I would say that has to be Helen Hanes."

Aggie told herself all afternoon that it didn't matter. That no matter what happened if and when Helen caught up to Brooks, he would still come home. He would *probably* still come home? Was this his home? Or was his North End cabin going to end up as a place he visited two weeks out of the year? Or never? Despite everything he said about wanting to stay here, maybe he would change his mind. Aggie closed her eyes, forced herself to put this out of her mind. Her first guests were arriving in mere hours. The breakdown she so rightfully deserved was just going to have to wait.

Four o'clock that afternoon found Aggie showered, dressed, and standing on her front porch all but bouncing up and down waiting for her guests. It was a day of late spring perfection, and the afternoon sunshine was bright and sparkly and not too hot. There was a light breeze coming off the water and Aggie was glad she decided to serve the welcome drinks out front. A long table held ice buckets with bottles of chilled French champagne ready to pop, perfectly polished stemware and platters of canapés. There were piles of gougers, those light miniature French puffs of savory pastry that went so well with fizz. Blinis with a swipe of cream and caviar, figs and melon wrapped in prosciutto, and a large round of camembert to be eaten with either apple slices or impossibly thin toast points made with Aggie's rosemary sourdough focaccia. Soft French music played from the blue-tooth speaker Sadie let her borrow for the weekend.

In the living room was a welcome gift for each guest. A French market style straw tote containing a handwritten welcome note, a linen apron with The Bean and Bun logo, a hand thrown ceramic coffee mug Aggie commissioned from a local potter also sporting the Bean and Bun logo, a Turkish style beach blanket in candy pastel colors, fancy sunscreen and a wide brimmed straw beach hat.

The guest bathrooms upstairs were stocked with luxurious bath products and fluffy white Egyptian cotton towels. Each of the bedrooms were carefully outfitted with Aggie's tasteful selections of light and bright bohemian beach decor. In the kitchen, the food was prepped, both to serve and for the cooking demonstrations portion of the weekend. She was ready.

At four fifteen, the ladies arrived en masse in two large SUVs. Aggie knew they were all from Houston, but other than the food allergies and birth dates requested on the registration form, Aggie didn't know anything about them. It occurred to her she should have asked for pictures or at least tried to look them up on Facebook to learn their names before they arrived. Oh well, she thought, and she filed that away in her mental notes for next time. She pasted a bright smile on her face, took a deep breath to calm her nerves and went down the steps to welcome her guests. As they stepped out of the cars, it was one fashion plate after another. It was as if they were competing for best dressed in flowing maxi dresses in all colors of the rainbow. They sort of reminded her of Helen with their perfect tans and long, fake lashes. Stop it, she commanded herself. She boxed up all thoughts of Helen and of Brooks and shoved that box on the top shelf of her consciousness, way, way at the back.

"Hello!" said Aggie and she introduced herself to the group. As the women began introducing themselves, Aggie thought again how she *really* should have learned their names beforehand. She tried the best she could to make the names stick to the faces. It didn't help that they all ended in 'y'. Hilary, Bethany, Jenny, Jamie, Lacey, Natalie. Couldn't they have thrown in an Elizabeth or a Jill? Emma was great with names, which would be helpful, when she got here. For the time being, she started passing out champagne glasses. The ladies oohed over the bubbles and the canapés and the sea view.

Aggie felt a little rusty during the cooking demo, but after tripping over her words a few times, she found her rhythm, and everyone had a rollicking good time watching her finish off the duck confit while they sipped more wine. They all enjoyed a family style dinner around the old farm table, and Aggie stopped counting how many bottles of champagne and wine she popped open. It also thrilled her to no end seeing the women posing for endless selfies and posting them to their Instagram feeds. She hoped they were tagging her.

The next day, after the morning cooking class, the women spent most of the day lounging at the beach until it was time for Amelia's wine demonstration. Aggie had been worried that after the night before the ladies wouldn't be in the mood for more wine, but these girls got right back into the swing of things. They loved Amelia and her quirky sense of humor, and they loved her wines even more. By dinner time, Amelia had orders for no less than half a dozen cases that she promised to have ready for pick up at the wine shop on their way out of town on Sunday.

Sunday morning, the women lingered over coffee and the beautiful buffet breakfast Aggie set out. They all hugged Aggie with air kisses, promising to be back. By noon, they were all piled back into the SUVs, on their way to Amelia's to pick up their goods before heading back to Houston. Aggie couldn't help but be grateful she wasn't the one heading back to the city after only a weekend at the beach.

Aggie settled herself on the porch with an iced coffee and her laptop. She hugged herself in glee and laughed out loud. It had worked! This crazy idea had worked. The guests were thrilled with their experience. And they *were* tagging Aggie in their gorgeous photos and her Instagram account was blowing up. Her bank account was also sufficiently plump. Even after all her expenses, including a hefty fee to Amelia for the wine demonstration and a generous bonus to Emma, the retreat was a financial success. The Bean and Bun Beachside Retreat was officially a proven concept.

She opened a text and typed a message to Shane. *"I'm going to stay. Officially. You can let Mark buy in if you want. But that guy is straight up bullying you. All decisions are yours now, but I'd let him walk."*

Thanks to the Instagram traffic, the last two spots for the next retreat were booked. There was even one person on a waitlist. If only her last room was ready. Aggie carried her coffee back inside and went upstairs. She took a hard look at the unfinished room. It desperately needed paint. She could paint, couldn't she? It couldn't be that hard. The floors needed to be sanded and refinished. She thought she could probably handle that too. The bathroom remodel was another thing, but maybe she could handle the demo part and just hire Ambrose to put it back together? If she started now, she might swing it, if not for this next retreat, then for the one after that. One more suite could make a big difference in her bottom line. And she had a smidgen more free time now that Emma was at the bakery. Aggie made a phone call to her new neighbor, Mr. O'Henry from the hardware store. Ten minutes later, kind Mr. O'Henry promised to deliver everything she would need, including the sander to prep the floors first thing the next morning. "Really?" Aggie said. "That's so generous. Thank you!"

"No trouble at all, Aggie girl. That's what neighbors are for. Although, if some of your chocolate croissants were to show up at the store, I wouldn't be heartbroken over it."

"Didn't Mrs. O'Henry say those were on the not-to-eat list?" Aggie asked skeptically.

"What Mrs. O'Henry doesn't know won't kill her."

"All right. It'll be our little secret. Just this once!"

That evening, Lillian brought Jude over for a full debriefing on the retreat and a home cooked meal. The two women sat on the porch while Jude hunted crabs on the beach. Lillian poured the rosé she brought over and toasted Aggie. "To you and your culinary brilliance."

"Why, thank you." Aggie clinked her glass with her friend's. The wind picked up and Aggie saw dark clouds on the horizon. "Looks like we're in for another storm." Her face fell as the clouds sent her mind racing back to the last storm and Brooks' fateful arrival on her front porch.

"That's okay. I'll take it over snow any day of the week." Then Lillian noticed the frown on Aggie's face. "What on earth is the matter? You should still be on cloud nine."

Aggie blew out a big breath. Part of her wanted to cry, but she didn't. But she did slowly, starting with the night of the last storm, tell Lillian about Brooks. She told her all of it, starting with the party the night before Lillian arrived, his arrival to check on her during the storm, the next morning in the bakery kitchen and her regrettable front porch nap that caused her to miss their dinner date. She relayed her conversation with Brooks on his front porch and the complete radio silence from him since. And she wrapped up with Helen's appearance at the shop the day before.

"Oof," said Lillian. "That's a lot. But, good for you!"

"Huh?" Aggie looked up.

"You have been severely lacking in the love life department for *eons*. I don't think you've had any fun since our sophomore year of high school. I'm just thrilled you made room in your schedule for something other than work for once! Hallelujah!" Lillian threw her hands up. "However, this ends, it calls for celebration."

"Well, not if he doesn't call or come back."

"From everything you've told me, I'm pretty sure he's coming back. Even if he doesn't call. I mean you did stand him up. Men have fragile egos. He'll go to Hollywood, people will fawn all over him and his manuscript for a few days, and he'll come back good as new. You'll see."

"Maybe. If Helen doesn't get to him while he's there," Aggie said for the first time voicing the thought.

"He seems like a good guy. Also, I have a confession. I knew you were going over there for dinner.

We met him on the beach that afternoon. Jude and I were out kicking the soccer ball. He seemed so nice, and he was really sweet with Jude. He even kicked the soccer ball around with him for a bit. I just wish I knew you needed a wakeup call. We could have avoided the business."

"That would have been nice."

" But I bet he comes back. And even if he doesn't, he ended your drought, so there's that."

Aggie didn't have a response to 'that'. At least not one she wanted to say out loud.

Lillian took another look at the sky. The storm clouds were piled thick and dark, and bolts of lightning were beginning to flash, illuminating one cloud bank after another. "Now, let me go get Jude off of the beach before he gets hit by lightning." The rain pelted down outside, and the three of them enjoyed a cozy evening in Aggie's kitchen. Aggie cooked a simple supper of red wine braised pork chops, a caprese salad and some of the leftover gougeres. "Don't worry," she said to Lillian as the pork chops simmered in the wine, "all the alcohol will cook off. I'm not feeding booze to your child."

"Shoot," Lillian said, "add another glug. Maybe it will help him go to sleep. The child has all the questions of the universe at bedtime. I need access to a paleontologist, an astronomer and a priest." Aggie laughed and in response, poured Lillian another glass of wine, and they all sat down to eat.

"Oh, my goodness, what are these!?" Lillian swooned, biting into one of the savory air-filled little French pastries left over from the weekend.

"Pretty good huh? I'll send you home with some. I have a ton in the freezer."

"Yes please!" Jude piped up as he reached for his fifth one. The three lingered over dinner, and Jude caught Aggie up on all his latest adventures on the beach, his new school friends, and his soccer team's ranking.

"Hey," Aggie asked Lillian as they finished eating "you want to come help me operate power tools tomorrow?"

"I'm sorry. What?" Lillian looked at her as if she suggested a quick shopping trip to the moon. Aggie explained her plan to start sanding down the floors the next morning.

"Um, yes. I think I should be here. I mean, someone should, right? Isn't it a little dangerous to operate something like that by yourself?" Aggie rolled her eyes. Lillian had had people to do everything for her for too long.

"It'll be fine. So, you're coming?"

"Sure, right after I drop Jude at school." The spring storm passed swiftly, and the air felt cool and fresh as

Aggie walked Lillian and Jude out on the front porch. The steps were slick with rain and Aggie was about to caution Jude to watch his step, but as only an eight-year-old boy will, he skipped the steps altogether. Before anyone could say anything, he climbed up onto the rail from the porch and was down to the ground in one gazelle-like leap, all legs and arms. "Jude, you are going to give me a heart attack," said Aggie. Jude just shrugged, waved, and hopped in the Land Rover.

"You and me both," Lillian called back to Aggie as she cautiously made her own way down the slick wooden steps. "I know when we hit the teen years, I will thank my lucky stars I have a boy instead of a girl. But I swear boys are harder to keep alive and in one piece."

"I think I believe that," said Aggie. And she stood on the porch and waved as they drove off for home. Then Aggie made her way up to bed and fell into a very deep sleep, happy to be back in her third-floor room.

Chapter Thirty

Brooks sat across the prime table of the very hip restaurant where his agent, Avery Jacobs, suggested they meet for lunch to discuss his next book and next steps. The waiter arrived with their drinks. A dirty martini for Avery and sparkling water for Brooks. He needed his wits about him today.

"Brooks, about this new manuscript," Avery started. "It's well, it's different."

"I know," said Brooks. "I like to think I'm evolving as a writer."

"It's certainly not bad, Brooks. In fact, the writing is wonderful, very mature. But it just seems like it doesn't fit with the others. I mean, you have Chester McCombs meditating and drinking coffee and eating scones. This is a bit of a departure from where we left him tossing back martinis in Jakarta at the end of book seven."

"I know, but I like it."

"I like it too Brooks, but I'm not sure your readers are going to be on board with this new Chester McCombs."

"He's still having a hell of an adventure, Avery. He's fighting the Columbian cartel for crying out loud."

"I get that. And again, it's not that I don't like it. But if you like having your books made into movies, I'm just not sure this one is going to make the cut."

Brooks had already sold the movie rights for the first four books to the studio. One of the meetings this week was to hammer out details for a deal to the rights for the next four, including the as-yet unfinished book eight currently under discussion. This new contract, considering the blockbuster success of the first movie, promised to be much more lucrative than the first.

"Brooks, this can be your Jack Reacher. Your double-oh-seven. This can be your golden ticket."

"Do you mean *your* golden ticket, Avery?" Brooks looked pointedly across the table, annoyed.

"I make no qualms about how this business works, Brooks. I don't work for free, but I do also want to see you succeed. You're a great writer and a hell of a good guy. One of the last of a dying breed, I'm afraid. It's your choice what you want to do, but if I let the movie executives read this," he waved the pages, "I don't think there's going to be another deal."

"I think I'm okay with that," said Brooks. And he set his Perrier on the table and walked out. He started to dial Aggie's number. He should have called before this, but he was embarrassed at the way he'd acted before he left. And now he was in a foul mood, and it wasn't fair to call her right now.

He considered the conversation he had just rudely walked out on in the restaurant. He could just re-write the book. Give Avery and the movie executives what they wanted, and quite frankly, what his readers probably wanted, do the deal, and move on. Avery expected many more Chester McCombs books. The contract for an additional four books was sitting in Brooks' email, unsigned. He didn't know what to do. He was getting a little bored with Chester and his jaunts to exotic locals and seductive intrigues with mysterious women, his taste for martinis and fast, expensive cars. But it was every writer's dream, wasn't it? A steady, dependable, lucrative stream of work. And movie rights as the cherry on top of this glorious literary sundae. He should be grateful. So why did he feel like a heel?

Brooks knew he had been a total a shit to Aggie when she'd come to apologize. A passive aggressive shit. He should have invited her in. He should have grabbed her and pulled her inside and kept her there with him until he had to leave for Houston. Hell, he should have canceled this trip. But he really couldn't. He'd already put this meeting off too long already. But he should have told her how disappointed he was last night and how his heart leapt when he woke up and saw her car parked outside. But in his hungover state, his bruised ego took center stage and stole the show. He would get back to the island, apologize to Aggie and then he would figure out what to do about Chester McCombs. Avery could wait. It wouldn't kill him. He parked the car and started towards the steps leading up to his second-floor apartment, but stopped cold when Helen gracefully unfolded her long legs and rose from her perch on the bottom step.

"Hi Brooksy," she cooed, standing still shaking out her hair, so he could fully appreciate her.

Brooks shook his head. "Helen, what in the hell are you doing here?" His voice was pure steel.

"Well, isn't it obvious? I've flown halfway across the country and back to apologize to you and fix this."

"You *what?*" Brooks was completely confused.

"Yes," she said with a coy smile. She was certain revealing the fact she flew all the way to freaking *Texas*, would demonstrate how serious she was about getting back together. She continued in a sing-song voice. "I found your little island. You think I don't listen Brooksy, but I do." She moved towards him, and he took a step backwards.

"You went to my house?"

"You know, I didn't make it that far. I stopped at this sweet little coffee shop and the barista there told me you were here."

"*YOU WHAT?* "Brooks was yelling now. He was furious, picturing Aggie putting the pieces together, which she surely had.

"Yes," Helen continued, completely unfazed by Brooks' volume. "She seemed to think it was strange that I asked where Brooks Jagger lived."

Brooks closed his eyes and counted to ten. He opened his eyes and looked hard at her. Where he used to see such beauty, such potential, he now only saw an empty shell. "Because, Helen. That's not my name. Please just go." He pointed at her car. Then he pushed past her and went up the stairs to unlock the door to his apartment.

"But Brooksy, I just flew halfway across the country and back. The second flight was in *coach* for crying out loud. Can't you see I want to fix this?" She followed him up the stairs.

He unlocked the door but blocked her from entering. "Helen, there is no fixing it. You broke it. As a matter of fact, I don't think there was anything to break in the first place. It's over. Please just go." He turned his back on her and walked inside, dropping his phone and keys on the entry table. Helen was right behind him and shot into the apartment. She shut the door behind her.

"Helen, get out of here." Brooks growled.

"Brooks, you would understand if you had answered any of my seventeen phone calls. I know you were pissed. But it wasn't what you thought."

"Helen, you were naked and kissing another man. I think it's exactly what I thought."

"Brooks, it was for the movie. He was coaching me on my next scene."

"Really, you expect me to believe that?"

"Yes, I do. Because it's true. I may be a lot of things, Brooks, but I am not a cheat!"

Brooks softened a tiny bit, the wall he built up around all things Helen starting to crumble the smallest amount. She was shallow, and she was calculating. But in her defense, he was never concerned about her fidelity until that day. Maybe she was telling the truth. His mind flashed back to his last birthday. They had spent it at the beach, a sun soaked, perfect day. It was the day he decided to buy a ring.

"Wait here," he said, heading for the bedroom.

Helen started to follow him, but then Brooks' phone buzzed on the table. A coy smile playing on her lips, Helen picked it up, and in a voice too quiet for Brooks to hear from the other room, said, "Hello" in her most seductive tone. The line was silent, and then went dead. She carefully placed the phone back on the table and turned around as Brooks re-entered the living room.

Chapter Thirty-One

Monday morning found Aggie and Lillian upstairs staring dubiously at the monstrosity of a machine in the middle of the unfinished bedroom. It looked like a jackhammer with a fourteen-inch round sander instead of a hammer on the bottom. The delivery guys were kind enough to haul it up the stairs. It was bigger than either one of them, and the guys chuckled as they left.

"Come on, we can do this," said Aggie.

"Okay," Lillian said doubtfully, her eyes still on the machine. "I'll plug you in. Here goes nothing."

Aggie and Lillian covered their faces with the masks Mr. O'Henry included in the box of supplies.

"I guess I'll start over here," Aggie said and held her breath as she turned the machine on. The sound was deafening, and Lillian clamped her hands over her ears. Aggie made her way laboriously across the room, pushing the machine in front of her and managed to turn it back the other way. The vibrations it gave off radiated right down to her toenails, but she held a tight grip on the handles and kept slowly moving forward. She made two more passes across the room and was feeling proud of herself. In the middle of the third pass, the machine jerked awkwardly and made a terrible sound. "*Turn it off!*" Lillian yelled.

Aggie flipped the switch to off and for good measure, Lillian unplugged it from the wall before they went to investigate. The lip of the sander had caught a loose board that now sat at an odd angle. Aggie kneeled and tried to tap the board back into place. When that didn't work, she tried to pull it out. It gave easily and Aggie set it aside. At least it was intact.

"Dammit!" she cursed, frustrated. "I'm going to need the guys to come back and fix this." She sat down, feeling defeated. Lillian came over to investigate. She poked at the board next to the hole left by the one Aggie pulled out. "This one's loose too." She moved it aside.

"Ags."

"What?" Aggie was laying on the floor on her back, one arm thrown over her eyes.

"There's um, there's something down here."

"What do you mean 'something'? Like an animal something? Or evidence of an animal something?" Aggie shuddered as she remembered some of the discoveries the guys found in the walls during the renovation. *What on earth was she thinking, trying to do this herself?*

"No. Come look."

"What?" Aggie sat up and scooched toward Lillian. In her lap sat a gunmetal gray box, about the size of a loaf of bread. The lid was rusted shut and didn't budge when the girls tried to loosen it. Aggie took the box and gently shook it. Nothing rattled and there was no smell. "Iz, will you go downstairs and see what you can find to open this? There should be a flathead screwdriver in one of the kitchen drawers."

"Sure." Lillian headed downstairs.

Aggie was unsettled. She should take this to Brooks, or even maybe to Nellie. But this was her house now. Brooks made it quite clear that everything that remained was hers. And when she tried to call him yesterday, a woman answered his phone. A woman who sounded a lot like Helen Hanes. There was no way she was calling him now.

Lillian came back into the room and if she didn't look so comical, she might have been frightening. Her hair was frizzed out around the bandana holding her bangs back and in her right hand she gripped the handle of Aggie's very expensive, ten-inch chef's knife.

"Are you crazy?" Aggie asked. "That won't work. And even if it would, that knife is worth more than whatever is in this box. Hold on." Aggie set the box on the floor, took the knife from Lillian and went downstairs to find the screwdriver.

She returned minutes later and while Lillian held the box, she carefully inserted the tip of the screwdriver between the box and lid and tried to pry it open. It didn't budge, but she kept trying. After several attempts the lid finally gave up its struggle with the pop of a sealed mason jar. Whatever was inside had been preserved airtight. Aggie set the lid down and the girls peered into the box. Inside, it was stuffed to the brim with yellowed papers. There was a stack of envelopes in the center and then stuck haphazardly around the stack were more. Some were folded in half giving the impression they had been shoved in as the box became overfull.

Aggie gingerly took the top letter from the pile and carefully extracted it from the envelope. It was postmarked October 1, 1943. Lillian sat looking over Aggie's shoulder and they both scanned the page.

Dearest Nellie,

I can't imagine why I haven't heard from you. We have finally arrived at the front. I'm not allowed to tell you much more than that. The weather is cold, colder than I've ever known it could be, and I dream of being with you on our sunny beach. The guys in my platoon are good eggs, they have become like brothers to me. But I miss you terribly and pray daily that this war will come to an end so I can come home to you. Please write to me, darling. Tell me about Sandcastle, about your gardens. Tell me how you are. Enclose the sun if you can.

All my love,
Billy

The girls looked at each other in stunned silence. "What do we do with these?" Lillian finally asked.

"I have to call Brooks. We obviously have to take these to Nellie. But I can't not tell him. Gosh I don't want to though."

"Why not?"

"Because when I called last night, Helen Hanes answered his phone. He's clearly made a choice. I blew it."

"Oh, boy." Lillian's pale eyebrows shot upward. She started to say more, but Aggie was dialing. Aggie's heart hammered in her chest, praying a woman wouldn't answer. She wasn't sure if she could handle that twice. The phone rang four times before his voicemail picked up. Aggie left a brief, impersonal message saying she needed to discuss something she found in the house and to please call her as soon as he could. The girls sat with the box for most of the morning. After reading a few of the letters, Aggie folded the one she was holding and put it back in the box.

"I feel like we shouldn't be reading these. I mean, it's like I'm reading someone's diary. It feels wrong."

"You're right." Lillian nodded and sat back leaning against the wall. "Should we try to finish in here?"

"I guess so." Aggie gave the sander the stink eye. "Let's try this again." The two women spent the next several hours wrestling with the sander. By the time they were done, they were satisfied with the result. They even managed to put the missing boards back, but not until after Aggie took a few pictures of the box's hiding spot on her phone. They cleaned up their mess, and Aggie arranged for Mr. O'Henry's crew to pick up the sander. They didn't even attempt to get the thing down the stairs.

Aggie put together a big salad for a late lunch. The girls sat down to fresh greens from the farmers market dressed with a garlicky vinaigrette and studded with juicy red garden tomatoes, herbed goat cheese, briny plump olives and strips of smoked salmon on top. The girls enjoyed the small but luxurious feast on the porch. They were lingering over a coffee when Aggie heard a car. But it wasn't just any car. Her ears instinctively perked up at the vroom-vroom of a 1966 Thunderbird. She looked up and there indeed was Brooks, zooming toward her driveway. Her heart leapt.

"Ah," Lillian said. "That's my cue."

"Don't be silly. You can stay right where you are."

"Oh, no ma'am. I need to get cleaned up before I pick Jude up from school anyway." She gestured at her get up of white coveralls and her messy hair.

"Okay." Aggie blew out a breath.

"Call me later, though, okay? I'm going to want a full report."

Aggie just nodded, her eyes on the car. Lillian waved at Brooks as she got into the Land Rover at the same time Brooks was putting his car in park. Aggie stayed seated as Lillian drove off. Brooks made quick work of the distance between himself and Aggie with his long legs. He stopped in front of her. "Hi."

"Hi. Do you want to sit?"

"Thanks." He sat down in the seat Lillian just vacated. "That looks good," he said, pointing at the leftover salad.

"Do you want me to make you a plate?"

"No, no." He looked her in the eye now. "Aggie, I am so sorry. I was such an ass. There's no excuse for it. My ego took a beating when you didn't show the other night, and I guess I don't handle that very well. I know it wasn't your fault, but I just kept thinking that even if it was subconscious, you had regrets or didn't want to come, or maybe you were just scared of my cooking."

At this, Aggie finally smiled. "Should I be scared of your cooking?" she attempted a joke. Then she looked him fully in the eyes. "I really, really am sorry I missed our dinner. I swear, if I could go back and change it, I would. I would never have sat down. I was just, so, so tired. Which, come to think of it, was partly your fault." She laughed nervously.

"Seems I do remember that. Except it was maybe you that kept me up," Brooks said with a smile.

"Okay, I'll take half the blame."

He took her hand. "You don't deserve any blame. For anything. This was all me. Next time I act like an ass, just hit me or something. Or maybe we can come up with a code word."

"Next time?" Aggie asked a little shyly.

"Yes, next time. There can be a next time, right?" he squeezed her hand. "You did promise me dinner."

"I did. I just wasn't sure if you were sure you were going to come back to cash in on the offer. Like, come back to stay. And um… your, well, Helen, came to the island."

Brooks groaned. "I know. I'm so sorry. She found me in LA. I was on my way back from meeting my agent, I was about to call the movers to send the rest of my stuff here, and there she was, sitting on my steps. But I told her, in no uncertain terms, that there was nothing left. That I live here now."

Aggie's mind was reeling with confusion. "But she answered your phone when I called yesterday?"

"She what?" Brooks pulled out his phone and scrolled through his calls. "Shit. She barged into my apartment. You must have called right when I left the room to gather up her stuff. I swear, I handed her a box of her things and told her to leave. I'm right where I want to be, Aggie. You believe me, don't you? I'm done with LA. I'm done with Helen. All I want to do is be here, with you, walk on the beach, eat your amazing food and write something more substantial than Chester McCombs books. Is that too much to ask?"

Aggie just shook her head and leaned into him. She rested her forehead on his strong, broad shoulder and shook it slightly. "No, it's not too much to ask. Not at all". Then she looked up at him and he leaned down to kiss her. That kiss lasted a very long time. Right before they crossed the line into indecency, just like the last time, he picked her up and carried her inside. But this time, he didn't stop to ask permission. He already knew the answer. He just carried her upstairs to the little attic bedroom. Hours later, they made their way downstairs.

"I did promise you dinner," Aggie said. "And lucky for you, I have some fairly decent leftovers." Aggie pulled out two servings of the duck confit and Potatoes Anna from the Friday night dinner. She had saved these back for herself and Emma, but they were both too busy to eat a proper meal that night.

"Wow," said Brooks. "You have been holding out on me. So, how was the retreat? Other than delicious?"

"It went well, I think. A few learning curves, but good. It filled the coffers, and the next two retreats are fully booked. I even have a couple people on a waitlist." At that, Aggie's fork clattered to the plate. "Oh my gosh. I can't believe I haven't shown you yet."

"What?" Brooks asked, around a mouthful of potatoes.

"You've got to come with me. Right now," Aggie said standing up.

"Really?" Brooks whined, pointing at his plate.

"Really."

Brooks reluctantly got up and at the last minute, picked up his plate and fork and carried them with him.

Aggie laughed. "I guess I'll take that as a compliment?"

"You should." He nodded emphatically. "What is so important?" He stuck another forkful of duck in his mouth.

"You'll see. Come on." Aggie headed for the stairs.

"Are we going back to bed? I'll put the plate down."

Aggie laughed and swatted at him. "No, not yet anyway."

As they went up the staircase, Aggie quickly filled him in on her plan to finish the remaining room so she could accept the last person on her wait list. She told him about the incident with the sander and finding the box as they walked into the room. She held Brooks' full attention now, and he set the plate on a side table on the landing before entering the bedroom.

"Here, you should just look at these." Aggie carefully picked up the box from where she and Lillian left it in the corner. She removed the lid and handed Brooks the letter on top. Brooks held the fragile, yellowed document carefully and scanned its contents.

"Oh, wow. What on earth?" He sat down cross legged on the floor and read two more letters. Then he put them back. "We need to take these to GranNell. It feels wrong just reading these."

"I know, we thought the same thing. Who is Billy Black?"

Brooks looked up from his spot on the floor. "I have absolutely no idea." He looked at his watch. "It's way too late to call tonight. We'll go tomorrow."

"I have to open up tomorrow, but I could get away by noon."

"That works, I'll pick you up."

They carried the box downstairs and finished their dinner. They lingered over their wine and almost ended up back upstairs, but Aggie pointed out she had to be up at 4:30am the next morning. He left reluctantly and promised to pick her up the next afternoon.

Chapter Thirty-Two

The following day, Aggie was in an excellent mood and went through her tasks with a spring in her step. As soon as the hour was decent, she called Lillian and filled her in.

"Can I please, please come with you guys? I know I don't know Nellie, but I did keep you from killing yourself with that sander."

"I'll ask Brooks, but I'm sure it's fine. She wants to meet you anyhow. She especially wants to meet Jude."

"Great, 'cause I'll have to bring him with us."

"Okay. Be here by noon."

"Will do."

Just before noon, Brooks parked the Thunderbird in front of The Bean and Bun. He wasn't perturbed by the extra company per se, but he had been looking forward to having Aggie to himself on the drive over. But he would roll with it.

"Hey, my man," he called to Jude as he walked in with his mom. Jude gave him a high five. He was thrilled to be picked up early from school with the promise of one of Aggie's monster cookies and an outing. "We were in the middle of math. Math is not my favorite."

"What is your favorite?" Brooks asked.

"Science. We're learning about dinosaurs. The Jurassic Period. Did you know that T-Rex and stegosaurus are always in movies together, but really didn't ever exist at the same time?" Jude delivered this nugget of information as if he was sharing the secret to time travel.

Brooks just laughed. "No way!"

Lillian moved over to the counter to talk to Aggie. "Are you sure it's okay if we come along? I mean, I'm dying to, but…"

"It's fine. I want you to come. It's an odd circumstance, but I'm excited for you to meet Nellie. She's wonderful. Speaking of, let me gather up some treats for her." Aggie only had one blueberry lemon scone left, so she added a chai cinnamon roll and a lemon square. Then she poured an Arnold Palmer into a to-go cup. She added a monster cookie for Jude and closed the box. The foursome piled into Lillian's Land Rover as it fit the four of them much more comfortably. Jude was bummed. He really wanted a ride in Brooks' Thunderbird. But Lillian was firm and insisted on driving. "No way, young man. That thing doesn't even have airbags."

"It doesn't?" Aggie asked, turning to Brooks.

"Of course not," he said.

The group found Nellie in the middle of her bridge tournament. She waved when they trooped in. They waited for her to finish the hand. The group took a break, and Nellie rose to greet her guests. "Who have we here?" she asked as she embraced first her grandson and then Aggie.

"Wait, don't tell me. I think you must be Jude."

"That's right." Jude's shaggy blonde head bobbed up and down. "And that must make you Lillian," she said as she took one of the younger woman's hands in both of hers. "So lovely to meet you both. Aggie has told me all about you."

"I've so looked forward to meeting you."

"What have you brought?" asked Nellie, eying the rusty metal box tucked under Brooks' arm. Her eyes were bright as she turned her gaze to Jude and put both hands on her hips. "Have you found buried treasure on the beach? My grandfather always swore there had to be some of Jean Lafitte's loot still around somewhere." Nellie took Jude's hand and started to launch into one of the many pirate tales that peppered Brooks' childhood, but Brooks laid a hand on her arm.

"GranNell, we need to talk. Can we go somewhere quiet?"

"Of course, dear. Whatever is wrong?"

"Everything's fine, but let's go find a place to sit." Brooks was once again concerned about giving her a heart attack. He waited until Nellie was settled on a bench in the garden. Jude sat cross legged in front of her, Lillian and Aggie on either side on the bench. Rather than squeeze onto the bench, Brooks sat down on the grass beside Jude and very carefully worked the lid of the rusty box open.

"Aggie, why don't you tell her?" Aggie proceeded to share the episode with the electric sander in the upstairs bedroom, complete with Lillian coming in with the kitchen knife. Her words were falling over each other. She was nervous and a little embarrassed about reading intimate letters meant for Nellie some seventy years ago. Aggie clumsily wrapped up her tale and Brooks handed Nellie the letter from the top of the stack.

Nellie took it and held it at arm's length. She reached down for the reading glasses hanging from a chain around her neck. Handwriting that was still familiar and dear after all these years came into focus. She gasped, so soft it was barely audible. "Oh. Oh, my." She was quiet for several long moments, staring at the envelope.

Brooks finally spoke. "Are you ok?" Nellie bobbed her head once, but still sat, staring at the yellowed envelope. "GranNell, who is Billy Black?"

Nellie shook her head, forcing her thoughts back to the present. She looked at Aggie holding the box and to-go cup from The Bean and Bun. "Is that for me, dear?" she asked, pointing to the drink. Aggie nodded and passed her the cup. Nellie took several long sips while the group waited silently. Even chatty little Jude sensing the solemn tone, was quiet. At long last she tore her gaze away from the envelope and smiled at her grandson. "Billy Black was my first love." Nellie seemed to have recovered from her shock and slipped into her comfortable role of storyteller. She told them about Billy giving her a ride home from school on the handlebars of his bicycle, and about his impulsive decision to join the army, of finding him the morning of the Sandcastle building competition standing on the beach in his army greens. She told them of the letters she wrote faithfully every night for months, of her heartbreak when she never received a single letter in return. Nellie paused and took a few more sips. Brooks said nothing. The girls were both dabbing at their eyes.

"So, the bastard just *left*?" Brooks was ready to fight someone, as if this horrible slight to his beloved GranNell happened last week, rather than almost three quarters of a century ago. "But wait," Brooks shook his head. "If he never wrote, then what are all these?" Brooks said, stating the obvious, gesturing at the box.

"Patience, darling."

Brooks was still sitting cross legged on the ground in front of her, next to Jude. Nellie leaned forward and placed her hand on his head, just as she did when he was a small boy no older than Jude sitting at her feet while she spun wild tales of pirate ships and buried treasure. She took a few more sips, as if the caffeine and sugar were giving her strength to get through her story.

"My parents did not approve of our relationship. And they weren't completely wrong. I was very young. Only seventeen when Billy went off to war. But it was a different world back then. There were girls younger than me getting married. Especially with a war on. Mabel Jenkins was in my year, and she got herself married and pregnant in between the time her beau was called up and the time he left. Two weeks after her baby was born, she got the telegram. She was barely seventeen years old and left to raise her baby girl alone. I can see how my parents were afraid the same might happen to me." She took a deep breath. "I never did receive any letters from Billy. After six months, I stopped writing to him, and after a year I stopped crying about it. Sometime after that, my father brought home a young man who moved to the island to expand his commercial fishing business. He was handsome and kind. Smart and a hard worker. He asked if he could take me to dinner and I said yes. We only dated a few months before he proposed, and I said yes again. I was happy. I was loved. My parents approved. Life was good."

"But one day, when your uncle was about a year old, Brooks…" Nellie's eyes misted over as she seemed to focus on some unseen object far in the distance and continued her story.

She could recall the day as if it were last week. She was a young wife with a baby in the cradle. Her husband, Martin Schmidt, was off on one of his many business trips adding more restaurants and fish shops to his ever-growing list of clientele. Martin's little fishing enterprise was booming. He now owned a small fleet of fishing boats that supplied seafood to high end restaurants all along the Gulf Coast, and he was intent on expansion.

Nellie had put the baby down for a nap and was sitting on the porch, planning her spring garden. When her mother passed away the previous fall, her father went to live with her sister's family. It was too hard for him, reminded of his wife at every turn in the big house. So, Nellie and Martin moved into the family home. It was an odd time in Nellie's life. The sadness of her mother's passing and the joy of being a young wife welcoming her first baby made for a complicated juxtaposition, her emotions occasionally warring with each other. But keeping up her mother's vegetable garden gave her a soothing sense of continuity. It was mid-March, and the sky was the sparkling sapphire blue you see in Texas in early spring, before the heat and humidity set in for the long summer. It was one of those days that reminded Nellie of the Dickens quote. *"It was March, when it is summer in the sun and winter in the shade."* She still remembered that line running through her mind when she looked up and saw a man walking alone down the beach, head down, hands in his pockets. She didn't know him, but something about him seemed familiar. Something about the way he walked. She tracked his progress along the shoreline. When he started to angle away from the surf towards the house, she started to move inside and lock the door. Possibly call a neighbor from the new telephone Martin recently installed in the kitchen. But as she got up to move toward the door, the stranger looked up. The light fell fully on his face, and she gasped, rooted in place. The stranger, who wasn't a stranger at all, eventually came to a stop directly in front of the porch. "Hello, Nellie," he said in a low, soft voice. Nellie just stood there, her hands covering her mouth, unable to believe he was standing in front of her. All the nights she cried alone in her room after waiting for the promised letters that never arrived. She opened her mouth to speak, but no sound came out. Instead, she just stood there. "May I sit?" Billy gestured towards the steps. Nellie just nodded dumbly. Billy sat and waited for Nellie to collect herself. Eventually she spoke and asked the one question she asked herself every day for months and even now still occasionally wondered.

"Why? Why didn't you write?" she asked, looking at him imploringly. At last, now finally, even though she was married to another man with a child of her own, at last she would know.

"*What*?!" Billy's mouth dropped open. "Why didn't I write? Nellie Anne, are you pulling my leg?" Nellie suddenly regained all her faculties and retorted with her hands on her hips. "Billy Black, I am most certainly *NOT* pulling your leg. What in heaven's name do you mean by that?"

"What I mean is, I wrote to you every day. Every single, doggone day for a *year*. Even though I never received one letter from you."

"You… you never received any letters from me?" The indignation left Nellie as quickly as it came.

"Nope. After I left, I wrote every day. Once we shipped out, I sent a letter every chance I could. For a year. After a year of no reply, I figured you decided you didn't want to wait for me after all."

Nellie's face suddenly felt very hot. A year. He kept the faith longer than she did. After six months, she had given up. A single, silent tear ran down her face. She quickly dashed it away.

"You wrote me?"

"Only a hundred letters or so."

"Oh, Billy. I'm so sorry. I thought you… I thought you must have decided you didn't want me…?"

"Not want *you*? Are you crazy? Thinking of you got me through most of that godforsaken war. Did you write to me?" he asked softly.

Nellie nodded. "So many letters. I would leave them with the mail to go to the post office. "Oh my, it was my parents. It had to be. My mother." Nellie closed her eyes. How could her parents have done this to her? Listened to her cry herself to sleep every night for months all the while hiding the very thing that would have alleviated the suffering of her young heart. She looked up.

"Dammit," Billy cursed. Then after a pause he slowly continued. "I came to find you after I got back. I wanted to hear from your own mouth that you didn't want me. But you were dating someone else, so it seemed crystal clear. And then I heard you went and got yourself engaged, so I figured it was better I just went on to Houston and finished school. And so, I did."

"And so, you did." Nellie looked down at her wedding ring and twisted it around her finger. She loved her husband. She truly did. He was a good man. A wonderful husband and a doting father when he was home. But there was a piece of her heart she never truly retrieved from Billy Black.

"Are you happy?" Billy asked softly.

"Yes," she answered honestly. "I am."

"So, there's no chance of you coming back to Houston with me then?"

"I have a baby, Billy. A little boy. I have a family. No, I can't go with you."

"I understand," said Billy standing up. "Anyhow, if you were the kind of woman who would have said yes to that, I wouldn't so desperately want you to. But I had to ask."

"I'm sorry, Billy. So desperately sorry."

"It's all right. At least now I know."

"At least now I know," Nellie echoed his words.

He reached out and delicately linked the tips of his long, strong fingers with hers, but he didn't trust himself to come any closer.. They stood there like that for a long time, looking into each other's eyes both wondering the inevitable question, *What if?* Tears were welling up in Nellie's eyes again, and before she did anything she would regret, she pulled her hand back, tucking both hands deep in the pockets of her apron.

"Goodbye, Billy."

"Goodbye, Nell."

She went inside then, closing the door firmly behind her. Safely behind the curtain, her eyes followed him until he walked over the far dunes and out of sight.

Nellie's eyes slowly refocused on Brooks as she brought herself back to the present. "Wow," said Brooks. "Did you ever tell my grandfather?"

"I did. He knew all about Billy. I told him about him on our first date. We didn't have any secrets."

"So, you never saw Billy again?" Aggie asked softly.

"Well, I never talked to him again, but I did see him once more. Your grandfather was a wonderful man, Brooks, but he liked his bourbon and his cigars a little too much." She looked at Lillian and Aggie. "Martin was older than I was. He suffered a series of heart attacks when our boys were young. I begged him to stop traveling so much. When he was on the road with clients, he would eat horribly, smoke too much, drink too much. And the boys and I wanted him home more. We didn't need the money, the Francis trust could easily have supported us, but he always had a bit of a chip on his shoulder about that. Wanted to make his own fortune, leave his own legacy as he used to say. He kept at it, and one day it all caught up with him."

"He died?" Jude asked quietly.

"Yes, sweet boy, he did."

"Just like my dad."

"Yes, honey, just like your dad. And my boys were heartbroken."

"Yeah, I get that," said Jude in a voice far too heavy for a child. Lillian reached down and even though he had grown too tall for it, pulled him into her lap. She buried her face in the top of Jude's head, and he snuggled in as if he were three instead of eight going on nine. But he looked up at Nellie, clear eyed, waiting patiently for her to continue.

"A few years after Martin passed, the boys were off at summer camp, and I went to Houston to visit Gladys for a few days." Nellie's mind slipped quickly back to 1958.

Gladys was out for the morning, fulfilling a Junior League commitment she couldn't get out of, and so she left Nellie to amuse herself for the morning. The Houston telephone book was sitting on the kitchen counter, and Nellie found herself flipping through the B's while she sipped an iced tea. There it was, in small print right there on the paper, halfway down the page. Theodore William Black with a telephone number and an address. She stared at the page for a long time and then firmly closed it and went to get ready to meet Gladys for lunch. The next day she should have been on her way back home. But she found herself parking down the street from the address she memorized from the phonebook. The house was neat and tidy. A little white craftsman bungalow with dark green shutters and potted geraniums on the porch.

"I hadn't seen him in so many years." Nellie said to the little group sitting on the Peach Tree lawn. "I felt like a schoolgirl with butterflies. More nervous than that first day he took me home on the handlebars of his bicycle. I finally worked up the courage to make myself get out of the car when the door to the house opened. And there he was, handsome as ever." Nellie smiled to herself even now, recalling the sight of him. "He stood tall and straight, and his hair was still thick and dark. He came out onto the porch. I pushed open the car door and started to go to him. I was positively giddy. But before I could call out, he reached back through the doorway and a blonde, curly headed sprite of a little girl toddled out onto the porch attached to his finger. A grownup version of the little girl followed behind her, carrying a tray with their lunch. I watched while she laid the food out on a table and settled the little girl in a chair. He had a family. A beautiful family, and I had no right to be there. So, I left."

"Oh, Nellie," Aggie gasped, bringing Nellie once again back to the present. "I'm so sorry."

Nellie took a deep breath. "Oh, don't be." Nellie patted her hand. "I won't lie; it stung a bit. I had allowed myself to fantasize about his return to the island. The same way he once wanted to take me back to Houston, I'm sure. But in the end, I was glad he had a family, that he wasn't alone. I'm sure he had a nice life. As have I," she said, looking at Brooks.

"And you never heard from him after that?" Brooks asked.

"No, my darling, I never did. Don't go feeling sorry for an old lady though. I've lived a beautiful life, and I don't regret one tiny little thing. I did always wonder what my mother did with the letters though. I guess now we know." She took another deep breath. "And now, my dears, I think I need to rest. Brooks, will you take the box to my room please? I do believe I'm going to need a sherry to read those."

"Okay. Do you want us to stay?"

"No, no. It's almost supper time. You all go on. I'll be fine. It's a nice evening. I'm going to sit here for a minute."

They rose to go, but Nellie stopped Jude. "You, young man. Do you play cards?"

"I'm pretty good at crazy eights and gin rummy," Jude replied.

"You might have to prove that. Why don't you and your mama come back this weekend and we'll see how good you are?"

"Okay," said Jude and he looked to his mom for confirmation.

"Yes, that's so nice. We'd love that," said Lillian and Jude nodded. "He has a soccer game on Saturday morning, but we could come after that."

"It's a date. On Saturdays" she said to Jude in a conspiratorial tone, "the cook lays out a fancy cookie and dessert spread." Jude's eyes got wide. "I mean," Nellie added with a sideways glance at Aggie, "they aren't Bean and Bun cookies, but they're awfully good."

"Okay, sure." Jude was smiling.

"All right, you all get on now. I'm sure this little man has homework or some other such nonsense."

Lillian looked at Jude. "That's right, I believe there is a multiplication worksheet with your name on it."

They all hugged Nellie, even Jude, and headed for home. Nellie sat back down on the garden bench. She still held the one letter Brooks handed her. She didn't read it again, she just lay her hand on the yellowed page, as if she could somehow connect with Billy through time and space by the words he so lovingly wrote so very, very many years ago. She stayed there until the sunlight faded and a soft, gardenia scented twilight crept into the garden. The cicadas were tuning up for the evening and a whippoorwill called out to its mate. One of the nurses walked toward her. "Mrs. Schmidt, you ready to come on in, honey? Supper's ready."

"Yes," she said. "Yes, I think I am." She gratefully accepted the woman's arm, suddenly feeling terribly tired and every bit of her ninety-one years.

Chapter Thirty-Three

The next morning, Aggie relayed the news to Emma and Sadie. Sadie was dabbing at her mascara by the time Aggie finished. "It's beautiful. And so sad. It's like they were just ships passing in the night their entire lives."

"It's like a real-life fairy tale. Except the ending is so sad," Emma added.

"Did you ever read Grimms?" Aggie asked. "Most fairy tales are positively tragic."

"Fair point," said Sadie. "I wonder if she ever tried to contact him again?"

"She says she didn't," said Aggie. "She didn't want to intrude on his family."

"Of course, she didn't," said Sadie.

Emma pulled her phone out and started tapping away. "Y'all, is this him?" A minute later, she held out a Facebook profile picture.

"I have no idea," said Aggie. "I never saw a picture".

Emma read the Facebook bio aloud. "*Theodore William Black. Workplace: Retired Golfing Grandpa, Professional Astros Fan. Birthplace: Sandcastle Island.*

There's no way this *isn't* him." Sadie and Aggie looked over Emma's shoulder at the Facebook photo. A smiling, tanned, lined face with a full head of white hair looked back at them from the screen. He was surrounded by four young adults who must be grandchildren and a gaggle of tiny humans, presumably all his progeny. "Does it list a marital status?" asked Aggie.

"Nope. But I bet I can find out. Can I borrow your laptop?"

"Aren't you not allowed to touch a computer for the entire year?" asked Sadie.

Emma rolled her eyes at her aunt. "I'm not going to hack anything, I swear." She crossed her heart with her index finger.

"Here you go." Aggie pulled her laptop from under the counter and handed it to Emma. She was more curious about Billy Black than she was worried about Emma's restrictions. She looked at Sadie. "That took her what, all of twelve seconds? I wouldn't even have thought to look online."

"Amazing, right?" Sadie shrugged. Sadie sipped her coffee and Aggie served a few tourists while Emma sat tapping away at the laptop at a corner table.

Brooks walked in and stepped right behind the counter. He wrapped an arm around Aggie's waist and dropped a kiss on the back of her neck. Sadie's eyes bulged and she came dangerously close to spitting coffee onto the counter. "Um, something you want to share with the class, friends?"

Brooks grinned at her and raised his eyebrows. "Whatever do you mean?"

Aggie just blushed. "Oh, yeah. We were so busy talking about other stuff, I completely forgot."

"You forgot?" Brooks turned to her, faking an indignant expression. "I'm hurt, Ms. Jeffries." Aggie swatted him with a hot pad. "You know what I mean. Now, get on the other side of the counter. What are customers going to think?"

"Probably that you're easy." Brooks teased and Sadie almost spit out her coffee again. Aggie really swatted him now.

"Move it, mister," she said playfully. Emma walked back up with the laptop.

"Find anything?" Sadie asked her niece. If her sister happened to walk in and see Emma with a computer, she would never hear the end of it.

"Yep, here he is. Theodore William Black. Born May 25th, 1924. Married July 3rd, 1955. Widowed in 1985. Two children. Lots of grandchildren and great grandchildren. Current address is 3360 24th Street, Pensacola, Florida." Emma looked up from the screen. "Sadie, *STOP* looking at me like that. It's all in public records. Anyone could find this if they knew where to look. It's not illegal."

"She's right," said Brooks. "I should have thought of that. I can't believe I *didn't* think of it. We have to tell GranNell."

"You're right," said Aggie.

"Are you going to contact him?" asked Emma.

"I don't know," answered Brooks. "I need to talk to GranNell. If she wanted to try to find him, she probably already would have done so. She may want to just leave it alone."

"I don't know," said Aggie. "She did try once."

"True. But that was decades ago. I can't go to Peach Tree today anyway. I have to head to Houston tomorrow to meet with my agent. He wanted me to fly to LA, but I told him if he needed to meet in person, he could come to me. He balked at the drive from the airport, so we compromised on Houston. I booked us a table at Brennan's so at least I'll get a decent dinner out of the deal."

"All right, when will you be back?" asked Aggie.

"Saturday or Sunday probably. We just dropped a big bombshell on GranNell. Let's let her sit with this for a few days, and we'll go over there on Monday after I get back."

Sadie left the shop to meet a client after extracting a pinky promise from Aggie to keep her abreast of all developments. Brooks followed Aggie into the kitchen. "Any chance you could come with me to Houston?"

"Really?" Aggie asked.

"Yeah, we could get a great hotel and lounge by the pool. Order room service. Also, you could run interference with my agent, so I don't throttle him."

"Ah, the truth comes out."

"Seriously, it would be fun. Can't Emma run this place for a couple days? I realize relinquishing control is hard for you. We could think of this as therapeutic practice."

"Hey, I'm getting better! I left Emma here all by herself twice this week. And yes, she probably could, but I need to finish getting ready for the next retreat, and I really need to get that last bedroom done at the beach house. Ambrose is coming out tomorrow to start work on the bathroom, but I'm doing the painting and stuff myself." Brooks made a sad puppy dog face and she almost caved. "Raincheck?"

"Sure," said Brooks. "But I'm not bringing back any Bananas Foster, so don't ask."

Aggie made a swoon face, recalling the famous and decadent Brennan's dessert of bananas flambéed in sugar, cinnamon and rum served over ice cream. "Bananas Foster. I would give my right arm for one, but I don't think one would travel well anyway."

"Okay, maybe I'll try to make you a copycat Banana Foster when I get back."

"Hmmm, don't they light it on fire?"

"Yes, what's your point?"

Chapter Thirty-Four

Late Saturday morning, Jude still in cleats and shin guards, he and Lillian arrived at Peach Tree House. The day was shaping up to be a warm one, but the table where they found Nellie shuffling cards under the big, leafy magnolia tree was shady and pleasant. "Well, hello my dears. Tell me, how was soccer?" Nellie asked, a bright smile on her lined face.

Jude was grinning, holding up a chocolate chip cookie that was more or less the size of his head. A pretty nurse manning a table stacked with cookies and cupcakes and pastel candy-colored petit fours offered it as soon as they entered the courtyard. "It was awesome. I scored the winning goal! I totally faked the goalie out. It barely made the net, and he barely missed it, but I made it!" Jude was clearly on cloud nine.

"Well, that is a wonderful start to a Saturday," Nellie said. She winked and started dealing the cards. "Let's see if that winning streak of yours holds." After a few hands of gin rummy, Jude was holding his own and making a giant mess with the cookie while Lillian relaxed in the shade with a cookie of her own. "Gin!" Jude yelled once more, winning the round. Nellie faked a groan. "My goodness, Lillian. You didn't tell me you raised a card shark." Jude's grin grew even wider.

"Must be his lucky day," said Lillian. She loved seeing Jude so jubilant.

"Mom, look!" Jude pointed across the courtyard. Someone had brought in a golden retriever and a couple of children were playing with the dog. "Can I go see the dog? Please?!!"

"Okay, for just a minute." Jude was off across the courtyard like a shot out of a cannon before she could say another word.

"He's a lovely young man," Nellie said to Lillian. "You are doing a fine job with him."

"Thank you." Lillian's face fell slightly. "I'm trying," she said softly. "It's so hard for him without his dad."

"And it's hard for you too," Nellie said pointedly. "I do know something about that."

"I know you do. How did you do it? Everything just seems so hard."

"It is hard, no bones about it, dear. You just keep moving. One thing at a time, one task at a time, one day a time, one pot of soup at a time, sometimes one breath at time. You just keep breathing in and out, putting one foot in front of the other."

"Do you ever come out the other side?"

"No, my dear. You do not. But eventually the hurt softens, and you smile more because of what you had rather than cry because it's gone. Give it time. Be gentle with yourself. The island is good for you. The sea, it heals."

Lillian was staring down at her wedding ring, twirling it around her finger with her right hand as she listened. But now she looked up at Nellie. "I think that's the truest thing anyone has said yet. I could have saved a bundle on therapy."

"You keep going to your therapy. In my day, there was no such thing. Loss was just a part of life. You swallowed your lot and went on about your business. I think there is something to examining a life though, rather than just passively moving through this existence. There is a lot of sorrow, but also so much beauty and joy. You don't want to miss it. So, if your therapy is helping you find a little more beauty, a little more joy, you keep going. But also, spend some time by the water. Listen to it."

"Yes ma'am," Lillian said and smiled a watery smile. Jude was making his way back over to them. Lillian quickly dried her eyes and pasted a bright smile on her face.

"Having fun?"

"Mom, that dog is awesome! It knows so many tricks. Can we please get a dog? Please, please, please?"

"Ha, we'll see." Lillian made eye contact with Nellie over Jude's head. "One thing at a time. Okay, kiddo. I think it's time to go."

"Yes, and I think I need a little rest before my bridge tournament later this afternoon. I have a title to defend, you know."

"Okay. Good luck on your tournament," Jude called, and he ran back for a final pat of the dog's head before he and Lillian headed for the parking lot. Lillian and Jude stopped by The Bean and Bun on their way home. Lillian placed an order with Emma for a grilled ham and cheese for Jude and a cold brew coffee for herself. Aggie walked in from the kitchen. "Hi guys! How was your card date?"

"It was great, Aunt Aggie. Oh my gosh I got a giant cookie, I played with a super cool dog and Mom might, maybe let me get a dog, *and* I won at gin rummy. *AND* I scored the winning goal at my game!"

"Wow," said Aggie, "that sounds like it should be celebrated." She was turning toward the glass case.

"Yes, celebrated with a sandwich and maybe an apple for now?" Lillian stopped her raising her eyebrows. "Sorry to be a buzzkill. He already ate a cookie the size of his head this morning. This kid needs some protein."

"Okay, okay," grumbled Aggie. "I'm telling you though, those monster cookies are chock full of protein. And fiber."

"Lunch first," Lillian said firmly.

"Okay, okay. Sorry, bud," She shrugged at Jude as if to say, *I tried.* Jude just laughed and bit into his sandwich. While Jude ate his lunch, Aggie filled them in on Emma's online Nancy Drew moves and their discovery that one William Theodore Black was, to the best of their knowledge, very much alive and well and living in Pensacola.

"Oh, my gosh. What did Nellie say? She didn't say anything about it today when we were there."

"That's because she doesn't know yet. Brooks gets back tomorrow and we're planning to run over there on Monday afternoon. You want to come?"

"Is the Pope Catholic?" Lillian deadpanned.

Chapter Thirty-Five

On Sunday evening, Lillian joined Aggie, Sadie and Amelia for book club while Jude spent the evening with Emma and the twins. Aggie had faithfully distributed the copies of the first Chester McCombs book to the group and they planned to discuss it, amongst other things over a new flight of New Zealand whites Amelia recently added to the bar menu. Half an hour earlier, unbeknownst even to Amelia, a tall man in a worn Rangers baseball cap quietly entered the bar, ordered an Oregon Pinot Noir and sequestered himself in one of the deep armchairs by a corner table. The chair faced away from the girls, shielding his presence. The girls took no notice of the man as they assembled at their usual table. Amelia laid out glasses and after she fetched a charcuterie plate from the kitchen, started to pour tastings for her friends.

"Aggie, how's the next retreat shaping up?" she asked as she deftly wielded the heavy bottle.

"It's completely full! I'm so excited. I even have a couple waitlisted and I think" she held up her crossed fingers "that Ambrose and I will have the last room ready to get them in."

"I was working on an Italian theme for this one, but I think I'll just repeat my menu from last time. It worked so well, and everyone loved it."

"That makes sense," said Sadie. "Who doesn't love French food? And surely, it's easier on you to not recreate the wheel each time."

"It is. I think I'll keep one menu for the whole season and next year do something different so if I do get repeat guests, they'll have something new. You guys, I can't thank you enough."

"For completely pushing you into this crazy idea?" asked Amelia.

"Yes, for that," Aggie responded cheerfully.

"To crazy ideas!" Sadie raised her drink and they all clinked glasses.

"Lillian, how is the house?" asked Sadie.

"It's coming along. I really like it, but it does need work. There are so many things I'd like to do, but they can wait. Jude and I love being on the beach. For now, it's perfect for us."

"Yay!" Sadie clapped her hands. She had a gut feeling that the house would be a perfect fit.

"Thanks." Lillian smiled. She fell right in with Aggie's group of friends. She was closer to this bunch she had only known a few weeks than to the women she spent time with for years in Colorado.

"So, what did we all think of Chester McCombs?" asked Sadie. At that moment the man in the baseball cap sat up a little straighter in his armchair and turned his head slightly towards their group. The movement, reflected in the mirror above the bar, caught Amelia's eye, and a mischievous grin crept across her face.

"What are you smiling at?" asked Sadie "You look like the cat that ate the canary." Amelia held one finger up to her lips while she hurriedly scribbled something on a napkin and pushed it to the middle of the table. The women passed it around, confused at first. But soon they were all grinning after they read Amelia's chicken scratch note that said "Spy in our midst? This could be fun." The girls all nodded at each other, even Aggie who felt a tiny prick of guilt, but went ahead with the unspoken plan anyway.

"So, what did we all think of the book?" Sadie asked again.

"Awful," said Amelia. "I couldn't get through it".

"Me either, I've never read such an unbelievable character," added Sadie.

"I was bored to tears," Lillian added. "Can we please go chick lit for next month?" Aggie couldn't bring herself to add to the impromptu roast. But she didn't stop her friends either. She just sat back with her wine and tried not to giggle. She couldn't help but look over at Brooks and he caught her eye. The look on his face was downright pitiful. Aggie couldn't hold it in anymore. She just pointed a finger at him and burst out laughing. "Busted!"

"Well, that didn't take long," said Lillian. It took all of thirty seconds for Brooks' full height to be towering over their table.

"Really, you hated it? All of you?" He looked at Aggie.

"Guess now you'll never know," she teased. "Serves you right for spying. I thought you weren't getting back until later?"

"I wrapped up early and thought I'd surprise you. Ladies, can I steal Aggie for a bit?" The three waved them off. Brooks surveyed the flight wines on the table. He looked at Aggie. "Which was your favorite?"

"The second one," Aggie pointed.

"Amelia, my dear, can I please have a bottle of that to go?"

"You bet. Get Ernest to grab you one. It's on me."

"Why thank you. But I'm happy to buy it."

"Ah, let her give it to you," said Aggie. "She feels guilty." She picked up the napkin with Amelia's chicken scratch note and handed it to Brooks.

Brooks examined the napkin. "Yep, I'll take that bottle on the house after all. Thank you, ma'am." He plucked two clean wine glasses from behind the bar, swiped a corkscrew, collected the bottle from Ernest and pulled Aggie out the door.

"Where are we going?" asked Aggie as he pulled her down a side street.

"You'll see," he said.

As they got closer to the beach, he said, "I thought we could check out the light show."

"Ooh, yes!" said Aggie, catching on.

Aggie couldn't help but compare tonight's playful stroll to the awkward one just a few weeks prior. Aggie was warm with gladness and wine. Her retreats were working out, Lillian and Jude were here, the shop was thriving. And Brooks was, well, Brooks was currently making thoughts of anything else obsolete as he pulled her down onto the sand. The magical blue green light was indeed dancing on the water. As if the merfolk of Nellie's tall tales were gliding about in sequined finery, showing off their best dance moves just inches below the crest of the waves. But it was lost on Aggie and Brooks as they were swept away on an entirely different ocean. Later, Aggie attempted to put herself back together the best she could, trying to tame her hair and brush the sand from every inch of her body. She finally decided it was pointless. She lay her head on Brooks' chest.

"Did you really hate the book?" He asked as he opened the wine and poured two slightly sandy drinks.

"Not even a tiny bit." She shook her head as she sipped her warming wine. "I couldn't put it down."

"Really?"

"Yes, but…"

"But, what?"

"Nothing, it was great. You're great. You're a wonderful writer. Such vivid imagery."

"But?"

"It's not a *but*. It's more of an *and*. Chester McCombs is fun to read. I can hear your voice through him. He's witty, and adventurous, and exciting. But I think there is so much more to you. There is a depth to you that doesn't come through in that book. But what do I know? You have what, five million or so other people that bought it?"

"Six million. Well, now six million and one. The thing is, right now I only care what that one thinks." And he kissed her again. Eventually, he pulled back. He looked down at himself. "I think we need to rinse some of this sand off."

"I know. I've got to go back into the bar. My car keys are in there."

"Here, come with me." Hand in hand, they walked down to where the calm waves were slowly lapping at the shore. They stepped onto the wide expanse of wet sand left exposed as a wave retreated into the sea. As their feet hit the wet sand, their footprints lit up in the same unearthly blue green glow as the waves.

"What on earth?" Aggie cried. "Oh, my goodness, look at this!"

"Yeah," said Brooks. "Watch this." He walked away from her. He left a trail of glowing footprints following him. Aggie followed him and soon they were dancing on the beach making up the steps as they went. At some point, they stopped dancing and got down to the serious business of rinsing the sticky sand from their arms and legs, without completely drenching themselves in the process. This was an impossible task. They didn't end up going for a swim, but they both resembled drowned rats by the time they retraced their steps up the dark path towards Main Street and The Twisted Cork. It was almost closing time and apart from Lillian and Amelia sitting at the bar and Ernest washing glasses, it seemed the place had emptied out. Aggie and Brooks pushed open the door and the girls turned. Lillian took one look at the pair of them and burst out laughing. Aggie's hair was still full of sand, her clothes were mussed and damp, and there was still a giant patch of sand clinging to the front of her right thigh. Brooks' appearance was a similar story.

"Well, well, well," she said through her mirth. "What have we, here? Agatha Christy Jeffries, what have you two been up to?"

Brooks ignored Lillian and turned to Aggie. "Your middle name is Christy? That is so awesome."

"It is not awesome. At all. But at least my mother had the decency to spell it with a "y"."

Chapter Thirty-Six

The next day, Aggie, Lillian, and Brooks headed to Peach Tree House armed with the notes Aggie had copiously copied down from Emma's online wizardry regarding Billy Black. Aggie carried a box of lemon petit fours along with one of her new almond-vanilla bourbon scones. She'd spent days playing around with the recipe, adjusting spices. The scones themselves were a concoction of dark brown sugar, Mexican vanilla extract, cardamom and a pinch of salt. They were sinfully decadent all on their own. But while they were still warm from the oven, she glazed them with a mixture of powdered sugar, cinnamon, orange extract and a little Kentucky bourbon. Aggie was especially proud of them.

The threesome trooped into Peach Tree House. They were now familiar faces around the place, and several of the residents greeted them with a wave and a smile. A few were eyeing the white paper bag Aggie carried. The steady stream of pastry deliveries did nothing to hurt Nellie's popularity. They walked out into the garden, but Nellie wasn't at the card table under the big magnolia tree, or anywhere to be seen inside or out for that matter.

"Maybe she went for her walk," Aggie suggested, and they started to head for the garden beyond the courtyard wall. Before they took more than a few steps, one of the nurses started striding purposely toward them. "Mr. Schmidt!" the young woman called. Brooks turned. "Mr. Schmidt." She paused to catch her breath. "We've been trying to call you." She looked quite distraught.

"What's wrong?" asked Brooks, fearing the worst.

"It's your grandmother. Mrs. Schmidt was just taken to the hospital."

"Why? What happened?"

"We're not sure. She went to lay down for a nap this morning, but when she didn't come out for lunch one of the other nurses went to check on her and couldn't wake her up. She was conscious by the time the ambulance arrived, but they took her to run some tests. They think she might have had a mini stroke."

Brooks didn't wait to hear much more. He put his hand on the young woman's arm and gently but firmly interrupted her. "Which hospital, please?"

"St. Elizabeth's."

"Okay, thank you."

He took Aggie's hand. "Let's go."

Lillian followed behind the two of them, feeling out of place. "Brooks, would you like me to get a cab back? I don't want to intrude."

"No, no it's fine. Come on." Lillian didn't even comment when Brooks broke pretty much every traffic law on the way to the hospital and parked illegally out front. He rushed to the nurses' station and was rewarded quickly with a room number.

"Well, that's good news, I guess," said Aggie. "She's in a room and not the emergency room."

"She's donated a lot of money to this hospital over the years. I'm sure they're taking good care of her," said Brooks. "They better be, anyway," he added, punching the button impatiently for the elevator. They exited the elevator into a cool, brightly lit hallway and followed the signs to room 418. Outside the door stood an older man in spectacles and a long white coat. "Excuse me," Brooks said. "My name is Brooks Schmidt. I think my grandmother is in this room? Nell Schmidt".

"Ah, yes. She certainly is." His jovial tone put them all slightly more at ease. He stuck out his right hand. "I'm Dr. Campbell. I'll be overseeing Mrs. Schmidt's care. Not to worry, young man. Your grandmother is going to be just fine. She's a feisty one."

"You're not wrong there," Brooks shook the doctor's hand. "What happened?"

"We're not entirely sure. At this age, it honestly could be a lot of things. She was a little disoriented and dizzy. It's possible she's had a mini stroke. I want to keep her overnight for observation, but I think she should be right as rain in no time."

"Thank you. Can we go in now?"

"Of course, son. I'll be back to check on her before I leave for the day. Here is my cell number if you need anything." He handed Brooks a card.

"I appreciate that," said Brooks. "Thank you".

"I've been around a long time," said the kindly old man. "I did my internship here over forty years ago. Your family has done a lot for this hospital and we're grateful. It's the least I can do. Please feel free to call if you or your grandmother need anything."

"Yes sir," Brooks said. "Thanks again." And he pushed open the door to the hospital room. Nellie was sitting in bed, wearing a hospital gown and a sour expression. But she perked up at the sight of her visitors. "Thank goodness. You've come to spring me from this joint." She made to get out of bed. "Brooks, hand me my things, please. I believe they're in that closet."

"Whoa, not so fast," Brooks stopped her. "Why don't you tell me what happened?"

"It seems I took a rather sound nap, and everyone is making a huge fuss about it. I am positively fine. Now, darling, please hand me my things, and let's get out of here."

"Sorry. No can do. Doc says you need to stay overnight. But I promise I'll get you out of here as soon as possible."

"This is preposterous. Do you know how many checks I've written to this hospital? They think they can tell me what to do. I think not, young man." And she made to get out of the bed again.

"GranNell." This time Brooks' voice was slightly raised, and his tone was firm. "We can't leave yet. They said you are going to be fine, but they need to keep you overnight for observation, just in case. You'll be back in time for your bridge game, I promise." Nellie harrumphed and leaned back onto the pillows, more pillows than Aggie had ever seen on a hospital bed. In fact, this was a lot nicer than any hospital room she'd ever seen. It felt more like a hotel. Aggie stepped forward. "How's your appetite?" she asked quietly, holding up the white paper bag.

"I'm famished. Thank you, dear."

"Why don't we go find some coffee to go with those?" Brooks asked.

"Sure. You guys go," said Lillian. "I'll stay with her."

Brooks and Aggie left to go find the cafeteria. Aggie leaned back against the wall of the elevator and looked at Brooks. "Well, we can't tell her about Billy Black now. I don't want to give her a heart attack."

Brooks nodded, but then had a second thought. "You know, if I was going to tell her something potentially upsetting, what better place than one with a full staff of medical professionals on site?"

"Your call," Aggie said as the elevator doors opened. They entered the cafeteria, but Brooks stopped, tugging on Aggie's hand. "Do you mind getting the coffee?" I want to go track down Dr. Campbell and ask his opinion.

"Sure. Although it shouldn't be too hard. You have his cell number in your pocket."

"Oh. Right. Be right back."

Aggie went in and ordered three coffees and tried to fashion a version of an Arnold Palmer for Nellie. The young man at the counter was tracking down a drink carrier for her when Brooks walked back into the cafeteria. He was wearing the first smile she'd seen since the nurse stopped them in the courtyard at Peach Tree house.

"Good news?"

"Yep. I gave him a condensed version of Billy Black's story. He said it should be fine. But he was so fascinated he asked if he could be there when we tell her.." They carried the drinks back to the room. Lillian managed to find a deck of cards somewhere and she and Nellie were into a second hand of gin rummy.

"Thanks," she said, accepting the coffee from Aggie. Then she took a sip. "Or maybe no thanks. I don't mean to sound unappreciative, but I think the Bean and Bun has spoiled me."

"Ugh, me too," said Brooks after he tried his own cup. "Next time, we'll bring coffee too."

"Excuse me, there will be no next time," piped up Nellie. "This is a one-shot deal. I am perfectly fine."

"Okay, deal. No next time. I'm fine with that." Brooks sat down on the bed. "We need to tell you something. And I hope you're not mad."

"Oh, dear. What is it?" She looked at the girls. "I never was able to stay cross with Brooks for long. He's probably safe." She sat up and sipped her drink. She patted his hand. "Out with it. It can't be that bad."

"Well, it's not necessarily bad at all. You see, Aggie was telling Emma and Sadie your story about Billy Black."

"I hope you don't mind," Aggie interjected. "I guess maybe it wasn't my story to tell. But it was so romantic and enchanting. Emma compared it to a fairy tale." Nellie just nodded and waved her hand, indicating the sharing of her most private life events didn't trouble her in the least.

Brooks continued. "Well, there's more. So, this kid Emma is Sadie's niece." Nellie nodded. "Anyway, Emma is some kind of computer genius, and she started poking around online looking for Billy. GranNell, we think we've found him. He was widowed quite a few years back and never remarried. He lives in Pensacola."

As the color drained from Nellie's face, Aggie was doubly glad Dr. Campbell was in the room. She glanced at the old doctor watching his face for signs of alarm, but he was just calmly listening near the door. Nellie didn't speak for a long time. Finally, she just blew out a breath no one knew she was holding. And she uttered one syllable, "Oh."

"Are you alright?" Brooks leaned forward. Nellie's eyes refocused as if she had been far away.

"Yes, sweetheart, I'm fine. I need a minute though. I could use some rest. I think I'll take a little nap. Why don't you three go find a decent cup of coffee and come back in a bit?"

"Okay," said Brooks, reluctant to leave. He looked over at Dr. Campbell and the old man just nodded. "Probably an excellent idea for her to have a little rest. Don't worry, son. She's in good hands."

"All right. We'll be back in an hour, okay?" Nellie nodded, her eyes already closed. After the entourage left, Nellie opened her eyes and sat back up. She wasn't all that tired, but she did want a little privacy. She pushed back the bedcovers and padded over to the closet where the nurse hung her clothes. She reached into the pocket of her skirt and took out a yellowed envelope, the first letter Billy wrote to her. She had sorted through the postmarks and put all of them in order before reading each one. This first letter she carried around with her, tucked in her pocket. She read it perhaps a hundred times, scoffing at herself occasionally for acting like a lovesick teenager. In this first letter, he wasn't questioning why she hadn't written him. In this letter, Billy was full of optimism. He pledged his love over and over, he talked of all their plans for their future together and of his faith that they would all come to fruition. She didn't even need her glasses to read it. She just held her hand over the crumbling paper as his words ran through her mind.

Exactly fifty-nine minutes after they left, Aggie, Brooks, and Lillian trooped back in, and Nellie slipped the letter into the pocket of the hospital robe. "We're back! And we brought sustenance." Brooks held up a bag of fried chicken. "This has to be better than hospital food."

"Goodness, yes dear. But don't let Dr. Campbell see that."

"Too late," said Dr Campbell as he knocked on the door. "I'll turn a blind eye just this once. How are we feeling, my dear?"

"Good enough to go home?"

"Nice try, but assuming nothing comes up, I see no reason you can't leave by lunchtime tomorrow."

"GranNell? How are you feeling? What do you think? I mean, about Billy."

"What I think is that it's been too long since I've visited Florida," she said with a small smile.

"Really?" Aggie and Lillian asked in unison. This was a real-life fairy tale unfolding before their eyes. Aggie had never heard of anything so romantic.

"Yes, really. How would we go about making that happen?" Nellie responded.

"I'll look at airline tickets as soon as I get home," Brooks said. He was a little surprised this was the road she wanted to take, but he would make it happen for her. The group said their goodbyes to Nellie, and Brooks promised to return to collect her the following day.

In the hallway, Dr. Campbell was waiting for them. He let the heavy door close before he spoke. "Excuse me, Brooks," he said in a low voice. "I couldn't help but overhear. I don't mean to be the party pooper here, but your grandmother, while in excellent health for a ninety-one-year-old, did just have an episode. I'm completely comfortable releasing her into the competent care of the staff at Peach Tree House. But I'm not certain I can recommend a flight. Commercial air travel involves a lot of stress that I'm not certain Nellie is up for right now."

Aggie elbowed Lillian. "Too bad we don't have access to that fancy private jet anymore," she said under her breath.

Lillian's eyes widened. She turned to face Aggie. "Wait a minute. We do! Ben paid the membership dues a year at a time. It's not up until October." She raised her voice. "Excuse me, Dr. Campbell. What if we flew private?" She ticked off her reasoning on the fingers of her right hand. "There would be no lines, no crowds and no germs. Easy-peasy and no stress."

"Hmmm." Dr Campbell tapped his chin with his ballpoint pen and thought for a few seconds. "I guess that would be all right. As long as she gets up and moves around some on the flight."

"That's settled then," said Lillian triumphantly.

"Thank goodness," said Brooks. "I really didn't want to be the one to tell her she can't go. Thank you, Lillian."

Chapter Thirty-Seven

Aggie, Brooks and Lillian settled on the following Tuesday for their Pensacola excursion. They all felt better giving Nellie a few days to recoup before they whisked her off to Florida. Aggie also had another retreat she needed to get through. But Emma could handle the Bean and Bun solo on Tuesday.

The preparation for this retreat, especially as she decided to keep the menu the same, took far less time than the first. She was starting to find a rhythm. The welcome bags were already assembled, the menus were written. She was expecting glorious weather for the weekend and was excited to give her guests a fabulous experience.

Her guests arrived right on time, and she met them on the porch with her spread of champagne and canapés. The women oohed and ahh-ed over the house and the beach. Aggie had taken a note from the first retreat and looked up the women on social media. Not only did she memorize their names, but on Emma's suggestion, also friended or followed them ahead of time. So, they all met like old friends. The first evening went smoothly and all the women went upstairs that night feeling pampered.

Around eleven o'clock, Aggie was putting the last plate in the dishwasher. She was eager to get upstairs to bed when a knock at the back door made her jump. She looked up to see Brooks standing in the small pool of light coming from the kitchen window. She smiled and unlocked the door. "What are you doing here?"

"Couldn't sleep. Thought I'd come see how your day was."

"You know, I do have a phone."

"Some things are harder to do over the phone." He grabbed her and pulled her to him. She stepped into his embrace and leaned into his kiss. "You know," she said a few minutes later. "I have to be up insanely early tomorrow."

"I know, I know. I just wanted to see you. Can't blame a guy for trying. Have a quick night cap with me, and then I'll leave." He held up two fingers.

"Yeah, yeah, I know. Scout's honor," Aggie laughed. "All right. Here you go." She poured him a small scotch and grabbed a Perrier for herself. She started to move out on the front porch.

"You sure we should go out there?" Brooks said. "We don't have a good track record of going to bed on time from that porch. I'm not sure I'll be able to keep my promise."

"Good point." She changed course to head into the library. She sat down on one end of the deep sofa. You can sit way over there," she said, pointing to the opposite end.

Brooks laughed. "I'd hate to have to shout and wake up that gaggle of girls upstairs."

"It doesn't sound like they're asleep," said Aggie. Muffled giggles and voices were wafting downstairs. "If I didn't know better, you'd think I had a teenage slumber party up there. They've come down twice to grab more wine. I think they're camped out on the upstairs deck."

"Excellent. Maybe they'll sleep late."

"Maybe. But I can't." Aggie stifled a yawn.

"I know. I'll let you go to bed soon. I just wanted to see you."

"I'm glad you did." Aggie yawned again and let Brooks pull her over to him on the sofa. She snuggled into his chest and closed her eyes. She loved how safe she felt ensconced in his arms. Like nothing could hurt her. Like nothing bad could happen. She closed her eyes and relaxed into him. "How was Nellie today?" she asked sleepily.

"Good. I think she's excited about Tuesday. This private travel thing is amazing. Don't even need to pack a bag. Up and back in one day, lunch provided." Brooks was quieter now. "What if Tuesday is a disappointment?"

Aggie opened her eyes. "What do you mean?"

"I mean, GranNell has built this guy up for decades in her mind. What if he's not everything she imagined or remembers? There are so many ways this could not go well. He could have dementia. He could be an old grump. He could have a girlfriend. And also, I hate to state the obvious, the guy has to be in his mid-nineties. Even if our info is correct and he is still alive, he could kick the bucket any minute."

Aggie lay a finger over his lips. "It's going to be okay. Nellie is tough. Even if one of those things does happen. Or, even if all of those things happen, she'll be okay. We'll be with her. She has a full life here, and if she has to simply come back to that, I think she'll be fine." Brooks was still distraught. "Do you want to stay?" she asked.

Brooks eyebrows shot up. "Well, Ms. Jeffries, that is an interesting proposition from someone who claims to have an early morning."

"You can go up with me, Brooks. To sleep. But just because I've got to go to sleep doesn't mean you can't stay."

He kissed the top of her head. "Yes, ma'am, I'll settle for that. You go on to bed. I'll lock up for you." Aggie kissed him, which lasted far longer than she intended, but in the end, she disentangled herself from his arms and headed upstairs. She was so tired she was practically walking with her eyes closed. She smiled as she passed the second-floor landing and could hear the women still laughing and talking out on the deck. *Good for them*, she thought and headed drowsily up the steep flight of stairs to the third floor. Ambrose and his guys had indeed finished the last bedroom and bath on time, so she no longer had to decamp from her little suite on retreat weekends.

Brooks followed shortly, thinking how strange and wonderful it felt to be in this tastefully modernized version of his ancestral family home, going upstairs to Aggie in the little room where he used to write and play. It was odd and different. And he liked it. A lot. And he was mostly certain he could keep his promise to let her sleep. But when he got upstairs, he realized he had no choice. Aggie was out cold, breathing rhythmically, her hair across her face. He turned out the lights and undressed, leaving his clothes on the cushy armchair by the window, and slipped under the covers next to her. Aggie turned over and snuggled into him but didn't open her eyes.

Aggie woke up the next morning before the sun, feeling refreshed. She looked over and saw Brooks next to her, softly snoring and smiled. She was tempted to wake him, but she had a long list of things to do before her guests got downstairs. Brooks found her an hour later, juicing oranges. "It smells amazing in here," he said as he walked up behind her and nuzzled the back of her neck.

"Mmm," she murmured. She leaned into him for a moment, but then busied herself again with the juicer. "Grab yourself some coffee. And if you want, there will be fresh croissants ready in about ten minutes."

"Not sure how I can pass that up." He took a seat at the island after pouring a coffee.

"And then you've got to get out of here before anyone comes downstairs."

"Too late." A husky, sleep laden female voice came from the doorway. A bleary eyed, barefoot woman in a floral silk pajama set padded into the kitchen. She had a silk eye mask pushed up onto her forehead, and her hair stuck out in a half dozen directions.

"Coffee?" she asked almost pathetically.

"Here you go, Fran," said Aggie. She poured the woman a mug of a freshly brewed Oaxacan blend with notes of milk chocolate and orange. It was one of Aggie's particular favorites from a roaster in Houston.

"Cream?"

The woman nodded.

"Why don't you take this out on the porch, and I'll bring you a croissant in just a minute?" She woman nodded again, wrapped her hands around the warm mug and slowly padded toward the front door. Brooks looked at Aggie. "How much wine did they go through last night?"

"I have no idea. I told them they had free rein in the kitchen."

"They need your magic sandwiches."

"I think you might be right." She pulled the croissants from the oven and Brooks made a reach for them. "Careful!" she admonished. "Those just came out of a three-hundred-and-seventy-five-degree oven. They're a tad warm."

Brooks pulled his hand back. "Can you blame me?" he asked. "Gah, they smell amazing."

"Give them five minutes." Aggie set out handcrafted raspberry preserves and freshly churned local butter from the farmers market and started to fry up several pounds of thick cut bacon. When she deemed the croissants cool enough to not give Brooks a second-degree burn, she passed him one. He tore the tip off and steam drifted upwards. He blew on it and then took a healthy bite slathered with the raspberry preserves. He closed his eyes, making appreciative noises. The aromas of coffee and croissants were drifting up the stairs and Aggie could hear movement above her in the bedrooms. "That's your cue. These women came here for a girl's weekend. Scoot."

"Fine, fine. I'm going to stop by later at Lillian and Jude's and make sure everything is set for Tuesday," he said, referring to their plans for Florida.

"That's fine, send me a text and let me know." Another silk pajama clad creature was entering the kitchen. "Now go on!" she said, waving a dishtowel towards the door.

"All right, all right, I can take a hint." On his way out, he kissed the back of her neck and while she wasn't looking swiped a second croissant for the road.

Aggie was in an excellent mood. Her guests were having a wonderful time. They all enjoyed breakfast on the porch and Aggie's combination of croissants, coffee, bacon and a giant plate of fresh fruit seemed to have fortified the women enough to make it down to the beach. They filed out the door, each with their woven straw tote Aggie filled with beach essentials, including towels she managed to get monogrammed with each of their initials this time. It was like a Spring fashion show as all ten women floated down the staircase. They were a synchronized rainbow of beautifully elaborate beach caftans and wide brimmed floppy hats. Aggie waved them off with a promise to bring down snacks later. Aggie was a whirlwind of activity all morning. Amelia would join her to orchestrate the wine tasting later in the afternoon. And Emma's arrival around five o'clock to help with dinner prep and clean up would be a godsend, but she was busy tending the shop during the day. So, Aggie was on her own for now. She promised herself she would hire more help for the next retreat.

She twirled around the kitchen, washing dishes, wiping countertops and sweeping crumbs. When every speck of dirt, dust, and food was banished from the downstairs, she raced up to the bedrooms and started making beds and tidying bathrooms. She was dizzy as she came downstairs and realized she hadn't fed herself even a bite of food. She grabbed herself a leftover croissant from the Tupperware container where she had stashed them and took bites of it in between slicing fruit for the morning snack spread. She carefully packed perfectly hulled bright red strawberries, raspberries, blueberries and cubed watermelon into pretty containers and set them in her cooler on ice. She added small white cardboard boxes filled with gourmet crackers, thin slices of bright orange mimolette cheese and a small wedge of brie. Then she grabbed a stack of plastic tumblers and filled two large thermoses with ice water flavored with fresh mint and sliced cucumbers.

She really, really needed to hire an extra hand for these days, but for now she devised a system to get this all down to the beach on her own. She placed the thermoses in a backpack and hoisted it over her shoulders. Once the backpack was securely in place, she picked up her cooler. To a passerby, she might resemble a drunken pack mule staggering down to the beach, but she managed to get everything transferred in one trip. Most of the ladies were lounging on the brightly colored Turkish beach towels Aggie provided in their totes, some with paperbacks they found in the library. A few were bobbing up and down in the waves, and another two were walking along the beach at a pace that made it clear they were getting their steps in for the day. Aggie couldn't help but think those two were kind of missing the point. But she waved cheerily and held up the boxes, indicating nourishment had arrived. The woman happily accepted their gourmet snack boxes and chilled cucumber water. Aggie was about to leave them to it and go start prep for a late lunch and the wine tasting when a figure clad all in black started walking towards her from the shoreline. The stick thin woman wore giant dark sunglasses, a black flowing dress that covered almost every square inch of skin, and a black straw hat the size of a small umbrella. It took Aggie a minute to recognize her new neighbor. "Hello, Angelica," she said with a smile. She would have waved, but her hands were weighed down with the cooler.

"Hello, Maggie. How are you?"

"It's Aggie. But I'm great, thanks. Are you all moved in?"

"We are. The construction crew we brought in from Houston worked wonders. You should come and see it. It doesn't even look like the same house."

Aggie thought that was a shame. She remembered thinking the house was positively stunning before Angelica got her hands on it and was kind of afraid to see the end result. "I'm so glad for you. Remodeling is a tough project." She pointed towards the beach house.

"Oh, is this your house? I'd love to see it sometime. I can see you have your hands full though. And aren't you just the hostess with the *most-est*? Catering to all your friends. So sweet of you." Angelical gestured at the group of women.

"Oh, these aren't my friends. I mean, they are all lovely people, but I'm hosting them for a retreat weekend. I've started a new business," Aggie said with the same enthusiasm she emulated anytime anyone asked her about the retreats. "These ladies come down to enjoy the beach for the weekend, and we do a few cooking classes. Amelia from the wine bar puts on a little wine tasting class in the afternoon. It's been so fun."

Angelica was quiet for a minute, taking in the scene, her gaze turning from the women on the beach to the house. Although you could barely tell behind her massive sunglasses. "Ah," she finally said. "That's very...interesting."

"Well, it's certainly a more entertaining way to make a living than my accounting practice was," Aggie said with a smile. "But now I have to get back up to the house. Feel free to stop by. Take care." As Aggie walked back toward the house, something about the conversation with her new neighbor bothered her, but she didn't know what.

Thankfully, Emma and Amelia showed up at the same time. The ladies, freshly showered and dressed in another collection of the latest in fashionable beachwear with their hair and make-up freshly done, assembled in the dining room. While Emma and Aggie set up for the cooking demo and dinner, Amelia walked the women through a guided tour of the French wine regions, tasting all along the way. The rest of the evening went swimmingly, and it gave Aggie great joy to see the women taking selfies with each other, along with photographs of the beautiful food, and posting it all to Instagram and Facebook. The music played, the wine flowed, the food was exclaimed over. Women who counted calories every day of their lives asked for second helpings of the decadent Potatoes Ana and absolutely no one passed on the chocolate mousse.

By the time she waved the caravan of luxury SUVs off the next day at noon, Aggie was bone tired, but happy. Her plan was working. It was really working. She needed to hire extra help for the retreats themselves, and at the price tag people seemed happy to pay for a few days of sunshine and her cooking, she could afford to hire help. For the first time since she arrived on island over a year ago, she was on solid footing, professionally, financially and personally. As much as she missed Shane, she didn't see herself ever going back to Houston or to crunching numbers for anyone other than herself.

Chapter Thirty-Eight

An excited foursome boarded the sleek, eight-seater private jet at the little airfield not far from Peach Tree House. Well, three of the four were excited. As they took their seats Aggie felt lightheaded and was concentrating on taking slow, deep breaths while counting to ten forward and backwards over and over in her head. It was a distraction technique a therapist taught her to deal with the intense anxiety that consumed her when she flew. Unfortunately, it didn't work and anytime she had flown in the last decade it had been with a little orange bottle in her bag. She had been so busy with the retreat; she hadn't even thought about making a call to her doctor's office for a refill. She tried to tell herself this was fine, she was a grown woman, this was far safer than driving a car down Interstate 10. Nothing would go wrong. The pilot greeted each of them by name and a flight attendant offered them everything from fresh fruit to filet mignon. Brooks nudged Aggie when she didn't answer the dapper young man. "Hmm?" She looked up at him.

"You okay? You look pale."

"Oh, I didn't mention? Air travel and I, well, we don't really get along."

Lillian turned to her. "Don't you have your happy flying pills?"

"Nope, I ran out. I was going to get a refill, but I haven't needed to fly in a while." She was looking straight ahead, concentrating on her breathing. "I'll be okay." Lillian and Brooks glanced at each other, concerned.

"I got this," said Brooks. He made his way to the little refrigerator at the front of the cabin. "May I?" Brooks asked the flight attendant, gesturing at the tiny fridge.

"Certainly, sir. Be my guest." Brooks inventoried the assortment of drinks on offer. He took a tiny bottle of gin and emptied it into a plastic cup. Then he added a generous splash of tonic water along with one of the pre-sliced limes he found in a little plastic box in the fridge and carried it back to Aggie.

"Here, sip this."

"What is it?" Aggie was skeptical.

"Trust me. Take ten sips of this and you'll be fine."

"Or I'll be drunk." Aggie sniffed the glass. The scent of gin tingled in her nostrils.

"I'll make sure you're okay. But we can't have you passing out in the air. Maybe we should have brought a nurse along after all."

"Okay, okay," said Aggie. She took the cup and took a small sip. "Wowza, that's strong." She coughed and handed it back to him. "If I didn't know better, I think you were trying to take advantage of me," she said, attempting a joke.

"Ah, a sense of humor, that's a good sign in any patient. Just take tiny sips. I promise, it will help." At that moment, the pilot revved the engine and the plane started to move. Aggie gripped the armrests until her knuckles turned white. Brooks slowly peeled the fingers of one hand off the armrest and placed the cup in it. "Tiny sips," he repeated. "Ten slow, tiny sips."

Aggie concentrated on forcing ten small sips of the potent cocktail down her throat. She would take a sip, then count to ten backwards and forwards. A deep breath, a sip, count forwards, a deep breath, a sip, count backwards. By sip eight she could feel the warmth of the gin start to spread through her releasing a small amount of the tension in her shoulders. She continued the process until she looked up and the cup was empty. She handed the cup back to Brooks. She continued her breathing. "I think I'll be alright," she slurred, and smiled at Brooks.

"I think you're a little tipsy. But that's better than hyperventilating. We'll find you a coffee when we land."

Aggie, in fact, had mostly sobered up by the time they landed, but Brooks found her a coffee in the little lounge anyway. "It's not a Bean and Bun brew, but it's probably not too bad," he said, gesturing at the elegant surroundings of the lounge. Aggie nodded and drank dutifully; grateful Brooks had refused to make her another cocktail when the pilot began his descent into Florida panhandle airspace. She shook her head, forcing herself to focus on the business of the day. She felt guilty as she looked at Nellie. Nellie was the one who should be nervous. But Nellie appeared cool as a cucumber in a pale turquoise shirtdress Aggie hadn't seen before, her white hair attractively framing her face and pink lipstick perfectly in place.

Nellie touched Billy's letter in her pocket. She indeed did feel calm, as if this was exactly where she was meant to be at this exact moment in time. She couldn't say she knew what the next few hours would hold for her, but whatever they did, it was predetermined and nothing she could do would change it. Her job was just to show up. And show up, she had.

Lillian had a car service waiting to take them to the Florida retirement village where in theory, there was one William Black in residence. Nellie took a deep breath as they entered the cool lobby. It was so different from Peach Tree House, but also quite similar. The lobby was an atrium with twenty-foot-tall glass ceilings. Palm trees in gigantic pots dotted the space. A musical trio was set up in the corner, playing tributes to Glenn

Miller and big band music. All of which gave the impression you walked into the place mid cocktail party instead of a run of the mill Tuesday morning.

The cast of characters moving through the huge room reminded Brooks of Peach Tree House. Everyone appeared well dressed and cared for. Just like at Peach Tree, there was no one shuffling along in dressing gowns and the place smelled of the gardenias that filled flower boxes along one wall. The effect made one feel as if they were inside a giant greenhouse and the whole vibe was extremely pleasant. Brooks took charge and walked up to an attendant at the welcome desk. "Hello!" He flashed his most charming smile. "We're here to see an old friend of my grandmother's. Billy Black in room 107."

"Are you on the list?" a kind looking middle aged woman asked. She wore a smile and she spoke pleasantly enough, but her undertone said quite firmly that they were going no further if their names were not on said list.

"Um, no, he's not exactly expecting us. But we're looking for Billy Black. Or he might go by William now. Room 107. It's a bit of a unique situation. We just want to visit with him for a minute."

"Exactly what sort of a unique situation?" the woman asked, raising her eyebrows and giving off a mama bear vibe.

Brooks turned back to Aggie and Lillian. "Why don't you girls take GranNell and get something to drink?" He pointed at a little cafe set up in one corner. "I'll get us situated here."

When the girls were out of earshot, he turned back to the woman at the desk. He looked at the name tag on her crisp white uniform. "Pearl? Is it ok if I call you Pearl? Such a lovely name."

The woman pursed her lips but nodded and let him continue. "Pearl, I'd like to tell you a story." And as only a professional storyteller can, Brooks unfolded the love story and the almost connections of Nell and Billy spanning three quarters of a century.

"So," he concluded, "we've come an awfully long way for my grandmother to simply say hello. Could you help us? Please, Pearl?"

Pearl looked up at him, dabbing at the corner of her eye. She looked at Brooks and over at the ladies sitting at a table in the cafe area. "Alright, honey. Let me see what I can do. Wait here." She slowly rose from her post and walked down the brightly lit hallway towards the rear of the building.

Brooks turned to the women and flashed Aggie two thumbs up. "Looks like we're in," Aggie said.

By the time Aggie tidied up their table, Pearl was walking back into the atrium. Aggie looked at Nellie. "I think it's showtime." The three women were standing behind Brooks when Pearl's gaze took in all of them, a pained expression on her face. "Y'all, I am so sorry to tell you this. I don't have a Billy or a William Black on my roster. But the gentleman in room 107 passed away two days ago." She laid a hand on Nellie's arm, compassion in her eyes. "I am so sorry, ma'am. Your story was beautiful."

Nellie was quiet for a long minute and then she responded. "Yes, I suppose it was, in its own way." Disappointment was etched on her face. She was fully aware there were a number of ways today might have played out. She was prepared for her old love to not want to see her, or perhaps to be remarried to someone who wouldn't enjoy the idea of him seeing her, or to have children who didn't want to see him upset and didn't want him to see her. She was prepared for any of these scenarios and would have accepted whatever fate dealt out. But this, this nothingness, this dead end felt hollow. Even though it should have been the most probable, she had guarded her heart against this possibility.

Brooks slid his hand under her elbow. "I'm so sorry. Are you alright?" Nellie closed her eyes. "I will be." She looked at Pearl. "Thank you for your help, dear. May we sit for a minute?"

"Certainly," Pearl nodded. "Take all the time you need." The collective spirit of their little group couldn't be more out of sync with their jazzy surroundings as they rested on a group of benches near the band. The opening bars of "*The Way You Look Tonight*" wafted over them. An elderly couple began to dance. Well, you could sort of call it dancing. They leaned against each other slightly swaying in time to the music, almost as if they were holding each other up. One got the impression they danced to this tune many, many times on many different floors over the long years of entwined lifetimes. That maybe they once had some enviable moves, but now contented themselves with a gentle sway so as no one broke a hip. Nellie watched them, suddenly filled with longing. Then she sternly scolded herself for even a moment of self-pity. She looked at her companions. "I think I'm ready. Let's get back. I've got a bridge tournament tomorrow and a card date with Jude on Saturday. We have things to do."

"Okay," said Brooks. "Yes," he agreed with an enthusiasm that didn't quite reach his eyes. "You're right. Onward, ever onward."

"I'll call the driver," said Lillian, taking out her phone. "He should be nearby. We'll be on our way in two shakes." Nellie just nodded, staring into space. Lillian stepped outside to make the call. The sweet couple on the dance floor were still swaying back and forth. The last notes of the song faded away and the band set down their instruments to take a break. The couple separated but remained holding hands as though for mutual balance and slowly left the impromptu dance floor. The old man raised his free hand in greeting to a friend walking in from the hallway.

"Hey there, Theo! You gonna watch the Astros game tonight?"

"Betcha bottom dollar," his friend replied in a strong Texas accent, and he gave him a jaunty salute with a rolled-up copy of the Houston Chronicle. At this Nellie sat up straight and in slow motion turned toward the voice of the dancer's friend. Aggie and Brooks silently followed her gaze. At the end of the room stood a tall, attractive man with an erect posture, a thinning, but full head of white hair and bright blue eyes. He wore khaki pants, a crisply pressed button-down shirt and a pair of neon orange running shoes. And he was standing completely still, staring straight at Nellie. They all instantly realized their mistake. Theodore William Black didn't go by Billy or William these days.

Nellie, moving in a trancelike state, slowly rose and walked towards the man. It seemed to take ages for her to reach him as Aggie and Brooks tracked her progress across the room. At one point, Brooks made to go help her, but Aggie put a hand on his arm indicating he should keep his seat.

"Wait," she whispered. "She's okay." Nellie finally came to a stop in front of the man. "Hello, Billy." Her voice was clear as a bell.

"Nellie. You're here." The man was utterly confused, as if he looked around and suddenly realized he woke up on Mars today, instead of the familiar comfort of a Florida retirement village.

"I'm here." The two just stood and stared at each other for what stretched into an eternity. At some point while they stood there, his hand reached for hers, delicately linking the tips of his long fingers with her small ones. He towered above her tiny frame. Finally, he shook his stupor. He tilted his head to one side. "Can I get you a cup of coffee?" Nellie beamed at him and nodded. He tucked her hand into the crook of his elbow and led her over to the little cafe stand in the corner.

"What do you take in your coffee?"

Nellie laughed. "I don't really drink coffee," she admitted. "But anything is fine."

"Ah, are you still a lemonade girl?" She nodded and Billy, aka Theo looked back at the attendant manning the little cafe. "One black coffee please, and a lemonade for the lady." Billy carried their drinks over to a table in front of a window along the side of the room. It had a view of an outdoor, covered swimming pool and a giant shuffleboard court.

"I remember you taking your coffee with buckets of cream and sugar," Nellie said as they sat down.

"No cream or sugar in the army," Billy/Theo replied. "I sort of lost the taste for it."

"That makes sense." Nellie just stared into her lemonade. Now that she was here, finally sitting in front of them, she didn't know what to say.

"Oh!" She exclaimed, remembering her manners. She turned and motioned to Brooks and the girls, who were all sitting still as stones, unabashedly staring, watching the encounter unfold.

"Ah, do these folks belong to you?" Billy asked, grateful for a conversation starter.

"They do, indeed," replied Nellie as the group arrived, hovering over their table. "This is my grandson, Brooks, his girlfriend Aggie and her friend Lillian." Aggie blushed when Nellie referred to her as Brooks' girlfriend. But she liked the sound of it.

"Hello, sir." Brooks said, pumping Billy's hand up and down when he held it out to shake. He noticed the old man still had quite the grip. "We are so happy to see you, sir. You really have no idea."

"Brooks," Aggie said quietly. She could tell he was about to launch into the long tale that brought them all to Florida. She moved her finger in a circle, encompassing herself, Brooks and Lillian. "I think maybe the three of us should go find some lunch and let these two catch up."

"Your girl is an astute one, Brooks," Nellie piped up. "You all scoot. I am fine. Billy and I have a lot to catch up on." Brooks seemed hesitant.

"I'll take good care of your grandmother, young man." said Billy with a broad smile that revealed a perfect set of white veneers. "Not to worry."

"Okay, we'll be back soon. I have my cell if you need anything." The three younger people took their leave. As they left, Pearl came back to her station.

"Well, I see your grandmother made a new friend anyway," she said. Mr. Theodore is a sweetie."

"No ma'am, Ms. Pearl." Brooks shook his head with a grin. "That there is her very, very old friend. One Theodore William Black, who apparently some seventy odd years ago, went by nothing but Billy." Pearl brought a hand up to her mouth.

"Get out! You don't say."

"Yes, ma'am, I do." He looked over at the pair. They were now engrossed in conversation, the awkwardness dissipating quickly. "We're going to get lunch. We'll be back to pick her up in an hour or so."

"Oh, that's fine. I'll go check and see if they need anything."

"You know Pearl, I think they have everything they need. Maybe let them be for now."

"Okay, okay, I can take a hint." Pearl laughed and moved back behind her desk.

An hour and a half later, the three walked back into an empty atrium. Pearl had gone on break and a young, attractive redhead had taken her place. As their names were still not on any list, Brooks had to explain their story all over again. By the time he finished, though, he had Janet, Pearl's replacement, wrapped around his little finger and half in love with him.

"Oh, my goodness. What a beautiful story," she exclaimed with stars in her eyes as she smacked a large wad of gum. She leaned forward with her elbows on the desk, putting her considerable cleavage on full display for Brooks. "You stay right here. I'll go see what they're up to." She winked at Brooks. "I mean, I'm not going to go barging into his room, if you know what I mean. But I'll see if they're around. I mean, what if they're like *really* catching up?" Her voice dripped with innuendo. "I mean, it happens more often than you'd think around here. It's downright scandalous," she tsked. "I'll be right back. Don't you move now." She fluttered her long lashes at Brooks and tucked a burnished bronze lock of hair behind her ear. Then she blew a bubble at him before sauntering off down the hall. Brooks clamped his hands over his ears and turned to the girls.

"Did she just say what I think she said?" The girls' shoulders were shaking with laughter.

"Yep, yep she did," said Aggie through her giggles.

"But look." Lillian pointed out the window. "I think Nellie's reputation is still intact." Through the plate glass window, they could see Nellie and Billy on the other side of the turquoise swimming pool. They sat close together on a bench, under a Japanese maple. "For heaven's sake, I don't think they'll arrest us if we just go out there. Come on." Lillian tentatively pushed open the door. No alarm bells sounded, and no troop of white uniformed nurses swooped in on them, so they entered the courtyard and made their way down a floral lined path that led to the other side of the pool. Nellie looked up as they approached. "Oh, pooh. It is time to go?"

Lillian answered for them. "I'm afraid it is. The plane is waiting for us." Lillian consulted her watch. "We can give you a few minutes though."

The three of them turned back towards the atrium and saw Janet's curvaceous figure advancing on them. Her hips swayed and she was twirling a lock of hair around her finger as she pointed her other hand at Brooks and said saucily, "Aren't you a naughty one, coming out here? I'm sorry, I will have to ask you to wait in the lobby."

"It's okay Janet, we found them. Thank you for looking." Brooks was polite, but he put his arm possessively around Aggie's waist and pulled her towards him. "We'll head on inside and be on our way shortly."

Janet took in his posture with Aggie which was sending its intended and very clear message. "Alright then, suit yourself." And she flounced off back behind her desk, smacking her gum ferociously.

Nellie and Billy sat quietly on the bench. After Nellie had told the long tale of how she came to be in the lobby today, they caught each other up on the bare bones of their lives since they last saw each other. But there was so much more Nellie wanted to say. So many things she wanted to ask. Billy echoed her thoughts. "I wish you had more time. This is so surreal."

"So do I," said Nellie.

"Can I call you?"

"I would love that." Nellie wrote her number on the little yellow paper pad she kept in her purse. She tore off the top sheet and handed it to him. "But Billy, before you call, there is something you should see. Before we came here, I had the opportunity to read all your letters to me. I feel like you should have the same privilege."

"Your letters were in that box as well? Well, I'll be…" Billy's voice trailed off into silence as Nellie reached into her bag again.

"Yes, Brooks and Aggie don't even know that. God bless them, they read the first couple of letters and apparently felt a little guilty reading someone else's mail."

"Well, I'll be…," Billy said again, stupefied.

"Here they are. All eighty-four of them. And on top is a letter from my mother to me. It apologizes to me. I figure she owes you an apology too, so go ahead and read that one as well. She passed him a stack of uniform envelopes, yellowed with age and tied neatly with a worn yellow ribbon. "You read those, and then you can call me."

"Your mother never told you? Not even years later?"

"No, not even years later. On her deathbed, she whispered she needed to tell me something, but she was in so much pain, and I just told her everything was fine and to rest. Then the doctor came in and gave her more pain meds. She said something after that, but I couldn't understand her. I assume this was her secret."

"Are you angry with her?"

Nellie half laughed. "No. Maybe if I was younger, I would be. It seems silly to be angry about anything at our age, doesn't it?"

"Oh, Nellie Anne. You always were a wise one. But, yes, it seems like a waste." Billy looked down at the stack of envelopes. He held them as if they were a priceless antique, which they sort of were. "Thank you," he said simply.

"So, I guess I just have one more question."

"Shoot."

"Do I call you Billy or Theo now?"

"You know, no one has called me Billy since I joined the Army, but Theo sounds a little strange coming from you. I'll tell you what. Whatever you call me, I reckon I'll answer."

Nellie smiled and looked down at her lap. Then she looked up and said softly. "I think I have to go now."

"I know. Come on, I'll walk you in."

****

The plane ride back was uneventful. Brooks, Aggie and Lillian were dying to hear about Nellie's conversation with Billy, but Nellie was exhausted and fell asleep in the comfy chair almost as soon as they boarded the plane. Brooks mixed Aggie a milder cocktail before they took off. And while she almost cut off the circulation in his right hand with her grip, they made it back to the little airstrip near Peach Tree House without incident. Lillian rushed off to pick up Jude from soccer practice. He had been a little indignant at being left out of today's activities, but Lillian insisted he go to school. Brooks and Aggie helped Nellie into the Thunderbird, and Brooks slowly drove back to Peach Tree House.

"Thank you, dears," said Nellie when they dropped her off. "I promise I'll call you tomorrow, darling. But I need to rest." The events of the day had worn her out.

"Okay." Brooks said, and they let a nurse escort her to her suite.

Chapter Thirty-Nine

Billy, or perhaps we should call him Theo now as that is what he has been called for the last seventy years or so, sat in his room alone that evening staring at the stack of envelopes on the dresser. He hadn't opened any of Nellie's letters yet. He wasn't completely sure he wanted to. He had loved two women in his life, and he had lost them both. The first to a war and to Nellie's mother's manipulations. And then he lost his beloved Elizabeth to a vile cancer when she was far too young. A few years after Elizabeth's passing, their grown daughters encouraged him to try dating. He still had a lot of good years left, after all. They were concerned he would be lonely. They both loved their father dearly, but they were busy with their own young children and their careers. They didn't want him to be alone. But Billy/Theo was having none of it. His heart had mended after both losses, but he was a sensitive soul, and he wasn't certain he could stomach any more heartache.

To appease his daughters, he kept busy, but he didn't date. He continued teaching Civil War History at the local university even though he was well qualified for retirement. He played a lot of golf. He attended every home Astros baseball game with a couple of his buddies, and he even contributed to the neighborhood potluck every once in a while. He learned to cook for himself and after a few laundry loads of pink socks, managed to teach himself basic household chores that Elizabeth always handled with effortless efficiency. In retrospect, he was grateful his girls had pushed him to stay social and keep busy. It carried him through that dark time when he might have easily ended up as one of those sad old people who never leave the house. Because in truth, that is who he wanted to be for a long time. So, he had recovered from not one, but two heartbreaks in his lifetime. Even at the age of ninety-three, he wasn't sure he wanted to open up that part of himself again. So, he left the stack of letters on the dresser, unopened, and spent the evening as he planned, eating peanuts and cheering on the Astros in the lounge.

Chapter Forty

Brooks dropped Aggie off at the bakery with a promise to pick her up for an early meal in a few hours. Neither one of them felt like cooking tonight. It was crazy to Aggie that she had started her morning in the same spot and in the space of eight hours traveled halfway across the country and back. The miracle of private air travel.

"Hey," she greeted Emma with a smile as walked in. "How was the day?"

"It was good. I think we've sold out of just about everything you left. Did Sadie get in touch with you?"

"Oh, I don't know," Aggie admitted, reaching in her handbag. "I haven't checked my phone." She pulled out her cell and saw two missed calls and a text from Sadie asking her to call as soon as possible. She was tapping the phone screen to call her back when the door opened and Sadie herself came breezing in.

"Oh good, you're back. Sit down, we need to talk." She added to Emma "Double Americano, please, sweetie."

"Is everything okay? Are the twins all right? What's wrong?"

"Oh, the twins are fine, nothing like that. It's your new neighbor. Remember Angelica?"

"The lover of all things chrome and giant designer sunglasses? Yes, I remember Angelica. What does she have to do with anything?" Aggie was completely confused and had no idea where Sadie could possibly be going with this.

"Well, you know Miranda in my office also serves on the Island Council. Apparently, Angelica paid a visit to the council office yesterday asking how to file a complaint against you. She is claiming that hosting the retreats at the beach house violates your HOA restrictions by running a commercial enterprise out of the home."

Aggie was stunned. "She what? Can she do that? People rent out houses every day of the year all up and down the beach."

"You're correct. Short term rentals are allowed, which is how I would categorize what you're doing. I mean, it's not like you're selling macrame in your front yard to tourists walking down the beach. But legally, it's probably a grey area."

Aggie sat down, dumbfounded. "Why? Why would she do this?"

"Who knows? She clearly has nothing better to do? Perhaps people were people having fun and that in itself is illegal? I'm telling you, I worked with this woman for months before they bought their house. Maybe she has some redeeming qualities somewhere, but she is a first-class pill. She can find something wrong with anything."

"What do I do? If I can't host the retreats…" Aggie's voice trailed off.

"Don't panic yet. And don't cancel anything. Let me work on this. I have a call in to a real estate attorney, and I'm going to go over those HOA restrictions with a fine-tooth comb. You sit tight, and I'll call you tomorrow."

Emma handed Sadie her drink and looked at Aggie. "Wow, I'm sorry," she said. "What a bummer."

"Yes," Aggie echoed. "Bummer is one word for it."

"Oh my gosh, I can't believe I didn't ask," gushed Sadie, switching gears quickly. "How was today? Did you find Billy?"

Aggie relayed the events of the day, skipping over her slight inebriation on the flight there. Both Sadie and Emma were on the verge of tears when she told them about Pearl telling them about the man in room 107 passed away the previous week and they rolled with laughter when she told of Janet's shameless gum smacking flirtation with Brooks.

"So, what now?" Sadie asked.

"I have no idea," Aggie said honestly. "I really have no idea."

Chapter Forty-One

The events of the day exhausted both Aggie and Brooks. As promised, he picked her up and they decided rather than going out to dinner they should just order a platter of grilled shrimp and french fries from Buster's Icehouse and have a picnic on the beach. The gentle rolling waves and calm overcast sky fit Aggie's mood. She was bone tired and worried sick about what she would do if Angelica shut down her retreats. Once they were settled on the beach blanket, she told Brooks what Sadie shared that afternoon. "Surely, she can't do that?" Brooks said.

"That's what I said. But apparently, it could be considered a 'legal gray area' according to Sadie. Is what I'm doing considered short term rental or is it considered running a commercial operation out of a residential property? She's supposed to talk to a real estate attorney for me in the morning and dig through my HOA restrictions."

"Hmm. How many people are in that HOA now?" Brooks asked. "I know it's not very many."

"No, it's not. Let me think." Aggie mentally went down the line of beach houses on her stretch of beach that were technically part of the tiny subdivision of Francis Beachside Estates. "Myself, the O'Henrys, the dreaded Angelica and her attorney husband, a nice couple from Dallas that I've only met once, and..." Aggie's heart sank. She buried her head in her hands. Until this moment she'd forgotten that the fifth house, the one further down from the Dallas family, belonged to none other than Flora Hernandez.

"What is it?" Brooks asked.

"Mrs. Hernandez. She wanted to buy my building when it was for sale. But I beat her to it. I swear she's on a mission to own all of Main Street. She would love to shut me down."

"Look, I know Mrs. Hernandez is the property mogul of Sandcastle Island, but she's not evil. If I were you, I'd aim for low hanging fruit first. Take something over to the O'Henrys - maybe your magic sandwiches or something. Make sure they know exactly what you're doing. I mean, you're not opening a hotel, you're running these retreats maybe twice a month during the season?"

"For now, yes."

"So, that's maybe eighteen weekends a year. And I saw your business plan. You're charging an arm and a leg for these weekends, so it's not as if you're attracting a rowdy, college spring break crowd. I don't see anything reasonable they would object to. And take something to Mrs. Hernandez too. Let Sadie run her traps but go ahead and just talk to your neighbors. People on this island like you, they respect you. There would probably have to be a vote to shut you down. I can't imagine it would be too hard to swing at least the local folks over to your side."

"Everyone except Flora Hernandez," Aggie grumbled. But she looked up at Brooks and couldn't help feeling a tiny bit better. He was on her team. That felt good. She leaned against him. "Look at you being all reasonable and pragmatic. I like this side of you. It's sexy."

His idea was a good one, and she would feel better if she could start knocking on doors right this minute. But the sun was setting, and the clouds were clearing, melting into streaks of purple and pink and orange. She settled against Brooks and let the sound of the wind and the waves roll over her as twilight softened the landscape.

But even tucked snugly in Brooks' arms that night, she couldn't sleep.

Chapter Forty-Two

Billy returned to his room after watching the Astros game in a great mood. The good guys won, and it looked like the Astros might have a shot at the World Series. He undressed for bed and his gaze fell on the stack of letters. He moved over to the dresser. He stood there in his socks and boxer shorts, his hand resting on top of the stack for a long moment. But in the end, he got under the covers and turned out the light. He lay in the dark as the minutes ticked by and his mind drifted back over his conversation with Nellie that afternoon. He still couldn't believe she found him. That she came all that way. To him, even with her white hair and lined face, she looked exactly as the girl he had known. He started to turn on the light and reach for the letters. Then he decided the letters had sat sealed in their envelopes for something close to seventy-five years. They could keep for one more day. He eventually fell into a restless sleep and dreamt of the summer of 1943.

As was his habit, Billy woke early the next morning, before the sun broke the horizon. He called the concierge and asked for breakfast to be delivered to his room. This was *not* his habit. Typically, he would much prefer to eat in the dining hall and rehash last night's game with his buddy, Shep Adams, the only other Astros fan in the place. He ordered poached eggs, crispy bacon, a fruit plate and black coffee. While he waited on breakfast, he dressed quickly in a freshly pressed plaid shirt and khaki chinos. He pulled on the neon orange running shoes. His grandson was in podiatry school and sent the shoes for him, the latest in orthopedic support. Billy raised his eyebrows initially at the color, but he had to admit the comfort made up for any fashion faux pas. Also, at his age who cared what anyone thought of his footwear?

His breakfast arrived and he moved the letters to the kitchen table. He sipped his coffee, a ritual he enjoyed and took his time with breakfast, staring down the stack of envelopes the entire while. When he finished, he washed the dishes and stacked them neatly. Then he sat back down, took a deep breath and opened the letter on the top of the stack.

Dearest Nellie Anne,

My darling girl, if you are reading this, then you have discovered my terrible sin. It broke my heart night after night, hearing your torment. A mother can physically feel her child's pain and it almost broke me, as I'm sure it almost broke you.

I have thought many times of confessing to you, as I have to the priest. But I see you with Martin and your darling son. You have a happy, full and wonderful life, and it may not have played out that way with your wartime love.

I still hold fast to the fact that what I did as a motherly duty in hiding these from you was the right, though painful choice. And I keep them from you now to protect the beautiful life and family you have built. Please know, dearest, that with every single thing I have ever done, I have acted from a place of great love.

Your loving mother, Anne

Well, he thought. Way to start the morning off with a bang. Decades of life separated him from these events, but it still hurt to think of Nellie, crying every night thinking he had forsaken her. A flame of anger at her mother flared, but passed as quickly as it came. With the perspective of age, he thought he could understand her reasoning, even if he still didn't agree with it. He slowly made his way through the letters. The hot Florida sun was dead overhead when he folded the last one and slid it back into its fragile envelope. Five hours and six months of time had passed since he opened the first envelope. That first letter was obviously written the day of his departure after he left her standing on the beach in her daisy yellow sundress.

In the first letter, she apologized for her hysterics and said she would be a proper Army girlfriend. She swore her fidelity and promised she would do everything she could at home to help the war effort. Subsequent letters were newsy, keeping him abreast of all the goings on of the island. She even included newspaper clippings for a few events she deemed worthy of his attention. In every letter, she told him how much she loved him and eagerly awaited his return. By roughly the tenth letter, the tone changed. She was concerned that she hadn't had any letters from him, and she was worried for his safety. He had to still be stateside, but was he ill? Could he have been injured in a training exercise? Run over by a bus? She was worried sick and if he could please just find a way to get word to her that he was alive and safe it would ease her mind and heart mightily, thank you very much.

Her last letter was the one that broke him.

Dearest Billy,

I have had no word from you in six months, not since our parting that fateful day on the beach. I know you are well because I finally gathered enough courage to pay a call to your mother. She shared with me what a wonderful son she has been blessed with as he is considerate enough to write to her faithfully every week. She is incredibly proud of you.

The only conclusion I can draw is that you have somehow moved on from our shared story. Perhaps you regret our lovely summer. Perhaps you have met someone new. Perhaps, perhaps, perhaps…. I have accepted that I may never know.

Please know that I do not regret one minute of our summer together. My love for you is as unending as the waves that roll in from the ocean. But I cannot continue to pine for someone who obviously does not return my affections.

I bless your journey and wish you well. I pray life is kind to you. My hope is that by releasing you in this way, my own heart will begin to heal, and my own journey can continue.

Lovingly,
Your Nellie

Billy sat at the table with his eyes closed for a long time after folding that last letter. When he opened them again, he was surprised to find his cheeks wet. Somehow, completely without his permission or consent, the part of himself he locked down deep inside so many years ago had ripped itself open, releasing a flood of emotion and tears were streaming silently down his lined cheeks.

Chapter Forty-Three

Aggie woke before dawn and tried not to wake Brooks. They brought her car back to his cabin the night before as she needed to be at the bakery by five. She was dressing in the living room, trying to be quiet as a mouse when he stumbled in from the bedroom rubbing his eyes, wearing nothing but plaid boxer shorts.

"Love 'em and leave 'em, huh? This seems to be a pattern with you," he joked, his voice thick with sleep.

"Only because I have got to be at work at an ungodly hour. You should go back to bed," Aggie replied as she stepped into his embrace. He was still warm from their body heat under the covers.

He walked into the kitchen. "Here, let me make you coffee."

"You're making me coffee? You do remember I own a coffee shop, right?" she said as she slipped on her shoes.

"Yes, but sometimes it tastes better when someone else makes it for you." He already had the kettle on the burner and the coffee grinder whined as it pulverized beans. He poured the hot water over the beans in a stainless-steel French press. "In four minutes, you will have a perfect cup." He pulled her toward him and whispered into her hair, "And I know just what to do with four minutes." She giggled and tried to protest as he pulled her back into the bedroom. Needless to say; at some point, quite a bit longer than four minutes later, Aggie drove away from Brooks' cabin late for work, with very strong coffee. She buzzed through her morning routine and decided to take Mr. O'Henry a basket of the chocolate chip scones he liked so much. But Mrs. O'Henry didn't want him eating treats, which posed a problem as she didn't want to alienate her either. She decided to cover all bases and include just one of the scones and also a bag of her homemade granola. Surely Mrs. O'Henry couldn't object to granola?

Flora Hernandez had come into the shop exactly once, and she had ordered a Texas Sheet Cake Brownie, so Aggie slid a pan of those into the oven. She doubted the Dallas couple was in town, but she put together a goody basket for them just in case. As soon as Emma arrived, Aggie left her in charge and went off to try and rescue her fledgling business.

She hoped she would find both Mr. and Mrs. O'Henry home at 8:30am. On her days off, she could see Mr. O'Henry, forced undoubtedly by Mrs. O'Henry, exercising on the beach. Keeping Mr. O'Henry in good physical condition seemed to be Mrs. O'Henrys full time occupation. She took a deep breath and rang the bell.

Mrs. O'Henry answered the door in a pristinely pressed blue and white polka dotted shirt dress. She was obviously on her way somewhere. Or maybe Mrs. O'Henry woke up this way. Aggie couldn't be sure. "Hello, Mrs. O'Henry," Aggie said in a voice more cheerful than she felt. Her stomach was in knots.

"Hello, Aggie. How are you this morning? And what have we, here?" She eyed the white paper bag Aggie held; eyebrows raised.

"I brought you some granola," Aggie said, reaching in and handing the cellophane package over. "All natural, no preservatives. Lots of soluble fiber."

"Ah," said Mrs. O'Henry. "Well thank you very much dear. Would you like to come in?"

"Yes ma'am, I would. Is Mr. O'Henry home?"

"He is, he's just showering after his walk. Can I get you a cup of coffee?" Aggie accepted the offer politely, even though she had caffeine jitters from Brooks' much over brewed concoction.

"It's decaf," the older woman said, passing Aggie a ceramic mug with pink hibiscus flowers painted on it. For once Aggie was grateful for Mrs. O'Henry's health-conscious habits. Mr. O'Henry came into the kitchen dressed for work, his hair still wet from the shower. "Well, hello there, Aggie girl. What brings you here? I don't suppose you've brought any scones?" The older man rubbed his hands together in anticipation.

"Well..." Aggie wasn't sure exactly what to do. She figured the safest move would be to give them to his wife. "I have!" she said brightly, but she gave the bag to Mrs. O'Henry who accepted it with pursed lips and set it aside.

"Frank, your breakfast is on the counter."

"Oatmeal?" Mr. O'Henry sighed, eyeing the bakery bag on the counter.

"Yes, with flax seed, bee pollen and honey." Mr. O'Henry shot Aggie a pained look behind his wife's back. Aggie just shrugged helplessly.

"So, what brings you by?" he asked Aggie as he sat down with his bowl of oatmeal. To his wife's credit, it did smell quite good, and he ate it without complaint.

"Well, it has to do with our neighborhood association. I'm not sure if you know about my new business and I want to make sure you know all the details before um, anyone else tells you." Aggie launched into her prepared speech, all about how she needed to increase her profits and had taken a leap of faith purchasing the beach house to host her very quiet, very tasteful retreats. She told them everything that went on at the retreats, including how many people were involved, how many weekends she was hosting them and what she was charging her guests. The husband and wife sat quietly listening, Mr. O'Henry obediently spooning up his bee pollen dusted breakfast.

She nervously sped through this entire speech without taking a breath. When she finished, took in a giant inhale and was quiet. Then she started up again. "Do you have any questions? Does anything about this make you uncomfortable?"

"No, I don't see any problem," said Mr. O'Henry between bites.

"I'm so glad to hear you say that. Because apparently our new neighbor from Houston is trying to shut me down. If it comes to a vote, will you two please support me?"

"You can count on it." Mr. O'Henry spoke for them both. His wife nodded her agreement and chimed in.

"I would much rather see you hosting your retreats than just renting it out willy-nilly to just anyone that would pile fifty people in that huge house."

"Oh, thank you!" Aggie was almost in tears she was so grateful. She impulsively hugged them both.

"There, there, my dear." Mr. O'Henry looked embarrassed. "Have you spoken to Flora Hernandez yet?"

"No, she's my next stop."

"It's possible she'll feel differently. And you may have to wait a couple days. I think she's out of town. Something about a sick aunt who passed away in San Antonio." Aggie's spirits sagged.

"I'll call an official HOA meeting if I need to," Mr. O'Henry continued, "but I think maybe I'll just pay a visit to little Miss Houston and see if I can smooth this over. As far as I see it, this whole business doesn't amount to a hill of beans."

His wife interrupted him. "You're right on that, dear, but I think this might better be handled with a softer touch. You go on to the store. I will pay a call to our new neighbor." Aggie thanked them both again and immediately headed for her next stop. She knocked on the door of the Dallas family's house. It was a long shot to catch them in town on a Wednesday. There was no car in the driveway, and no answer at the door. Aggie put their goody basket in the backseat of her car and headed back to the Bean and Bun, frustrated. There was nothing to do but wait for Mrs. Hernandez to get back to town.

She spent the afternoon in the kitchen. In her foul mood, she didn't trust herself with customers, so she left the front of the house to Emma. A storm blew in and rain pounded on the roof so there weren't many customers anyway. The weather matched her mood. She needed something tactical to do, something to keep her hands busy. She normally used the big commercial mixer to knead bread dough, but today she mixed flour, water, oil and sugar by hand and pounded the dough over and over until the gluten was probably far over developed, but she didn't care. She was so frustrated. This was so unfair. She worked so hard, risked so much, done everything right, cut no corners. Everything was finally going her way and now this. Her insides felt hot, and she wanted to punch things, so she just kept punching the dough. And then, all her anger and frustration at the complete unfairness of it all boiled over and started filling up her eyes until the dough shimmered and hot tears of frustration were free falling into the bread dough.

Emma walked into the kitchen near closing time and found Aggie red faced, weeping, still pounding away at the dough.

"Whoa, what is going on in here? Are you okay? What's wrong?" Aggie just looked up at her, her fingers embedded in the dough. Aggie's eyes were red rimmed and puffy. It took her a minute, but she took a deep breath and tried to speak. "I'm just so tired, Emma. I feel like I've been fighting this uphill battle for over a year. I've been knocked down a hundred times, but I keep getting back up. And this is just one more time. I'm trying to fix it, but I'm stuck at this standstill and it's making me nuts."

Emma quietly left the room and in a wisdom beyond her twenty-one years, went next door and asked Amelia for a bottle of wine. She and Amelia returned momentarily to find Aggie sitting on the floor, her head resting on her knees. Amelia sat down on the floor beside Aggie, bottle and glasses in hand.

"Alrighty, friend. Here we go. Honestly, what you probably need is a shot of bourbon, but I don't have a liquor license, so this will have to do."

Aggie looked up at her friend and accepted the wine glass. She held it with both hands and took a large gulp, her hair falling into her face. "Thank you," she said quietly.

"There you go, just take a couple sips. I'm not trying to get you drunk, just to chill out a little." Aggie took another gulp and hiccupped. Amelia poured a small glass for herself and handed one to Emma. But Emma set hers down and went back out front to finish closing up.

"So, what's up? It's not Brooks, is it? I'll climb a ladder and kick his ass if I need to." Aggie let out something like a snort at the image of petite, tattooed Amelia climbing a step ladder in order to bring a fist even with Brooks' nose.

"No, not at all. Brooks is wonderful." She hiccupped again and wiped her face with the back of her hand. Aggie filled Amelia in on her last two days of drama, while Amelia listened silently.

"Oh, man. She wants your building bad. This isn't good."

"I know. But if I can convince her, she could ensure me a majority vote, even if that crazy vampire lady, Angelica, does file a formal complaint."

"I'd say that's a long shot, but would it be helpful for you to know I saw Flora walk into the Painted Bunting an hour ago?" Aggie looked up from her wine. "What? I thought she was in San Antonio. Something about a sick aunt."

"I have no idea. All I know is I was setting out the bistro tables on the sidewalk less than an hour ago, and she waved to me as she walked in."

"But I can't go over there now. I'm a mess. Look at me."

Amelia surveyed Aggie's puffy face and swollen eyes along with her messy hair. "Come next door. We'll get you cleaned up first." Aggie hiccupped again. But she let Amelia lead her next door. She sent Aggie to wash her face. She loaned her a hairbrush and some concealer to tame the red around her eyes. Aggie surveyed her reflection in the mirror. Not her best effort, she thought, but it would do. She hugged Amelia and went back next door. Emma was just finished with the tidying up. "Sorry," Aggie said. "All better."

Emma smiled and handed her the box of brownies. "Ready for these?"

"Ready as I'll ever be," Aggie said, accepting the box. Then she took a deep breath and dashed through the downpour across the street.

Flora Hernandez had run her successful gift and dress shop, The Painted Bunting, for as long as anyone on the island could remember. She had also, over the years, quietly bought up half the buildings on her side of Main Street. Aggie walked in and a small bell dinged in the back. The air conditioner felt icy on her wet skin and she shivered. The assortment of luxury candles Flora stocked gave the shop a pleasant herbal scent - a blend of lavender, and rosemary, and something Aggie couldn't quite identify. Cardamom, maybe? There was a tasteful display in the front window of striped pale blue and yellow beach umbrellas. Carefully arranged under the umbrellas was a colorful array of children's sand pails and shovels. As this island in particular is famous for its sandcastle building contest, alongside the children's toys there were all kinds of additional, intricate tools for carving gloriously elaborate creations out of sand. There were giant plastic shovels and buckets in all sizes. There were small scrapers and combs for finer detail work. There was even one small wooden tool that reminded Aggie of what she might use to frost a cake. Along one wall were home goods, mostly tea towels and throw pillows that said things like *Life's Better at the Beach* and *Vitamin Sea*. Further back, there was a selection of beautiful beach wear and colorful sundresses. Aggie had to admit, the place had a vibe.

"Hello," she called. She tried to sound cheerful and more confident than she felt, but it came out hollow and hoarse. She wove her way among the display tables towards the back of the shop where Flora sat peering over her laptop. If pressed, Aggie would guess Flora was somewhere in the neighborhood of a well-cared for fifty. She was beautiful with dark, shiny hair threaded with silver that fell all the way down her back. Her caramel complexion was complemented by the bright colors of the clothes she sold and wore.

"What do we have here?" She looked over rimmed spectacles to examine the box Aggie held out like a peace offering. Flora accepted the box. "What's this for?"

Aggie opened her mouth but nothing came out. Her mouth was sawdust. Her practiced speech abandoned her. She couldn't tell if the expression on Flora's face was confusion or annoyance. Aggie exhaled. Maybe just the truth. The very raw truth. "Um, honestly it's a bribe." She shrugged; her hands palms up. "A big brownie bribe."

Flora pursed her lips. "A bribe for what? You don't strike me as the political type."

"What? No! Not that kind of bribe. Sorry, I'm doing a really bad job at this." She took a breath and tried again. "So, I don't know if you know about my retreats?"

Flora set the brownies down and held up her hand. "The whole island knows about your retreats."

"Ah. Yes. Okay. Well, our new neighbor filed a formal complaint to shut me down. And I know you want to buy my building and probably would love nothing more than for me to be shut down and be forced to sell, but…" Aggie paused. Hot tears threatened, but she took a deep breath and forged ahead. "You see, the thing is I love it here. Moving here was like coming home to a place I didn't even know I was aching for. Do you know what it's like to feel as if you're living a life meant for someone else? Like you're trapped in four-inch heels that are a whole size too small?" A rogue tear escaped, and Aggie dashed it away with the back of her hand. "I've made a home here; I've built a business here. I've built the life I was meant to live."

Aggie was about to play the only card she had. She hadn't told even Brooks or Lillian her plan. It was the only card she had to play, and if Flora didn't go for it she was totally, completely screwed. She thought about Brooks, and about Lillian and Jude. About Nellie. Sadie and the twins. Amelia. Emma. Her regular's faces and the way they smiled when they realized she knew their order before they asked. Her retreat guests who so appreciated all the love she'd poured into the beach house. Her darling apartment on the third floor that felt like the top of the world. Her heart literally ached at the thought of leaving all that behind.

"I can't go back to Houston. I just can't." And then she laid it all on the table. "If I have to sell you the Bean and Bun building, I will."

Flora's eyebrows shot into her hairline, but Aggie didn't stop. She held up a finger. "But on the condition that you agree to lease it back to me without any rent hikes for at least ten years." There it was, she'd said it. There was nothing to do but pray Flora gave her an answer that let her keep everything she'd worked for.

Flora took off her eyeglasses and stood. Aggie's heart sank as Flora turned and ducked into the back room without a word. Aggie bit her lip, and despite her resolve, hot tears filled her eyes. The image of Flora's geometric patterned kaftan shimmered in front of her. She almost couldn't see when the older woman turned and pointed to Aggie and then to the bakery box. "Grab those, and come on back here." Relief and hope filled her like helium rushing into a balloon. She wiped her eyes again, picking up the box, and walking around the counter into the back room. Flora gestured for her to sit at a simple wooden table. She lowered herself into a chair and watched while Flora pulled two mugs down from a cabinet, placed tea bags in them and poured hot water from a black ceramic kettle sitting on a hot plate. She looked over her shoulder. The scent of jasmine wafted in the air. "Do you drink tea?"

"Yes, of course," Aggie said.

"I wasn't sure. You don't sell it in your shop. Some people don't drink coffee, you know."

"I sell iced tea."

"Not the same."

"Is that why you never come into the shop? You don't drink coffee?"

"Mostly."

"What's the other reason?" She might as well know. Flora picked up the tea mugs and sat down opposite Aggie pushing one to her. Then she opened the bakery box, broke the brownie in half and handed half of it to Aggie. Aggie accepted the brownie with a shaking hand. She set it down on the napkin Flora passed her and wrapped her hands around the mug to stop them from shaking. The smell of chocolate and cinnamon intertwined with jasmine scented steam calmed her nerves. Sort of.

Flora took a bite of brownie and stirred her tea. She smiled slightly and nodded towards Aggie. "These really are good."

"Thank you." She didn't know what else to say.

Flora chewed and swallowed, sipped her tea. Aggie thought she might burst.

The older woman finally focused her gaze on Aggie and sat back in her chair. "Do you know where we are?"

"Um, in your shop?" What a strange question.

"When I first came to Sandcastle from Mexico City, I had absolutely nothing. I was twenty years old when I opened this shop, and I lived in this tiny little room for three years. This space was my entire home. I slept on a mattress on the floor in the corner. I scraped and saved every single cent until I could buy this building. And then I scraped and saved and bought the building next door. And then I did it again. I came from nothing. Zero. And with every building I purchased, I felt a little more secure. Yes, I wanted to snap up your building. Partly because it's beautiful. Partly because now I comfortably can. But what I've realized is that I don't need to. I am financially secure. I am successful. And my season is a new one. I'm not going to buy your building."

Aggie was dumbfounded. "You're not?"

"No, I'm not. I know what it's like for a woman trying to build a business on her own. I'm at a point when I should be helping others who are walking the same path. Making sure it's a little smoother for them. And you know what else?" Flora smiled. "That gaggle of women stopped by here on their way to the beach house and put a nice dent in my inventory."

Aggie thought back to the ladies' multicolored kaftans floating down the beach house stairs like a kaleidoscope parade. "Oh my gosh, all those beautiful dresses! They were so gorgeous. They were from here."

"They most certainly were, and you know what else? They made another sweep through on their way out picking up stuff for their kids." Flora broke into a full smile. She held up her hands as if in surrender. "You don't need to worry. You will hear no argument from me."

In an instant, the weight Aggie was carrying fell from her shoulders, and she was light as a feather. "Oh my, gosh, Flora, thank you! Thank you so much!"

"A rising tide lifts all boats. This is a small island, and what's good for one of us is generally good for all of us." Aggie had tears in her eyes again. She had already done the easy math. There were five houses in their subdivision and even if only Flora, the O'Henrys, and herself were in favor of her retreats, Angelica couldn't stop her. She couldn't wait to tell Brooks.

Flora gestured toward the front of the shop.

"So, while you're here, do you need a new dress? Something to wear out with that handsome young man I see going into The Bean and Bun every morning?" she asked, wagging a bejeweled finger.

Aggie couldn't help smiling. "Ah, that's Brooks. You might say we're seeing each other," she confided, a small flush rising in her cheeks.

"Then you do need a new dress!"

"You know, I think I do. I may have a date tonight."

Flora rose and Aggie followed her over to a row of colorful dresses. Flora looked Aggie up and down, flipped through a few and pulled on from the rack. "This one." She handed it to Aggie and pointed to a dressing room. In the room, Aggie shed her wet jeans and button down and stepped into the silk. It was a deep orange with a print of tiny blue birds. A silk strap tied around her neck and another around her ribs. The back dipped low, and the full skirt swished around her ankles. It was a perfect fit. She stepped out of the dressing room and twirled. Flora nodded her head and smiled. "Yes, that is perfect. I'll wrap it up." She was an excellent saleswoman, Aggie thought. No wonder she's so successful.

Aggie tore her gaze away from the full length mirror. "Flora, I think I need one more dress."

Even weighted down with colorful packages from The Painted Bunting, Aggie practically skipped the two blocks to Sadie's office. The rain had stopped and the wet sidewalk glistened in the sun. She walked in and Sadie's co-worker, Miranda, waved her back. Sadie was on the phone, and motioned Aggie to sit. Aggie deposited her packages on the floor and sank into the leather armchair in front of the desk. Sadie hung up and looked at her.

"Shopping spree? Keeping your mind off things?" Sadie was obviously peeved. "I spent all morning poring over your deed restrictions, and on the phone with the real estate attorney trying to save her patootie while you're out shopping?"

"Well, sort of." She gave her a play by play of her morning.

"Well, I guess that's one way to do it," Sadie admitted. "The good news is I think we've both arrived at the same conclusion. According to the attorney, there would have to be a vote banning all short-term rentals in your subdivision to shut down the retreats. And if you look here," Sadie flipped to a page halfway through the thick document on her desk. "It defines commercial activity as the property being used fifty percent or more for business. I can't imagine you having retreats more than six months out of the year, can you?" Aggie shook her head.

Sadie continued "And if you ever did want to rent out the property part of the year just as a short-term rental or B&B when you're not having retreats, that's still allowed under the short-term rental policy. So, I think you're good. Although, I really did want to be the one to save the day." She pouted.

"You most certainly have saved the day," Aggie assured her friend. "And I have something for you." She pulled the box with the dress she had asked Flora to choose for Sadie. "Flora chose this one for you."

"I trust Flora implicitly. Let's see it." Aggie lifted a silk, halter style maxi dress out of one of the bags. This one was a red and orange geometric pattern, and Sadie squealed in delight. "Awe! Thanks, Ags!" she said with a big smile, and just like that, her irritation was completely forgotten. "This is gorgeous. Thank you!"

Aggie headed back to check on Emma at the Bean and Bun. It was a busy afternoon and she busied herself in the kitchen, but not before calling Brooks with her news. Aggie couldn't see it, but Brooks punched the air in triumph when she told him.

He was thrilled for her for so many reasons, none of which had anything to do with the fact he held her mortgage. She worked so hard. He loved her passion for her shop and her customers and her cooking. He loved how sweet she was with Nellie and her friends. He had never met anyone quite like her. He promised to pick her up from the beach house and take her out for an early dinner to celebrate. Her early mornings still put a cramp in their dating schedule, but maybe now her retreats were on solid footing, she could hire some more help. He would mention it at dinner, but for now, he settled back into the world of Chester McCombs. He was liking where the current story was going, although he anticipated an altogether different reaction from his agent.

Chapter Forty-Four

Nellie laid her cards on the small table positioned under the generous shade of the century old magnolia in the Peach Tree House courtyard. "Gin!" she cried.

"Awe, rats." Jude threw his cards on the table.

"Now, young man, don't be a sore loser. Why don't you run get us a couple lemonades and see if the cook has set up his cookie spread yet?"

"Okay." Jude brightened at the prospect of sweets and took off to the refreshment table. Lillian had dropped him off that morning. She needed to run a few errands on the mainland that Jude deemed boring, so they arranged for him to spend the morning visiting Nellie. The old woman and the young boy were becoming quite chummy, and Jude didn't mind hanging out there one bit.

A few minutes later, Jude walked carefully back to the table balancing giant chocolate chip cookies on top of two paper cups filled with ice cold, hand squeezed, lemonade. One of the reasons he didn't mind hanging out at Peach Tree House, other than the fact he genuinely liked Nellie, were the top-notch treats. And as the only youngster, the residents and staff spoiled him rotten. He handed Nellie her cookie and lemonade and took a giant bite of his own. Around a mouthful of cookie, and with all the impetuousness of youth he asked the question even Brooks was afraid to ask. "So, what happened with Billy? Is he coming to visit you?" The question caught Nellie off guard. Over a week had passed since their Florida trip, and she hadn't heard so much as a peep out of Billy. She was like a ridiculous teenager, constantly checking her messages. But there had been no word.

"Don't talk with your mouth full, dear." But then she sighed and answered the question. "I guess not. It was probably silly to think he might."

"I don't think it's silly. He should come visit you. You visited him. It's polite."

Nellie laughed and changed the subject. "Have you decided what you're going to build for the sandcastle contest? It's coming up, you know." Jude grinned, showing chocolate stuck in the gap where he was missing a tooth. "I have an amazing beyond amazing idea. But it's a secret."

"Ah." Nellie sat back in the wicker chair and raised her eyebrows. "I'm quite a good secret keeper. Excellent, in fact. You can ask Brooks. I have a very good track record. It's ninety-one years long." She crossed her heart with her fingertip. Jude considered this and decided ninety-one years was an ample amount of time for someone to get good at keeping secrets. He leaned in and whispered in her good ear. When he finished, he leaned back into his chair, reaching for his lemonade. "Well," Nellie said, bobbing her head. "That is different. Have you told your mother?"

"Nope, I'm going to surprise her."

"Alrighty then, secret's safe with me." She smiled at him and ruffled his blonde hair.

"Oh, look Nellie. That golden retriever is back! Can I go play with him? Please?"

"You bet. Go ahead." Nellie laughed and shooed him off. The sight of him playing with the dog struck her as a sweet scene. Every boy needs a dog, she thought to herself.

"Nellie?" Lillian appeared behind her.

"Hello, dear," she said, not turning her head, continuing to watch Jude. "Your son is just darling. Look at him with that pup. Don't you think he maybe needs a dog? I'd love to get him one, but I'd want your blessing first. I know a wonderful breeder in Houston." Jude was wrestling with a mop of fur.

"Uh, sure, Nellie, I think that's probably fine. But um, I sort of found someone hanging out in the lobby." Nellie turned toward her. Slightly behind Lillian, hands in his pockets but standing tall with a straight military bearing, staring at her with those familiar blue eyes was Billy.

"Oh," Nellie said softly. "Hello."

"Hello," he said. "May I sit?" Nellie couldn't speak around the sudden lump in her throat. She just nodded, moving aside Jude's cup and cookie. Lillian stepped in quickly. "I'll take those for you. I'm just going to grab Jude and we'll be on our way." Again, Nellie just nodded, incapable of speech. The two sat in the shade of the big magnolia. They sat quietly for a long time, but even a passerby might have noticed an almost palpable energy flowing between them, connecting through time and space, all the way back to 1943 and back again. All the *what if's* thought of and instantly discarded. The only thing that mattered was right here, right this minute. Nellie finally found her voice. "It is very, very nice to see you."

"It is very, very nice to see you too. Although nice seems like a terribly inadequate word."

"Yes. Yes, it does." Billy lay one of his large arthritic hands palm up on the table. It was a question, and Nellie answered it by placing her small hand in his. "I'm so glad you came."

"Are you?" Billy laughed, looking abashed. "I hope so. I'm not just here for the afternoon, Nellie. I've got a moving truck outside." Nellie was once again rendered speechless, something that had happened very few times in her long life, most of them in the last two weeks.

She blinked several times and shook her head as if in disbelief.

"Really?"

"Yes, Nell, really. And I hope you don't mind, but I've requested the suite right next to yours. And I'm not saying you have to open it, but apparently there is an adjoining door." Nellie just nodded, words still proving difficult. She almost pinched herself. She must be dreaming.

"Yes," she finally said. "I would like that. I would like that very much."

"I'm so glad. Nellie, I've only loved two women in my life. I lost them both. One is lost to me forever. I don't want to lose you again if I have a chance to be with you. Who knows how much time either of us have left on this Earth? I want to share every day I have with you."

Nellie just kept nodding. A single tear escaped, running silently down the deep lines in her face. One of the nurses hurried over, concerned. "Mrs. Schmidt, honey, are you alright?"

Nellie collected herself, sitting up straighter and quickly wiping her face.

"Yes, thank you, Dedra. I'm fine. More than fine to tell you the truth. Dedra, I'd like you to meet my Billy. Billy Black. He'll be moving into the room right next to mine."

"Alrighty then." Dedra smiled and held out her hand. "It's lovely to meet you Mr. Black. You let Ms. Dedra know if you need anything now, you hear?"

"Yes ma'am, nice to meet you as well. I think I'm going to be very happy here." His comment was directed to the nurse, but his gaze never left Nellie's face.

"Are you sure you won't miss Florida?" Nellie asked after Dedra had walked back inside.

"Nah," he replied with a generous laugh. "They were all a bunch of Miami Marlins fans."

This got a giggle out of Nellie too. An old woman with a cane and a floral dress hobbled over. "Who have we here?" she asked Nellie.

"Gladys, you are never going to believe this," Nellie started. But Gladys interrupted her, staring. "Billy? Billy Black?"

"At your service, Gladys." He gave a little salute. "It's nice to see you too."

Chapter Forty-Five

Aggie was ready for dinner when Brooks pulled in the drive at six o'clock. "Wow," he said as she twirled the skirt of her new dress across the deck. "We may have to go to the mainland. I'm not sure Buster's Icehouse is worthy of that dress."

"The day is worthy of this dress. Also, I just this second hung up with Lillian. She didn't have your phone number, or she would have called you first. You will never believe who was sitting in the Peach Tree lobby when she went to pick up Jude today."

There was only one person Lillian would have called him about. "No way!" he exclaimed "Really? Billy is at Peach Tree House?"

"Yes, she said she left them sitting in the garden making goo-goo eyes at each other. She also said that she didn't ask any questions, but there was a moving van in the drive with Florida plates. Do you think he's here to stay?"

Brooks shook his head. "I have no idea. I won't bother them tonight, but I'll call her in the morning. Tonight, I'm taking you and that dress out on the town." Aggie let him help her into the passenger seat of the

Thunderbird. The top was down, and her hair would be wrecked, but she didn't care. Even though the calendar claimed the official start of summer was still weeks away, the pleasant cool of a Texas winter and early spring was swiftly becoming a distant memory as the heat and humidity of the long summer season settled in.

Brooks was joking about Buster's Icehouse. Buster's offered live music and cold beer, a rough planked floor with picnic tables dotted around the sides and a makeshift dance floor in the middle. It was never a bad time, but Brooks didn't feel it suited the mood for tonight's celebration. He pulled up to a little shack on a plot of land just north of the nature preserve.

"What is this place?" Aggie asked. From where he parked the car, she could see a narrow path winding between waving palm trees.

"You'll see." They walked hand in hand down a path. The path eventually widened, and they stepped out onto a wide expanse of beach. In front of them sat an open-air shack set back a short way from where the shoreline would reach at high tide. Tiki torches lined the perimeter. A constant sea breeze would keep them comfortable and the mosquitos at bay.

The new restaurant was small, only eight tables in the open-air dining room with a few stools next to the bar. A young woman led them to their table and asked what they would like to drink. Aggie ordered a Chablis and Brooks asked for a local IPA. "Isn't this place fantastic?" He asked. "I came down to run the trails at the preserve yesterday and found this. They just opened. Look." He pointed down the beach to two young guys manning a giant steel fire pit. "There's no menu, just the catch of the day. It's brilliant."

"And it smells amazing." Aggie nodded her approval.

Their drinks came, followed quickly by a first course of tail-on gulf shrimp marinated in a spicy curry paste and roasted over hot coals. Aggie was tempted to lick her fingers and laughed when Brooks did. "I can't help myself, it's so good," he said. The shrimp was followed in short order by a plate of red snapper coated in a lemon butter and caper sauce and served on a bed on herbed rice dotted with toasted pine nuts. "Do you want dessert?" Brooks asked. Aggie nodded. They chose the key lime cheesecake and asked for two forks.

"So," Aggie asked, popping a bite of cheesecake in her mouth, "How's the book? Brooks nodded, smiling as he looked up at her.

"It's just about done."

"That's great, congratulations!"

"Well, you can congratulate me next week after I meet with my agent. I'm not so sure what he'll think of it."

"Why?" Aggie had finished books one through four. "The others seem pretty formulaic." She backtracked. "I mean, they're wonderful. I don't mean that in a bad way. I can't put one down once I pick it up, but they all kind of follow the same pattern. Is this one different?

"Don't worry, you're right on the money. I'm not offended. They are formulaic. It's what my readers expect. But this one is different, in a way. I'll let you read it soon. I'm meeting with my agent in Houston in a couple days. Want to come? I'll let you cash in your raincheck on Brennan's and a five-star hotel pool."

"That sounds like heaven. I really want to, but now that I know I can still host retreats, I've got to get ready for the next one."

Brooks paid the bill, and they promised their host a return visit soon. They walked back down the path, arms entwined around each other. After the short drive back to the beach house Brooks dropped a very tired Aggie off at home. He walked her to her door and made a good case for coming in, but she eventually shooed him down the steps. She had an early morning, and she was exhausted.

"All right," he said, nuzzling her neck. "I'll call you when I get back from Houston."

"Okay," she said, backing into the house as he walked to his car. She started to call him inside, to hell with her early morning. But she didn't, she just stood

there with a smile on her face and waved as he got in
his car.

379

Chapter Forty-Six

Brooks sat down across the table from his agent at the swanky downtown Houston bar Avery chose. The lights were too low, and the music was too loud in Brooks' opinion, but Avery seemed to like it. Brooks handed him a sheaf of papers containing the anxiously awaited ending of the new book. Avery dispensed with pleasantries and dove into the manuscript, dirty martini in hand. Brooks ordered a Dos Equis and the truffled popcorn appetizer. He nursed the beer for the next half hour while watching Avery's practiced eyes skim quickly across the pages as he sipped his martini. He kept an eye on the turning pages and braced himself when Avery was about ninety percent through the ream of paper. Brooks set his beer down on the table when Avery choked on a martini olive and went into a coughing fit. A waiter hurried over, but Avery waved him off. Once recovered, Avery sat up straight, pushing his drink aside. His eyes raced across the page, and he flipped furiously to the next.

Here we go, thought Brooks, *in three, two, and one. Showtime.*

Exactly on cue, Avery erupted. "What the hell, Brooks?! You've incapacitated your main character!"

"You don't like it? I think it's some of my best work."

"Well," said Avery, still staring at the pages in front of him. "I'm obviously skimming for plot here, but yes, the writing itself is superb. It's damned eloquent. But you've got Chester recovering from a near fatal fall, resulting in a below the knee amputation. I'm all for inclusivity, but I'm not sure how you are going to keep going for four more books if Chester can't jump out of helicopters, or race down mountains? And he is obviously madly in love with our new heroine, but what are they going to do? Go run a goat farm?!"

"I'm not a hundred percent sure yet. I was thinking they might buy a piece of land and settle down. Maybe grow coffee beans. Or start a vineyard? I like the idea of leaving Chester tending some vines. Can you grow grapes in Columbia?" Brook casually tossed a piece of truffled popcorn in the air and caught it in his mouth.

Avery looked at him, exasperation shooting out his eyeballs. "Brooks, there is a very lucrative contract for four additional installments of the Chester McCombs series sitting in your inbox, just waiting for you to ink it. And you are putting Chester out to pasture."

"I am."

"Brooks, you can't do this."

"Yes, I can." Brooks looked Avery square in the eyes. "Look, Avery. Odds are the studio will still want to produce the rest of the series. You are good at your job, and you have guided my career well. Please don't think I'm not grateful. But hear me when I tell you I am done with Chester McCombs. He's been my safety net for a decade. I'm ready to take a risk, write something different. Something with a little more substance. I feel like there is more in here." Brooks stabbed his chest with his forefinger. "You have a choice. You can stay on my team and work with me on my next project. Or I can go shopping for a new agent." Brooks leaned back in the booth and reached for a handful of popcorn. "What's it gonna be?" Avery sank back into his side of the booth as if admitting defeat. He took off his round, tortoise shell glasses and kneaded his eyes. Then he looked up and with the crook of finger signaled the waiter for another round of drinks.

"All right, Brooks." He held up his hands in surrender. "I give. It's been a good run. A great run. And you're right. I also think there is more in you. And you are still one of the good guys. I want to be the one to represent you whatever it is you decide to do next." The drinks arrived, and Avery raised his martini glass. "To new projects." Brooks grinned and clinked his beer bottle against Avery's delicate glass a little too enthusiastically, almost spilling the martini into his lap. "To new projects," he repeated.

Chapter Forty-Seven

Aggie's phone was buzzing in her back pocket as she reached in her bag for her house keys. She inserted the key in the back door lock of the beach house and answered the phone at the same time. "Hello," she said a little breathlessly as she set her bag down on the kitchen island.

"Hello, Aggie. This is Clara O'Henry."

"Oh, hello. How are you?"

"I'm fine dear, thank you for asking. However, this is a business call. I wanted to see if you have any open spots for your July retreat."

"Um, I think I do, let me pull it up real quick." Aggie walked over to her laptop sitting on the desk in the pantry. She made a few quick taps. "Yes, I have four spots open. Do you know someone who wants to book? I can take care of that for you."

"I do. I paid our new neighbor a visit this morning and brought her a little housewarming gift. Some of the local bee pollen I've been using and my favorite wheatgrass I get on the mainland. We had a lovely chat. I feel a little sorry for her, though. It seems her husband works constantly in Houston, and she's been spending a lot of time on the island alone. Also, her husband, who sounds like absolute jackass by the way, pardon my French, dear, promised her a tour of Southern France this summer. But he has taken on a big new client and made her cancel the whole thing. So, while it's obviously not the Riviera, I suggested a staycation and told her I might enjoy coming along as well."

"Wait, so you and Angelica are coming to the retreat?" Aggie was trying mentally to catch up. "So, she didn't mention trying to shut me down?"

"No, and neither did I. And if you are as smart as I think you are, you won't bring it up either."

"Maybe I should have taken her a housewarming gift."

"Emily Post says you have three months to deliver a housewarming gift. I think you're within the window."

"Roger that. I'll pick up something for her from the Painted Bunting tomorrow."

"That's a good girl. So, you have us down for the second weekend in July?"

"Yes, ma'am, I've got you down. But wait, Mrs. O'Henry. Have you taken a look at the website? I mean, the menu is pretty decadent. I can make some substitutions if you like." Aggie had no intention of modifying the menu for just anyone but was willing to do quite a lot to please Mrs. O'Henry at this point."

"Oh, no dear. Whatever you are serving will be perfectly fine. Just no need to tell Mr. O'Henry." Aggie swallowed a giggle, thanked her again and hung up, shaking her head. Wonders never cease. She went back into the kitchen and put together a simple dinner. Brooks should be by soon. She tossed a green salad with a bright vinaigrette of whisked sherry vinegar, grated shallot and a grassy Italian olive oil. She threaded shrimp marinated in herbs, garlic and lemon and more of the fruity olive oil onto kabobs for the grill. Then she popped some of her hatch cheddar biscuits into the warming oven. Brooks walked in the back door without bothering to knock. He walked right up to her and held out a very expensive bottle of Champagne.

"What's this for?" Aggie said.

"We're celebrating," he said and kissed her on the mouth.

"Clearly, but what exactly are we celebrating?"

"The retirement of Chester McCombs," he said, beaming. He was more excited to tell her than anyone else. He wrapped his arms around Aggie and kissed her again. It was her and her alone who made him confident he could write something with more depth and more substance. He would always be grateful to Chester. But it was time to part ways, and he was itching to start something from scratch.

Aggie set the table out front while Brooks grilled the shrimp. They carried their plates out onto the porch. They toasted with the champagne and let the effervescence tiptoe over their tongues. Brooks told her about Avery almost choking on his olive when he read the new ending. And she told him about her call with Mrs. O'Henry. Brooks had stopped off at Peach Tree on his way home to pay Nellie and Billy a visit. "It's crazy. I swear, they both look ten years younger than they did two weeks ago. They were acting like horny teenagers. They couldn't keep their hands off each other. He's in the suite next to hers, and they're talking about asking the owner to let them knock down the wall to make one big apartment."

"That's amazing, to have that kind of love. The kind that will endure that kind of time and distance. It's so rare."

Brooks set his fork down and took her hand, looking into her eyes. "Is it? I think it's maybe not quite as rare as you think." And with no prelude, he just simply said, "Aggie, I love you."

Aggie smiled with her whole face. "I love you, too." He pulled her into his lap, kissing her yet again. They sat like that for a long time, watching the sky turn colors, finishing the champagne. After the first stars came out, he set her back on her chair and carried the dishes inside. Then he took her hand and led her up the stairs to the room where he had played as a child and now as a man, had most definitely found a place that felt like home.

Chapter Forty-Eight

The morning of the 78th Annual Sandcastle Island Sandcastle Contest dawned bright and hot. At some point in the contest's long history, some bright soul made a motion to move the contest from the swelteringly humid, pavement melting heat of August to the slightly more tolerable second week of June. The population of the little island doubled overnight. A constant stream of tourists flowed into The Bean and Bun, and Aggie and Emma worked a line at least ten deep all morning. A selection of artisan tea bags now sat on the counter next to the glass pastry case. They served Iced Americanos, lemonades and pastries hand over fist. Also, thanks to Emma's salesmanship, almost no one left without a t-shirt, coffee mug or bag of coffee beans. By noon, their inventory of baked goods as well as merchandise was depleted, and Aggie and Emma were both exhausted. There was no way Aggie could bake any more stock, but they stayed open and served drinks to a steady stream of customers until closing time. At four o'clock, Aggie flipped the sign to *Closed,* and they both collapsed against the door.

"Today was bananas! Someone certainly has put us on the map. Have you eaten anything?" Emma shook her head. "Me either. I'm not sure there's a scrap of food left in this place, but I'll see if I can cobble something together."

"I've got a better idea," said Emma. "Let's clean up super-fast and head down to the beach. We can catch the judging and I'm sure they're selling food and stuff down at the contest site."

"That is a much, much better idea."

"I'll start cleaning up. I can wait to eat, but I could definitely use a caffeine infusion before we head down there."

Aggie nodded. "You are full of good ideas today. The last two Iced Americanos of the day, coming right up. Three shots each!" Aggie made the coffees, and the two made quick work of sweeping up and wiping down counters and tabletops. Aggie cleaned the coffee machine, and Emma set the kitchen to rights. Then the two women carried their coffees down to the beach. The beach felt like a carnival today, the sounds of music and merriment growing louder the closer they got to the center of the event. They passed every imaginable kind of sandcastle on the way, ranging from the standard to the theatrical. They passed traditional castles taller than a man with turrets, and spires, and moats with flowing water and little toy boats floating along pushed by the breeze. Some of the more notable sights included a dragon with intricately carved scales, a Tyrannosaurus Rex with giant bared teeth, a life size dolphin pod and a scene out of ancient Egypt complete with a pyramid and a mummy.

Aggie was amazed at the amount of delicate labor people put into their creations that in a few days would be blown and washed back into the beach as if they were never there at all. But today they *were* there, and it felt like a different land.

The breeze carried not only the briny scent of the Gulf, but also the aroma of cotton candy and hot dogs mixed with coconut sunscreen. Small children with sticky faces ran amuck, shrieking with laughter, chased by exhausted but happy looking parents. There were vendor stands selling everything from cold drinks and sandwiches to homemade jewelry to tacky t-shirts in various shades of neon.

And there, smack in the middle of all those enterprising souls sat a small table with a blonde eight-year-old boy behind it. He was selling lemonade, a typical eight-year-old activity, but the genius was in his additional items for sale. Neatly stacked on Jude's long table were plastic buckets and shovels, beach balls and frisbees, and pretty much anything a small child would beg his parents to buy for him when spending a day at the beach. Aggie walked up to the table. "Well, hello there, young man. I think I know you," she teased.

Jude grinned up at her. "Hi, Aunt Aggie! Would you like a glass of ice-cold lemonade?"

"I certainly would." She loved that the fact that she was already carrying one cold drink didn't deter him one iota from trying to sell her another one.

"Here you go! That'll be four dollars." Aggie fished in her wallet for cash and handed over bills which immediately became damp from the humidity. "Thank you very much, ma'am." Jude shoved the bills into a bulging money bag. "Nice doing business with ya. Are you sure you don't need anything else?"

Aggie laughed and looked at Emma. "What do you think? Should we hire him?" Emma grinned and nodded.

Lillian walked up and passed Jude a cone of blue cotton candy.

"How's business?" she asked him.

"Phenomenal!" He surveyed his dwindling piles of colorful plastic beach gear. "I think I'll close up shop soon and go play though." He eyed a group of boys kicking a neon green soccer ball back and forth across the sand down the beach.

"Sounds reasonable. I think you've had a pretty successful day." Lillian said, following his gaze. "Why don't you go ahead and play? I'll man your table for a bit."

"Okay! Thanks, Mom!" Jude was off like a shot. Lillian scooted behind the table and started straightening Jude's wares.

"He didn't want to build a sandcastle?" Aggie asked.

"Nope. And I tell you what. I am a smidge sad we're not building a sandcastle together today, but I'm so proud of this kid. Do you remember when we were at Peach Tree, and he played with that golden retriever?" Aggie nodded "Well, he's been begging for a dog ever since, but I told him he needed to save some of his money to help pay for it."

"Are things that tight?" Aggie asked.

"Oh, no," Lillian waved her hand. "I'm just trying to teach him how to save for something he wants. God bless Ben," her gaze flicked heavenward for a second. "He was generous to a fault with his money, but he was also an impulsive buyer. Remember the time he took Jude on that fishing trip to Cabo and came back with keys to a beach house because I complained about being cold? I want to teach Jude some delayed gratification is all. Which is ironic, because the last time we visited Nellie, she asked me if she could buy him a puppy. Anyway, all that to say, he has been saving up all his allowance. What is impressive is that rather than wait to save up all the money, he hatched this plan to multiply his cash. He bought all this stuff online for pennies and has a tenfold markup on it. And he's sold almost everything."

"Well, he chose the right inventory," Aggie said.

"That he did," Lillian replied.

"Maybe I should be taking business lessons from Jude." And more softly, Aggie added. "I guess the apple doesn't fall all that far from the tree, does it?"

"No," Lillian said, her voice soft, but strong. "No, I guess it doesn't. He has so much of Ben in him." She turned her gaze towards the beach where Jude was kicking the ball and laughing with a group of kids that he didn't even know a few short months ago. She fingered her wedding rings hanging from a chain around her neck. "I think we're going to be okay."

"I think so too." Aggie linked her arm through her friend's. Brooks was ambling up the beach. He stopped to kick the ball with the boys for a minute and then continued toward Aggie, grinning at her under his Rangers cap with those ridiculously white teeth. She couldn't believe he was hers. For so many years, she buried herself in her studies and then in her business. There had been a few men along the way, but they were always too much work. And they never understood her work. Brooks just folded himself into her life and her into his. It was so easy.

The judges announced the winners. First prize went to the ancient Egypt scene and runner up to the massive castle with the moat. Aggie led her crew over to the beach house where she had a cold supper waiting. They were joined shortly by Amelia, weighed down with bottles of cold rosé. Sadie, her husband Mark, and the twins followed shortly after.

Dinner on the porch was lively as the sun sank behind the house. Aggie passed out beach blankets, and they all trooped down to the sand to watch the island council's fireworks show. Jude and the twins ran around on the beach, and the adults sipped more rosé, lounging on the blankets. Momentarily, music drifted toward them, and the first whiz of color shot skyward from the contest site. A starburst of oranges and yellows and reds filled the night sky. The children came rushing back to the blankets. A tuckered-out Jude settled against his mother's shoulder. Emma pulled the twins into her lap so Sadie and Mark could enjoy the show in peace on the next blanket. The little ones pointed in wonder to the sky, their mouths hanging open. Amelia stretched out like a cat on her blanket, eyes towards the heavens.

Brooks pulled Aggie close to him, and she settled back against his chest. Instead of watching the show above though, Aggie watched the light play on the faces of the people surrounding her on her own personal piece of the beach. It didn't seem all that long ago she was grinding away in Houston, moving dutifully from one task to another, moving between her sterile apartment and her office.

Aggie gazed around at her little island family, feeling happy and content. She snuggled back against Brooks. He whispered into her hair, "I love you." She tipped her head back and turned her head on his shoulder to meet his eyes. "I love you, too." He kissed her then as the fireworks continued, exploding color all around them.

Epilogue

It was one of those glorious Texas fall days. The ones that feel like a Colorado summer. Days warm enough for a sundress, yet cool enough for an evening fire on the beach. The actual summer on the Texas coast that year was horrendously hot with temperatures hovering in the triple digits for weeks on end. The Gulf was like tepid bath water. Brooks broke down sometime in late July and bought a treadmill. No matter how early he woke for his morning run, he was gulping in warm soup for air as he struggled to breathe in the oppressive humidity. Despite the weather, it was a productive summer. Aggie's retreats were growing in reputation, thanks, surprisingly enough, to Angelica. After she and Mrs. O'Henrys little staycation, during which by the way, neither one of them turned down a morsel of the food and were exceedingly pleasant guests the entire time, Angelica submitted an article to an old contact at a major travel magazine. Aggie's Instagram following grew overnight to tens of thousands of women all dreaming of a weekend at The Bean and Bun Beachside Retreat. Aggie was fully booked well into the following summer.

Aggie also allowed several weeklong rentals for previous retreat guests wanting to bring their families back to Sandcastle Island, which didn't hurt her bottom line. During those weeks, Aggie vacated and played house with Brooks, a situation neither minded. Aggie's schedule improved as she learned to loosen the reins more at the bakery. She hired a talented young baker who came in every morning and got the ovens started. Aggie went in at seven rather than five, an hour Brooks found much more civilized and conducive to seeing Aggie every night. Emma was still a huge help, but she had received a letter from the university. They were officially offering her place back to her for the spring semester if she promised to only use her powers for good. Aggie would need to find a replacement for her by January.

Aside from Shane and Gregory, who were due to visit next month, Aggie still missed very little about Houston. When she spoke to Shane, he seemed to have grown into his own at the practice. He had let Mark walk. And even though it was an empty threat, he had his attorney send a terrifying letter reminding Mark of the full scope of the non-compete agreement he had signed. Rumor was Mark had opened a shop in a small suburb an hour north of downtown, but not one of Shane's clients had followed him. The shoes Shane had to fill when Aggie left were larger than he had anticipated. He hadn't realized how much Aggie had handled and when he was shouldering it all, it was heavy. But he slowly made a few more hires and was delegating a lot of tasks Aggie should have let go of years ago. He and the firm seemed to be flourishing.

Brooks was knee deep in a new project. It was a period piece about a young boy adventuring alongside the infamous Jean Lafitte's rough and tumble, Robin Hood-esque gang of pirates. The story was loosely inspired by tales heard at Nellie's knee, shelling peas on the porch of the beach house.

A blessed cool front had blown through overnight, pushing out the humidity and heat, leaving behind the sensation that everything had been scrubbed clean. A high-pressure system sat over the Gulf, and there wasn't a cloud to be seen in the sparkling, cerulean sky. Aggie opened the window of her third-floor bedroom and let the clean, cool air sweep into the room. She thought of the Anne of Green Gables quote *"I am so glad I live in a world where there are Octobers,"* as she sat at her dressing table and carefully applied mascara.

"Knock, knock."

"Come in." Lillian walked in the room looking lovely and fresh in a new dress from the Painted Bunting. It was a flowing paisley print in autumn colors that hung beautifully from her tall frame. Long gone was her awkward, bony stature. From Aggie, and from

YouTube, she was learning to cook and had become quite adept at feeding herself and Jude nutritious, delicious meals, and it showed on her frame.

"Are they all set up outside?" Aggie asked.

"Just about. Take a look for yourself." Lillian gestured at the open window facing the ocean. Aggie screwed the mascara wand back into the tube and padded over to the window. From three stories up, they could see a floral arch constructed entirely of the deepest pink bougainvillea set up on the beach. In front of it sat a handful of cane chairs. Off to the side was a string quartet and there was Brooks standing at the front, speaking to the minister.

"It's perfect!" Aggie squealed. "They did an amazing job." Aggie turned her back to Lillian. "Help me with this zipper, will you?"

Lillian quickly did up the last few inches of the dress, and Aggie spun in the middle of the room. The bodice of the dress fit her like a glove, but the skirt floated dreamily through the air. Aggie stopped to slip on a pair of flat, strappy gold sandals. Lillian nodded her approval and smiled at her oldest and dearest friend.

"You look amazing. Brooks is absolutely going to die when he sees you in that dress."

"You think?" Aggie grinned.

"Yep. If you don't need anything, I'm going to go find Jude and get down there."

"I think I see him," Aggie said looking out the window. She pointed to his little blonde head sitting in the front row. Next to him, on a leash sitting obediently was Jacks, his six-month-old golden retriever puppy. "He brought Jacks!" Aggie exclaimed.

"Is that okay?" Lillian asked.

"Is he potty trained?"

"One hundred percent potty trained."

"Fine by me, then."

"Ok, I'll see you in a bit." Soon after Lillian left, there was another knock on the door.

"May I come in?" Brooks' deep voice came through the door.

"Well, I was hoping to make a grand entrance downstairs, but yes, I suppose you can

come in." The door opened, and Brooks just stood there, taking her in. Aggie twirled

once more. "What do you think?"

"I think you look like an angel."

"You look pretty spiffy yourself."

"I clean up every once in a while."

He did indeed look quite dapper, clean shaven in a cream linen suit and crisp white shirt. He held out his arm and she took it and let him lead her down the stairs and across the beach. As soon as they came outside, they could hear the music. Every pair of eyes turned towards them as they crossed over the old wooden walkway and down the aisle to the floral arch, thinking what a handsome couple they made. When they reached the front, Brooks deposited Aggie in her seat and walked back down the aisle. A few minutes later, he returned in a golf cart with Nellie. He parked the cart at the back of the crowd and helped Nellie down out of her seat. On cue, the music changed tune, and Nellie took her grandson's elbow with one hand. In her other, she lightly held a bouquet of magnolia blossoms. She wore a silk shirtdress with a full skirt the color of the deepest indigo of a bluebonnet. More flowers were tucked in her white hair. She may have needed Brooks' arm for a wee bit of balance, but she felt much younger than her most recent birthday indicated as she walked down the aisle.

Billy stood tall and proud under the floral archway as his bride approached. They spoke their simple vows with clear voices. The ceremony didn't take long. Nellie and Billy said they had waited over seventy years to marry each other, and they didn't intend to drag out the process. Afterward, Brooks ferried Nellie, Billy and several Peach Tree guests back to the house on the golf cart. Inside, the house was positively bursting with flowers. Between the flowers and the buffet lunch Aggie set up in the dining room the place smelled like heaven. The musicians also moved inside and soon the place was filled with the sounds of big band and swing music, some of it the same tunes Billy and Nellie danced to at the old VFW hall back in 1943.

Everyone feasted and danced and enjoyed the jovial spirit of the day. Jude danced about with Jacks' paws on his shoulders. The twins got caught sneaking cookies off the desert table and hiding underneath it. As there was no tablecloth, they were in plain sight of their parents. However, Sadie and Mark decided if it bought them enough time to enjoy a dance, they would deal with the sugar crash later.

The party was winding down and Aggie handed out little cloth favor bags filled with lemon drops as guests started to leave. Billy and Nellie danced slowly in the middle of the room. They reminded Aggie of the dancing couple at the retirement home in Pensacola. Even though Billy and Nellie had spent such a small percentage of their long lives together, the way they moved gave off the vibe that they had been dancing together, holding each other up, moving to the same music for a lifetime. And in a way, they had.

Finally, the last of the guests waved their goodbyes, and Aggie and Brooks sank onto the front porch steps with a bottle of champagne. Aggie kicked off her sandals and moved one step below Brooks so she could lean her back against his chest. "It was a beautiful day." She said, staring out at the waves.

"It really was. You know," he said slowly, "if I was ever to get married, I think this is just the way I'd want to do it."

"Really? Me too, I think. This was beautiful. It felt special and authentic."

"Well," he said, resting his chin on her head, "I'm awfully glad to know you feel that way. I'm thinking maybe sometime in the Spring?"

He rose and moved below her on the steps. He bent down on one knee and pulled a small box from his pocket. He opened it and held it out to Aggie. On a pillow of purple velvet, sat a perfect, round diamond solitaire on a simple, thin gold band. "This belonged to my great grandmother. Aggie, you are the most incredible human I've ever met. I still don't know how you manage to do everything that you do, but I want to spend the rest of my life figuring it out. You push me to do better, to be better, and I want you to keep doing that. I don't want to live one day of the rest of my life without you. Will you marry me?"

Aggie just stared at him. His image and the ocean beyond blurred with her tears as she finally nodded her head. "Yes. Yes, I so, most definitely will." He slipped the ring on the ring finger of her left hand. It was a perfect fit. Then he took her hand and led her back into the home that raised four generations of his family. God willing, it would raise another.

The End

Nellie's Favorite Lemon Blueberry Scones

- 2 1/2 Cups Almond Flour
- 1/2 Cup Coconut Sugar (can sub white sugar)
- 2 1/2 Teaspoons Baking Powder
- 1/2 Teaspoon Kosher Salt
- 1/4 Teaspoon Cinnamon
- Zest of 2 lemons
- 1/2 Stick Butter
- 2 eggs, beaten
- 3 Tablespoons Heavy Cream
- 2 Teaspoons Vanilla
- 3/4 Cup Dried, fresh or frozen Blueberries

1. Heat oven to 400 degrees F
2. Place butter in freezer for 30 minutes-remove from freezer right before using
3. Line a cookie sheet with parchment paper and set aside

4. In a large mixing bowl, combine almond flour, coconut sugar, lemon zest, baking powder, salt and cinnamon. Set aside
5. In a small mixing bowl, whisk together the beaten eggs, vanilla and cream
6. Using a box grater, grate the frozen butter into the flour mixture and combine with a spoon or your hands.
7. Pour egg mixture into the flour mixture and combine
8. Gently fold in the blueberries
9. Turn out the dough onto the cookie sheet lined with parchment paper. The dough will be wet and sticky.
10. Form an 8 inch disc
11. Using a large chef's knife, cut the dough into eight triangles, just like a pizza. Clean the knife with a damp paper towel after each cut.
12. Carefully work the knife under each scone and separate them slightly.
13. Bake for 12-14 minutes until the tops are barely golden brown.
14. Transfer to a cooling rack to cool.
15. Store in an airtight container.

Acknowledgements

Golly, there are a lot of thank you's to be said.

First, to my friends and family who believed in me and didn't say (to my face at least) that I was nuts for spending precious, toddler nap-time hours writing a BOOK - thank you for the kind words, encouragement and for all the coffee.

To my early readers: Jenny, Linda-aka-Mom, Tana, Pam, Patty, Aimee, Amanda, and Hilary, thank you for slugging through those atrocious first drafts.

To my cover designer, Ashley Santoro, I'm grateful for your amazing creative gifts and your immense patience with my one-gazillion revisions.

To Amanda Armstrong and the Publify publishing team. Amanda, when we met I literally had goosebumps and knew you were put in my path for a reason. Thank you for bringing The Bean and Bun to life.

To my sister, Jenny, (who lucky for me, also happens to be the best audiobook narrator), thank you for nerd-ing out on plot lines and giving the most sound feedback. Side note - pretty please finish YOUR book. I'm dying to know how it ends.

To my Mom, who doesn't have it in her to tell me to axe a chapter but will save me from the tragic embarrassment of comma misuse.

To my Dad, for never telling me there was anything I couldn't do or be.

To Witter and Lucas. You two inspire me endlessly. To indulge in creativity, to hold things lightly, and to pursue something purely for the joy it creates. I love you to the dinosaurs and back, and I will be ridiculously grateful until my dying day that God chose me to me your mama.

To Alan. My husband, my rock, my favorite human, and the first person to read this book in its entirely. You already made all my dreams come true, so thank you for being my biggest cheerleader when I stumbled on a new dream. Sorry for all those times I woke you up when I was trying to quietly sneak out of bed at 4am to spend time on Sandcastle Island with Aggie. Also, I will forever consider the fact that my big, tough husband teared up reading something I wrote as one of my biggest accomplishments. I love you forever.

About The Author

Amanda lives in the Texas Hill Country with her husband, two rambunctious little boys and a spoiled golden retriever named Waffles. She sells real estate by day, but on evenings and weekends you can usually find her on one kids sports field or another and/or refereeing nerf gun fights and light saber battles. She writes in fifteen minute increments from the carpool line.

9 798899 190729 3